NIGHTTIME PASSES, MORNING COMES

DAYS OF WAR

BOOK TWO

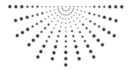

JONATHAN CULLEN

LIQUID MIND PUBLISHING

All rights reserved. No part of this book may be reproduced, distributed, or transmitted in any form or by any means, including photocopying, recording, or other electronic or mechanical methods, without the prior written permission of the author, except in the case of brief quotations embodied in critical reviews and certain other noncommercial uses permitted by copyright law.

Copyright © 2023 by Jonathan Cullen

www.jonathancullen.com

Liquid Mind Publishing

This is a work of fiction. Any resemblance to actual persons, living or dead, or actual events is purely coincidental.

ALSO BY JONATHAN CULLEN

The Days of War Series
The Last Happy Summer

Nighttime Passes, Morning Comes

Onward to Eden

Shadows of Our Time Collection
The Storm Beyond the Tides

Sunsets Never Wait

Bermuda Blue

The Jody Brae Mystery Series
Whiskey Point

City of Small Kingdoms

The Polish Triangle

Love Ain't For Keeping

Sign up for Jonathan's newsletter for updates on deals and new releases!

https://liquidmind.media/j-cullen-newsletter-sign-up-1/

CHAPTER ONE

M*arch 1942*

Thomas sat on the bed beside the small Bakelite radio, his boots untied and his police cap and coat hanging on the door. With his brother George working nights at the shipyard, he would often listen for hours to the news from Europe. But much like his life, even the war moved too slowly for him. He hated being alone knowing Connie was just next door. Sometimes they would smile between the windows or wave from the porch. But unless they planned to meet somewhere in secret, they had to pretend they weren't together.

Connie still hadn't told her aunt, worried that she would panic. Mrs. Ciarlone was Italian, and with America now at war, she and Connie were classified as *alien enemies*. The only ones who were safe were her daughter Chickie and her older son Sal, who both had been born in the country. If Connie agreed, Thomas would have married her anyway, but he wasn't even sure they could. With all the new rules and restrictions for immigrants, no one knew what was allowed and what was not.

He couldn't even tell his mother they were engaged because she was in the state mental hospital. Mrs. Nolan had taken her husband's death harder than anyone, and no one blamed her. But in the months following that terrible summer, she had stopped bathing and going out. Most nights after dinner, she would sit on the couch listening to the radio, drinking until she couldn't stand.

Now that Thomas was on the police force, he could have afforded an apartment, finally getting away from his brother. But George had been better since their father died, working steadily and staying out of trouble. And with their mother sick, Thomas could never leave. If the tragedy had done anything, it was to bring them all closer together.

Sometimes the family's misfortunes were too hard to think about, and as a cop, he already had enough stress. News of the war only made him anxious, so he turned the dial, searching for stations through the static. When he stopped at WBZ, he told himself it was because it was the best signal, the tower only a couple of miles away in Medford. But the truth was, while he preferred the hip sounds of bebop and blues, classical music reminded him of his father.

Someone knocked. When he rolled over, Abby peeked in.

"The hospital called," she said, breathless.

"I didn't hear it ring."

"Because the radio was too loud."

Sitting up, he reached for the knob and turned it down.

"And what'd they say?" he asked.

"It was Doctor Berman. He wants to see us. He thinks she can come home."

Thomas felt a wave of relief.

"When?"

"Friday."

"I'll get the day off. Do we have to bring anything?"

She pursed her lips and shook her head. With her brown hair cut to her shoulders, she looked older, somehow more mature. Her first year of college had turned her from a timid girl into a woman.

"George will drive us," he said.

"I'll ask him when he gets home."

"There's no *ask*. He'll drive."

As she lingered in the doorway, he felt a draft and knew he had to put on more coal.

"What is it?" he asked.

"Will she be okay?"

When their eyes locked, he could feel her anguish, and as twins, they always had a close bond. Out of everyone, she was doing the best, and yet he worried the most about her.

"She'll be okay," he said, finally.

"Promise?"

"I promise."

With a smile, she closed the door, and he lay back down. He was glad their mother was coming home, but he was nervous too. She had been admitted in November, only weeks before Pearl Harbor changed everything. The country had only been at war for a few months, but in many ways, she was returning to a new world.

After working ten hours, Thomas was exhausted. He knew he should eat, but he wasn't hungry, and one of the benefits of being a patrolman was that every shop or restaurant owner would try to feed him. For lunch, he had spaghetti in the North End; in the afternoon, he ate pierogies in Scollay Square. By dinner, he was so full he had to turn down apple pie from a diner on Cambridge Street. So he put his hands behind his head and shut his eyes.

Sometime later, he was awoken by a noise. Abby burst in.

"Thomas!"

She sounded upset, but he didn't panic because, much like their mother, she was always frantic.

"What's wrong?"

"Something is going on next door."

"Next door?"

"The Ciarlones—"

Thomas was up before she could finish. He ran downstairs, and she followed behind. When he opened the front door, he saw two black cars on the street.

"Wait here," he said.

She ignored him and grabbed her coat, and he knew he couldn't stop her. They slowed down when they reached the sidewalk, which was still covered in ice and snow from months of cold.

Suddenly, someone shrieked over at the Ciarlones' house. As Thomas ran toward it, two men came out of the shadows and stopped him.

"What're you doing?"

One was younger, the other overweight and smoking a cigar.

"Get back in your house," he said.

"Like hell."

Thomas darted to go around them, but they got in his way.

"Not so fast—"

"Thomas!"

He looked over and saw Connie on the porch, her niece Chickie close beside her in pajamas.

"That's my girlfriend!" Thomas shouted.

When he tried again, they grabbed him, but he shook them off and jumped back. Reaching for his wallet, he took out his badge and held it up. The men paused and looked at each other.

"We've been informed this house is occupied by alien enemies," the younger guy said.

"And who the hell are you?"

The fat one stepped forward, his hat so low Thomas could barely see his eyes.

"FBI. Now move along."

After months of experiencing the power and respect of his new job, Thomas felt like a civilian again. The Boston Police had no authority over the feds. If anything, they were subservient to them.

"Pardon the disruption, sir," the younger one said, a politeness Thomas didn't expect. "We'll be on our way soon once we finish our job."

Thomas had learned from being on the force that, in every law enforcement duo, one was reasonable, and one was not.

"Which is what exactly?" he asked.

"Confiscation of prohibited items."

"Prohibited?"

"Anything in violation of Proclamation No. 2537."

Thomas didn't know much about wartime regulations, and he was embarrassed he didn't. When he glanced over at Abby, she was shivering. She had put on her coat so fast that the buttons were uneven.

Hearing a commotion, they all turned, and Mrs. Ciarlone was on the porch. In her black dress, she was hard to see, but Thomas could tell she was sobbing. With Connie and Chickie next to her, she pleaded in broken English with the three agents, who listened but seemed indifferent.

Thomas stood helpless, something he hadn't felt in a long time. The temperature was near freezing, but he wasn't cold, steam billowing from his mouth as he watched in a quiet fury.

"She's a widow for chrissakes," he said.

The younger guy nodded, some small show of understanding, while his partner shrugged his shoulders. One of the men came down the stairs with something in his arms.

"Just a radio," he said.

"Any cameras?"

"No, sir. Finnerty found some binoculars, but they look like children's."

"How about their registration status?"

"The young lady is her niece. She registered last week, but she says her aunt can't write."

"Not our problem," the agent said. "She needs to get down to the post office by Monday. If she don't register, she'll be arrested."

Thomas shook his head and turned away. It was the first time he had ever felt true sympathy for Mrs. Ciarlone.

Since moving in five years before, the family kept to themselves and didn't talk to anyone. Mrs. Ciarlone's twenty-two-year-old son Sal was friendly, but he was always working so no one ever saw him. The only outgoing one was Chickie, who at thirteen acted half her age due to some mental deficiency. Thomas never blamed them entirely, knowing that, as foreigners, they were looked down on, even by other Italians.

By now all the neighbors were out, people watching from their porches in the dark. With a *dim-out* order across the city, no one could let out any light, or they would be fined.

Thomas knew it was humiliating for Mrs. Ciarlone, and he remembered the time his father was taken from the house by the police after a drunken fight with their mother. At five years old, he realized he wanted to be a cop, the comfort he got in knowing they were safe from his father's violent outbursts. But seeing how the Ciarlones were treated made him wonder about authority.

Headlights came up the street, and they turned. George pulled over in his black Chevy, the tires spinning in the slush. He opened the door and stepped out.

"What's this all about?"

One of the agents glanced back, but the others didn't notice.

"Ma's getting out of the hospital," Abby said, random enough that George squinted in confusion.

"Who are all these guys?"

Thomas didn't answer, knowing his brother could always make a bad situation worse.

"Let's talk inside," he said, and they started up the steps.

By the time they reached the door, the men had gotten back in their cars and driven off. The raid had only lasted fifteen minutes. Next door, Connie stood with her arms around her aunt, patting her back while Chickie looked on frightened from the shadows. When she peered up, Thomas smiled, and to his surprise, she smiled back.

CHAPTER TWO

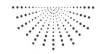

Leaning over the sheet pan, Abby dipped the brush into the glaze and wiped it across the hot donuts. When she got a bob cut the week before, it was for style as much as function because she was tired of getting powdered sugar and flour in her hair. The older ladies wore hairnets, but they were too frumpy. With America now in the war, there were fewer young men around, and girls had to look good.

Some days she felt like a grunt, sweating in the bakery three mornings a week before going to class. The manager had asked her to work at the counter, which they reserved for young women because teenagers didn't know how to deal with customers. But Abby declined. She liked the seclusion of the kitchen, where the work was dirty but simple and she didn't have to see people.

"Abby, quick with those damn bombolonis!"

Eve stood in the doorway, her arms crossed and a ribbon in her hair. With her dark hair and full lips, she could have been attractive if she had better manners. She swore like a sailor and was the only girl Abby knew who chewed gum in the morning.

"They're called donuts," Abby said.

"What would an Irish girl know anyway?"

Abby glanced back with a frown, but they always joked around, something that made the job fun as well as tolerable.

Reaching for the spatula, she piled the pastries onto a white tray and brought them over.

"That doesn't look like two dozen," Eve said, keeping one eye on the front. The rush was over, but it was impossible to know when it would get busy again.

"What would an Italian know?"

As they spoke, Loretta walked in the back door, her bag over her shoulder, her shoes damp from the snow.

"More prejudice against the Italians?" she remarked.

"What prejudice?"

"The police were at our neighbor's house last night. They took Mr. Baglioli's radio antenna. Can you believe it? The man is almost eighty."

"You can't tell who to trust."

Abby and Loretta both looked at Eve.

"What makes you so high and mighty?" Loretta asked, taking off her scarf and hanging it beside the freezer.

"With a name like Baglioli, maybe he's a spy."

"Italians are more loyal than Japs, that's for sure. And aren't your parents from the old country?

"My grandparents. But they came here a million years ago."

"You're still Italian."

"I'm an American."

Loretta's expression sharpened. The two girls always bickered, but it was usually over fashion or boys. Eve had barely finished high school, and Abby always suspected she was jealous of Loretta, who was studying to become a nurse. Out of a dozen women who worked at the bakery, Loretta and Abby were the only ones pursuing a real career.

"It happened on our street too," Abby said, hoping to calm them.

"What did?"

"The police. FBI, actually—"

"FBI?" Eve said, her eyes widening.

"They searched our neighbor's house, looking for illegal things."

Loretta got a clean apron from the pile, tying it on with particular force.

"What a disgrace," she said, shaking her head.

The bell over the door jingled—a customer had come in. Before Eve went out to the front, she asked, "And did they find anything?"

Abby looked first at Loretta and then at her.

"No."

She didn't know why she lied, other than to prove her neighbors were decent people. She understood Loretta's outrage, and if she was ashamed about the raid, she could only imagine how Mrs. Ciarlone felt. Abby hadn't seen her since, and while she never got involved in gossip, she was sure the whole street was talking about it. She worried most about Chickie but realized she was probably too young and too impaired to understand what happened.

The country had only been at war for three months, and already the government was doing all it could to root out traitors and saboteurs. Once the shock of Pearl Harbor subsided, it had been replaced by a quiet suspicion, and no one knew who to trust.

Half of Abby's friends in high school were Italian, and she never thought of them as foreigners. But in a neighborhood where most people were immigrants, the war brought out tensions that had always been hidden under a veneer of politeness and civility. And while there were hardly any Germans in East Boston, Abby did fear for the old man who owned the grocery store on Bennington Street, knowing the local gangs were ruthless.

She finished icing the last tray of cinnamon rolls and took off her smock. Glancing over at the clock, she saw it was 8:15, and she had to get to class. As she got her coat and bookbag, Carlo walked up from the basement with a 40-pound bag of flour over his shoulder. Short and wiry, he had been working there since Abby started, quietly making dough and managing the oven. He never said much, smiling at the counter girls in a way that was tender, not creepy.

"Toodle-loo, Carlo."

"Go to school," he said. "School is everything."

Abby was touched by the advice, which somehow sounded more

sincere with his accent. Since her father's death, she found herself drawn to the wisdom of older men.

"Thank you."

She put on her wool hat and gloves and walked out to the front, where one of the employees was smoking.

"You can't do that in here!" she said, and the girl quickly put it out.

She laughed to herself and stopped at the window, which had just enough reflection for her to check her hair. Then she reached for the door and went out into the cold.

......

When Abby got off the trolley, she looked at her watch and cringed—she had three minutes until class started. Panicked, she rushed up Commonwealth Ave., stepping around people, dodging patches of melting snow. She had been commuting to Boston University now for eight months and still couldn't time it right. A trip that should have taken twenty minutes was twice that long.

Like a lot of people, she blamed any change or inconvenience on the war. With the threat of a German attack, she had somehow expected the city to get quieter, like those desolate Polish villages she saw in the newspapers. But it was even busier than before, the sidewalks crowded and traffic at a standstill every morning. Aside from the civilian activity, there were more police on the streets, and in Kenmore Square, she saw a column of Army trucks drive by.

She got to the building and went up the steps, reaching for the door an upperclassman held open for her. Inside, the air was stuffy, and by the time she got to the third floor, she was sweating from both heat and nerves. She ran down the corridor, and when she got to the end, she slid to a stop.

GERMAN II CANCELLED
UNTIL FURTHER NOTICE

Taped to the door was a small note. As she stared at it, she felt a mix of surprise and concern. Of all her professors, Mr. Bauermeister had been the kindest, encouraging her when she was struggling, once letting her retake an exam she'd failed. In some ways, he was a mentor and was the only teacher who had asked her about her life.

With classes now in session, the hallway was empty. She walked up to the sixth floor, the department of Foreign Languages and Classics. At the end of the hallway, she came to the professor's office, and when she turned the knob, it was locked. His mailbox had been removed from the wall, but on the door, she could still see the traces of what someone scrawled the previous semester: *Nazi Go Home, Kraut,* and something about Hitler she couldn't make out.

The words had been carved into the wood, a canvas of slurs and accusations, and Abby remembered the horror she felt when she first saw it. Mr. Bauermeister had let it stand, telling her that the only way to fight hatred was to expose it, and she admired his courage. The graffiti had been smoothed over with lacquer, some attempt by the administration to hide the secret prejudices of the staff and student body.

She walked away, down the empty hallway, the only sound the clank of the radiators. Unlike the city, the campus had gotten quieter as every week young men, and even some professors, left for the service. As separated as universities were from the problems of the world, the war affected everyone and everything. There were rumors that the dormitories would be used to house soldiers.

"Abigail?"

She looked into the supplies room and saw her English teacher turning the drum on the copier. In her ruffled blouse and skirt, she looked feminine, almost pretty.

"Hello, Ms. Stetson," she said.

"Can I help you?"

Ms. Stetson smiled, but she always seemed serious, with a tense forehead and beady eyes. Abby didn't know if it was bitterness over being one of the few female professors or because she liked women and couldn't admit it.

"I was going to see Professor Bauermeister."

Ms. Stetson stopped what she was doing and turned to her.

"Come in, please," she said, waving. "Close that."

Abby walked in, but she didn't shut the door. While the copy room was more public than Ms. Stetson's office in the basement, the last time they met alone, the professor had gotten a little too close.

"Miss?" Abby said.

"You've not heard?"

"Heard what?"

"Mr. Bauermeister has been arrested."

"Arrested? For what?"

"Something about his status as a foreigner, I believe."

As she said it, she arched her back, unusual pomp for a woman who had been born in Canada.

"That's terrible news."

Ms. Stetson pursed her lips, tilted her head. It was obvious she didn't agree.

"Anyone who is not a citizen must register, Ms. Nolan. It's the law."

If the war had done anything, it was to make everything a debate about politics and policy. Abby didn't know enough about the government to have an opinion, but after seeing how the Ciarlones were treated, she had some private concerns.

There was a short pause, an uncomfortable silence. Abby never liked the way Ms. Stetson looked at her, and not because she was a lesbian. The professor always had some faint expression of disapproval, a condescending smirk. When she continued making copies, Abby turned to go.

"Oh, Miss Nolan?" she said, and Abby stopped. "Have you any extracurricular activities?"

"Pardon?"

"Any sports? Clubs?"

Abby had played volleyball the previous fall and enjoyed it. But added to the stress of work and school, it almost broke her, and she didn't have the leisure time a lot of her classmates had.

"Not this semester, Miss," she said.

"Why don't you consider joining the *Massachusetts Women's Defense Corps*? We're forming a local battalion."

Abby struggled not to frown. *Forming a battalion* didn't sound like anything women would be involved in.

"It's a volunteer organization," the professor added. "We work with all the other civilian defense organizations."

"What type of work?"

"Whatever is required. Air raid wardens, canteen workers, drivers, medics. Have you any siblings in the service?"

Abby shook her head.

"Good. Then it'll be an opportunity to prove your family's commitment to the war effort."

Abby had heard of the organization, seen its posters in the hallways and lobby.

"When—?"

"We have a recruitment drive tomorrow evening. 238 Beacon Street. Make sure you have tennis shoes."

Abby didn't have a chance to say no because Ms. Stetson acted like she had already agreed. It seemed late in the school year to start a new activity, but she realized the MWDC wasn't a sewing circle, and the war didn't run on semesters.

"Yes, okay," she said, nodding.

"Be there promptly at six."

"Thank you, Miss."

CHAPTER THREE

They all sat in silence as George sped down Blue Hill Avenue. Thomas had offered Abby the front seat, but she said no, sitting in the back with her arms crossed. The ride seemed like a quiet reflection on all that had happened, and no one knew what to expect.

Maybe they had gotten used to their mother being gone, Thomas thought, and their lives had been easier knowing she was safe and being cared for. But she couldn't stay in the hospital forever, her caseworker explaining that her mental state was "grave" but not "dire." The distinction sounded more like bureaucratic babble than any kind of professional evaluation. Either way, after five months of rehabilitation, she was getting out. And despite all the fears and uncertainties, their family would finally be back together again.

In some ways, Thomas blamed the war for her breakdown, and for his father's death, although the country wasn't in it at the time. The shipyard had expanded so fast to keep up with aid going to Europe and Russia that one of the new cranes hadn't been installed right. Thomas was on guard duty that day, and the collapse shook the entire waterfront. At first, he thought it was an explosion, and with all the artillery around, that wouldn't have been a surprise. As a government contractor, East Boston Works was, by that time, operating around the clock, and Military Police had been assigned to help guard the sensitive freight.

Once the shock of his father's death was over, Thomas finally accepted that it was an accident, but he was still angry. Mr. Nolan had worked there for two decades without an injury, and it was a shame he had to lose his life as a result of sloppy construction and haste.

However hard it was on their mother, no one ever thought she would try to take her own life. Out of everyone in the family, Mrs. Nolan was the most religious, and the Catholic Church's position on suicide was clear. So when Thomas walked into the house that night and saw Abby leaning over her on the floor, he thought she had fallen again after a few highballs. But the gash on her wrist was no mishap, and it was bad enough that, had she been home alone, she could have died. George had an Army tourniquet, which was a bitter irony. Thomas had known for months his brother was stealing from the shipyard and had warned him to stop. So it was humiliating to know that his contraband was what saved her.

"Bet they're glad to be in this country," George said.

As they waited at the traffic light, Thomas looked over and saw three old ladies at a bus stop. Dressed in heavy coats, with scarves over their heads, they looked like immigrants. Since their father's death, George had been less obnoxious, but the remark was harsh enough that Thomas said, "Who the hell isn't?"

All his life, he never cared about where people were from. Everyone they knew seemed to have some connection to another place. But now that he was engaged to Connie, it was something he had to think about. With America at war, anyone who looked or sounded like a foreigner was viewed with suspicion. She had registered as an *alien enemy* and just in time because the U.S. Attorney was cracking down, threatening prison for those who didn't. For now, she was safe, but Thomas worried about how it would affect their plans to get married.

They turned onto Morton Street, past massive triple-deckers with peeling paint and sagging porches. The area had always been vibrant, but after ten years of depression, even the nicer parts of the city looked worn out.

They drove through the gate of Boston State Hospital, following the winding road up to the main building. The grounds were covered in snow, the trees gray and bare. Thomas thought back to how the grass was still green when their mother arrived, which now seemed like a lifetime ago.

As he glanced back to check on Abby, they hit a rut.

"Can you watch where you're going?!" he snapped.

George looked over with a grin.

"It ain't a Cadillac."

Thomas scoffed and looked away, more from irritability because he was proud of his brother. George was the first in the family to get a license and the first one to buy a car. The Chevy may have been a jalopy, but it made all their lives a little easier.

They parked out front and walked to the doors. Inside, the lobby looked more like an atrium with high ceilings and crown molding. Like any government building, it had a shabby elegance, the floors scuffed, the walls yellow from age and cigarette smoke.

They went over to the desk, and a woman looked up, her glasses hanging on her nose.

"May I help you?" she asked in a monotone.

As Thomas went to speak, George did too, and they looked at each other. With their father gone and their mother hospitalized, it wasn't clear who the head of the family was. George was the oldest, but it was hard to trust someone who had been in trouble all his life. And while Abby was the most reliable, she got easily flustered and could never make a decision.

Finally, George nodded, which Thomas took as a sign of deference.

"We're here for Katherine Nolan."

"Visitation?" she asked, reaching for the phone.

"To take her home."

Thomas' voice cracked as he said it, the emotion that had been building for the whole ride over. He looked at Abby, and she was biting her lip.

The woman dialed and pointed to a waiting area, which was nothing more than a circle of mismatched chairs by the window. They walked over, but none of them sat down.

Moments later, the double doors opened. A young nurse brought their mother out in a wheelchair, Dr. Berman walking beside them in a white coat.

"Ma," George said.

"Mother," Abby said with a smile.

As excited as they were, the reunion was subdued. The lobby was no place for a big show of joy and exaltation. When Mrs. Nolan looked up, her skin was smooth, her smile accentuated by light lipstick. Thomas didn't know if it was the makeup, but her face seemed to glow.

At fifty, she was still a beautiful woman, with high cheekbones and hazel eyes. She always kept her hair short, some relic from her days as a flapper. While she had always been thin, she had put on weight, which was now more obvious that she wore a dress, not the hospital gown.

As Thomas leaned over to kiss her, he flinched when he saw, behind her temples, red sores from the shock therapy. At first, they had been against it, as electrocuting someone seemed a gruesome way to help them. But they were told it was the best treatment for depression.

"Your mother is doing fantastic," the doctor said.

"If this is fantastic, I'd hate to see terrific," Mrs. Nolan said.

"She'll still need plenty of rest," Doctor Berman said.

"All I do is rest."

"Ma, stop interrupting," George said, and for once, Thomas agreed with him.

"Now," the doctor continued, "she needs to get out, too. Plenty of fresh air, sunlight. We're like plants..."

Thomas listened, but it sounded strangely naturalistic for someone who had been dousing her with amphetamines and electricity.

"Once it gets warmer, I advise daily walks. Continue with the Benzedrine, one a day, ten milligrams. If she's feeling unwell—"

"I'm right here," Mrs. Nolan said, peering up.

"Yes, Katherine. You've always made your presence quite clear. Which is why we are all going to miss you dearly."

"It's nice to be missed."

"Any concerns, phone the office. Do you have any questions?"

Thomas looked at George and Abby, and they shook their heads.

"No. Thank you," he said.

"Very well."

The doctor called the nurse, who stood a respectful distance away.

"I can walk," Mrs. Nolan said.

She handed George her pocketbook, as well as the bag with her things. As she struggled to get up, Thomas and Abby each took an arm.

"That's what I like to see, Katherine," Doctor Berman said. "Persistence."

Mrs. Nolan didn't respond, instead staggering across the lobby like a child learning to walk. Before they exited, Thomas turned back and thanked the doctor with a wave.

"He has a daughter at Boston University," Mrs. Nolan blurted.

They all looked at each other.

"Who does, Ma?" George asked.

"The Doctor. Maybe you know her?" she said to Abby. "Her name is Sarah, or was it Sandra?"

Thomas looked at his sister, who smiled sadly.

"Maybe, Ma, maybe."

As they led her to the car, Thomas heard something and looked over to see two men by the corner of the building, watching him with blank stares. For a moment, he thought they had escaped until an orderly yelled for them and they walked off.

George held the door open, and Thomas and Abby lowered their mother onto the seat. They all got in, and he started the car, making a wide U-turn in the driveway. As they drove off, Thomas looked back at the building, its brick walls and barred windows, and got an eerie chill. Whether his mother was recovered, he didn't know, but he never wanted her to return.

......

For the first twenty minutes, Mrs. Nolan walked around the house with a vague and sentimental wonder. Her grandfather had built it, and she had grown up there, the legacy of a family that had arrived from Ireland when East Boston was still farmland and pastures. For a woman who had never strayed far, leaving only for groceries or church, her five months in Boston State Hospital probably felt like a lifetime.

She examined all the furniture, ran her hand along the bookshelf. She wound the pendulum clock and picked up the souvenir plate her great aunt had brought back from the St. Louis World's Fair in 1904. She even looked at the floors and rugs, but she couldn't complain because they had cleaned everything, sweeping, dusting, and mopping. They did the laundry too, hanging it in the back hallway to dry.

In the kitchen, George was making liver and onions, and Abby was at the dining room table doing homework. Thomas stood in the foyer, and even with his siblings around, he was afraid to leave his mother alone.

"I'm not a toddler," she said with her back to him.

She was looking at the framed picture of her and her husband, the only photograph of Mr. Nolan they had.

"Ma?"

"Take your coat off. I'm sure you've more to do than mind me."

She turned around with a disappointed smile, and he felt embarrassed for being so overprotective. So he hung up his coat and went down to the basement, crouching to get to the furnace. Their father used to shovel the coal, but now it was his job because Abby was a woman and George had bad eyesight.

He came back up, dusting off his hands, and he gasped when he saw his mother trying to pour a drink.

"No," he said, grabbing the bottle.

"Thomas?!"

"No alcohol, Ma. Please."

"What's wrong with a little hooch?" George said.

Thomas gave him a sharp look and then gently pulled the jug until his mother let go.

"You heard what the doctor said, Ma."

"I'll make you some tea," Abby said, rushing over to fill the kettle.

"Tea, phooey!" Mrs. Nolan said.

When George took the frying pan and walked out, Thomas followed him.

"What the hell was that?" he asked as they went down the steps.

George pushed the lever on the ground with his foot and poured the grease into the garbage bin.

"She's as much of a right to drink as any of us," he said.

"That's what got her into this mess!"

Once George was done, he looked up.

"She's got more problems than booze."

Thomas' temper surged, but he didn't want to start a fight, knowing it would upset their mother. So he stayed calm, and George walked away, leaving him standing alone in the cold.

Hearing a tap, he looked over to the Ciarlones' house and saw someone in the window. As he walked over to see, the back door opened, and Connie stepped out. She came toward him, her figure swaying, and even in the darkness, she was beautiful.

She had arrived the summer before from Italy, a county that had already been at war for two years. She never spoke much about her past, and the most Thomas knew was that she had been married and her husband was killed in Greece. The mystery of her previous life was something that consumed and sometimes haunted him.

They met at the fence, and she peered up, her eyes sleepy and sensual.

"You'll catch flu," he said quietly.

"Won't you keep me warm?"

She was the only woman who could make him blush. But he didn't respond to her flirtations, knowing he would only get frustrated. In the warmer weather, they had made love at the cottage, on the beach, and even in the shed. But for a couple whose relationship was a secret, winter stifled any intimacy, and until they were married, they could only be together if they got a hotel room.

"Your mother? Is she home?" she asked.

"We just got back an hour ago."

"Is she well?"

"She seems better. The drugs make her woozy."

Connie frowned in confusion. Although her English was good, there were some words she didn't know.

"Like, dizzy," he explained.

"Ah."

"How's your aunt?"

"She is still sad. My uncle bought her that radio."

Thomas was still angry about the raid, which seemed even crueler because Mrs. Ciarlone was a widow. Her husband had died in an accident while working for the WPA during the Depression, and while she had gotten a small pension, it wasn't enough to raise two kids. She had never been friendly, but after Mr. Nolan's death, everyone was a little more sympathetic. Even Thomas' mother, a woman who could hold a grudge for life, had said *she's got more trouble than the rest of us*.

Still, he couldn't understand why she never became a citizen. But it wasn't unusual, and many immigrants failed to apply, probably thinking their work and families were proof enough of their patriotism.

"Salvatore was very mad," Connie said. "It made Chickie scared."

"Does he have to register?"

She shook her head.

"No. He was born here."

The door opened, and he glanced back to see Abby. With the new war regulations, they couldn't turn on outdoor lights, and sometimes it felt like they were living in a world of shadows.

"Are you having dinner?" she called over.

In her voice, Thomas heard a hint of sarcasm. They both hated liver and onions, something only George and their mother ate.

"I'll be there in a moment."

Abby waved to Connie, who smiled back, and then she went inside. Maybe it was because they were twins, but they always supported each other in love. When Abby met a Jewish guy the fall before, Thomas was the one who convinced their mother to give him a chance. As it turned out, they all liked Arthur Gittell, even George, and Abby hadn't been the same since he left for the Army.

"I should go," he said.

As Connie stood waiting, he leaned forward and they kissed, the warmth of her lips filling him with yearning. Then he quickly pulled away and looked around. Even in the dark seclusion of the backyard, he worried the neighbors would see.

"Have you told her yet?" she asked.

"Not yet. Soon. I promise."

Each time they met, she asked him. They had been planning to get married for months, and the war no longer seemed like a reason to postpone it. They were both nervous, and she hadn't told her aunt yet either. The truth was, neither of them knew what the reactions would be. With everything going on in the world, love seemed like an extravagance.

"Goodnight, my dear," she said.

With a smile, she blew him a kiss, and he watched her as she tiptoed across the yard, up the back steps, and then disappeared into the house.

CHAPTER FOUR

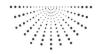

Like most colleges, the majority of students at Boston University were male, a number that was quickly declining as men joined the Army, Navy, and Coast Guard. So Abby was surprised when she walked into the basement cafeteria Friday morning to see a dozen soldiers in uniform. She got in line behind them, waiting quietly while they ordered. When a private in front of her winked, she responded with a cute smile. It was more out of sympathy than flirtation because she knew some of them would never come back.

She got to the counter and ordered a ham sandwich and coffee, reaching into her purse for her last five dollars. While she got paid the next day, money was always tight, and since their father died, she and her brothers had been helping with the bills. With war shortages, the cost of everything was up. The only one who had to worry about gas prices was George, but coal was high too, and there was even talk of rationing.

As Abby got her change, someone called her name. She looked over to see Frances, or *Fran*, waving with long white gloves. They had met at the college book fair the summer before freshman year. Beside her was Harold, dressed in a pinstripe suit, one leg crossed over the other. Out of thousands of students, the three of them had somehow been brought together, which was proof enough of fate for Abby. They were the best of friends, a tight-knit group that Harold liked to call his *band of rogues*, although she never considered herself mischievous or daring.

"Is there a battle I should know about?" she asked as she walked over with her tray.

"Aren't they dashing?" Harold said, taking a drag on his Pall Mall and staring at the line of soldiers behind her.

Abby raised her eyes but didn't reply. Even if it was obvious to some people that he was queer, they never acknowledged it for his safety.

"*You're* the dashing one," she said, looking at his outfit. "Is that new?"

It seemed early in the year for teal blue, but he set styles and didn't follow them.

"I got it in Bermuda when I went to see Papa."

"It's lovely."

"A bit tight around the tush, but it'll do."

"Please tell us your mother is home safe," Frances said.

"She came home Friday."

"And is she feeling better?" Harold asked.

Abby nodded, too emotional to speak. Growing up, she always thought she had friends, but in East Boston, people were more interested in gossip. Whether it was envy or ignorance, everyone seemed to get some private thrill from the struggles and failures of others.

"What're all the soldiers doing here?" she asked Harold.

"Better ask blondie. I live off campus."

"The Army has requisitioned some of the dormitories," Frances said.

"So the rumors are true?"

"Yes, and luckily it's not my building."

"And *unluckily*," Harold said, "it's not mine."

Abby grinned and bit into her sandwich.

"What're you doing here so early?" Frances asked.

"My German class is canceled."

"Cancelled? Like the professor is unwell?"

"No. Permanently, or…I don't know."

Looking around, she lowered her voice and leaned in.

"I was told Professor Bauermeister has been detained."

"Detained?"

"By the police."

"Good heavens," Harold said. "I hope it doesn't have anything to do with all this alien nonsense."

"Shhh."

Frances smiled at three soldiers who walked by.

"I'm worried," Abby said.

"I'm sure it beats teaching Goethe to freshmen."

"Or Siddhartha," Frances said, pretending to shudder. "We read it in high school. A dreadful book—"

"Serious! He's been good to me."

Whether it was her tone or expression, they stopped. She had started college right after her father died, and it had been one of the hardest times in her life. Meeting Frances and Harold had saved her from loneliness, but it was the professor who had encouraged her to stay in school.

"Darling," Frances said. "Maybe I can help. My father works for the OCD."

Abby didn't want to sound stupid, but since the start of the war, she had heard the names of so many government organizations she couldn't keep track.

"The OCD?"

"Office of Civilian Defense. How do you think he heard about Pearl Harbor so early?"

Abby smiled, but the memories of that day were painful. She was staying at Frances' parents' house for the weekend, a sprawling estate on Duxbury harbor. What she thought was a small get-together to celebrate the end of the semester was, in fact, a full-on party with catered food and a bar with a bartender. For the first time, Abby felt important, and she even danced with two Army officers. The magic ended early Sunday afternoon when Frances' father rushed home from playing golf to tell them what had happened in Hawaii. She always wondered how he had heard so soon.

"You think he could help?"

"I could ask. I'll see him this weekend."

"But you have to come out with us tonight," Harold interrupted, lighting another cigarette.

Confused, Abby looked over at Frances.

"We were just talking about going to the Cocoanut Grove. Won't you come?"

With her mother home, Abby felt guilty about going out. George worked later at the shipyard, and Thomas sometimes didn't get back until after dinner. Over the months, their lives had gotten busier, and the house was empty for hours at a time. Abby could be there some of the time, but she could never be there all the time. One of the hardest parts about being an adult was realizing that, while she could help her mother, she wouldn't always be able to protect her.

"Sure," she said, finally. "Let's go to the Grove."

......

They got to the club just after nine, and there was a line out front. They would have arrived earlier, but they stopped by Harold's apartment. He lived on the second floor of an elegant brick building outside Kenmore Square. Abby didn't know if he was rich, but he acted it, always dressed in the finest suits, wearing polished wingtips. He was the only person she knew with a "watch collection," and he talked about places like St. Moritz or Monaco as if everyone had been.

Unlike Frances, who was close to her parents and sister, Harold didn't have much of a family. While he was away at boarding school, his mother drowned in her swimming pool after drinking all day. His only brother had dropped out of Cornell and was trying to make it as an artist in New York City. Harold never dwelled on the past, and one of his favorite lines was, "What bringeth the new day." He was cheery and smiling at the worst of times. But behind all that optimism, Abby sensed something tragic, and part of her pitied him.

Finally, they got to the front, where a stocky man in a black coat stood watching the door.

"Ladies," he said with a nod.

As he stared at them, Abby got nervous until Harold reached between them and slipped him a ten-dollar bill. The drinking age had been twenty-one since Prohibition ended, but she and Frances were still a few months shy.

"Enjoy your evening," the guy said, then he turned aside.

They went through the revolving doors and into the lobby, where Harold took their coats and checked them in. A maître d' waved and led them through a grand archway into the ballroom. The tables were set with white linen and had flower centerpieces; fake palm trees lined every wall and walkway.

They sat near the dance floor, and Harold pointed at them.

"What's your pleasure?"

Abby looked at Frances.

"Maybe just a Martini?" she said.

"I'll have the same—"

Suddenly, the lights dimmed, and the band began to play a Latin number.

"Martinis are for accountants. Tonight we're in Havana," he said, then he called a waiter over. "Three Daiquiris, please!"

With a smile, the man bowed and walked away. Harold adjusted his tie and lit a cigarette, so excited he looked ready to burst. A few couples were already on the dance floor, and he didn't seem to like being outdone.

"Whaddya say? The Rumba calls!"

Leaning over the table, he held out a hand to each of them.

"You two go," Abby said. "I'll wait for the drinks."

Frances looked at her as if to make sure. Then she took Harold's hand, and they went out to the floor. Abby watched as they started to dance, hands clasped and jerking to the rhythm. And while she couldn't tell the rumba from the mambo, they were a striking pair. When they all first met, she used to get jealous until she found out Harold had no interest in women. Now she liked seeing them together, knowing that their connection had as much to do with friendship as it did with social class because they were both from wealthy families.

The waiter returned and put down their drinks. As Abby took a sip, she reached for Harold's cigarette, which lay smoldering in a gold ashtray. She hadn't had one in months, maybe longer, but something about the atmosphere made it appealing.

"Abigail?"

Startled, she looked over and saw Salvatore, Mrs. Ciarlone's son.

"Hi-ya, Sal."

"I didn't know you smoked."

"I don't...usually," she said, stumbling.

For years, he would come home late at night, and everyone in her family wondered what he did for work. Then she and her friends came to the nightclub after their high school graduation, and she learned he was the head waiter, something that even impressed her mother.

"Are you here with friends?"

Before she could reply, Harold and Frances came dashing back.

"Sal, meet Harold."

With a gracious nod, Harold said, "My pleasure," and then reached for his drink.

"And Fran," Abby said, before correcting, "*Frances*."

It didn't matter because they were already looking at each other. When Frances held out her hand to shake, he kissed it instead, and it was the first time Abby ever saw her get flustered.

"Are you enjoying the band?"

"I love Spanish music," Frances said, still winded. "But I don't know the moves too well."

"You should join us for our Latin Night next week. D'Arnez and his Cuban orchestra are playing."

Frances looked over at Abby and Harold, her face glowing with anticipation.

"I'd love to go," Abby said.

Harold just put up his thumb, always available for a good time.

"We'd be delighted."

"Very well," Sal said, and it was obvious he was glad. "I'll have tickets for you at the door. You'll be my guests. Enjoy your evening."

As he walked away, Frances craned her neck and watched until he disappeared under the archway.

"How do you know him?" she asked.

"He's my neighbor."

"He's from East Boston?"

Abby chuckled. As sophisticated as Frances and Harold were, they knew nothing about the working-class parts of town and were always intrigued.

"He seems so debonair," Frances said.

Abby agreed, although she never thought of him that way. With broad shoulders, a square jaw, and dark eyes, he had traditional good looks. His charm seemed more sincere than his manners, which he had probably learned on the job.

"Oh darling," Harold said, raising his glass and draining the last bits of slush into his mouth. "Be smitten on your own time. We're here for action, not love."

The horn section blared, the drums rolled, and the MC called everyone to the dance floor. By now, the room was almost full, and people were still coming in. As the band started to play, Harold stood up and looked around.

"Garçon," he said, waving to the nearest waiter. "Another round, if you please."

CHAPTER FIVE

It was the largest blackout so far, an area covering six hundred square miles and affecting 1.7 million people. The public was told it could happen anytime between 8 pm and midnight, but the actual time and duration were kept secret. Most people had gone home early to avoid any inconvenience, and over two thousand air raid wardens were on the streets to enforce the rules. Once it started, all vehicles had to stop—including buses, trains, and streetcars—and could only continue once it was over. No one knew what to expect, and the test seemed as frightening as an attack itself.

By the time Thomas got to Maverick Station, it was past eight o'clock, and he knew the sirens could sound at any time. Afraid of getting stuck on a trolley, he decided to walk the mile and a half home. The streetlamps had already been put out; the only light was from a corner pharmacy, one of the few businesses allowed to stay open. Preparations had been good because, by the time the alarm went off, all of East Boston was dark.

He continued up Bennington Street through Day Square, the shops all closed and not a single car on the road. With his hands in his pockets, he walked quickly, and not because he was cold. There was something eerie about the silence, like the aftermath of a catastrophe that had ended humanity but left the buildings standing. He had never seen the city so dark or so quiet.

As he passed the cemetery, he saw a faint glow, more like a flame than a light. He wanted to ignore it, but he had only been on the job for four months, and it was too early to start slacking. So he went through the front gate and followed the path between the tombstones. He wasn't spooked, but he unsnapped his holster just in case.

When he reached the end, he realized it was only candles, scattered around a grave and flickering in the breeze. On the headstone, it read FRANCESCO IPPOLITO: 1889-1942, and he knew it was just a vigil for someone who had recently died. It was an Italian tradition, and something the official blackout orders had failed to account for. He wasn't going to put them out, and even if there ever was an air raid, he doubted a dozen small fires would alert the enemy.

Hearing a noise, he walked over to the fence and saw three men by a storage building, its loading door open.

"Hey!" he shouted.

He grabbed the iron slats and jumped over, landing hard on the street. When he walked over, the men fanned out.

"What're you doing?" he asked.

"Mind your business."

He looked at them and then at the door.

"Is this your place?"

The one in the middle stepped forward, and there was just enough moonlight that they could see each other.

"Oh, you again?" he said.

Thomas cringed when he saw who it was, a local thug who, while not quite an enemy, had become a nuisance. He reached for his badge, and the guy lunged and hit him. Thomas jumped back, his arms up and ready. His years of boxing at East Boston High had given him good reflexes, but he knew he was outnumbered.

Another man punched him from the side, and Thomas covered up. In seconds, they were all around him, and he grunted with each blow. Cornered against the fence, he was starting to lose consciousness. He reached into his coat, groping for his pistol, and when he finally got it, he raised it and fired three times in the air. Instantly, they scattered and disappeared into the darkness.

Stumbling over to the building, he saw crates of frozen meat on the sidewalk, beef, lamb, and pork.

"You there!" someone shouted.

Thomas looked and saw two air raid wardens running toward him. Dizzy and in pain, he took out his badge and showed it.

"Robbery," he said, gasping for breath. "Pull the alarm box."

One of them ran back towards Bennington Street.

"You alright?"

Thomas nodded, although he wasn't sure. When he wiped his face, there was blood on his hand, and he heard a ringing in his right ear. He had been pummeled before in the ring, but it was humiliating when it came from three thugs.

A minute later, two cruisers raced up, and one of the advantages of the blackout was that cops were everywhere. They drove with their lights off, but it didn't matter because the moment they got out, the all-clear sirens rang out. Slowly, lights started to come on in the houses. The test was over.

"Son of a bitch," a sergeant said, walking over.

Thomas showed them his badge, and they acknowledged him as a fellow officer.

"Looks like they timed it right," he said.

"They sure did. You need an ambulance?"

"I'm alright."

"You get a look at them?"

Thomas hesitated. After a long day, he didn't want to go looking for suspects, and he also wasn't sure he wanted to snitch.

"Not really. It was dark."

"Hey, Sarge," one of the officers called, holding up a pair of bolt cutters. "Should we take these?"

"Yeah. You can dust them for prints."

Thomas laughed. Even as a rookie, he wouldn't have asked such a stupid question. On the back streets of East Boston, burglaries were common, and the culprits were hardly ever caught unless it was at the scene. The men hadn't taken anything, and with all the meat still sitting in crates, the most they could be charged with was breaking and entering.

"You gonna write a report?" the sergeant asked, but he didn't sound enthusiastic.

"Maybe in the morning."

"Boys," the man barked, "get this stuff back in the building. Find out who owns it, let 'em know."

Thomas waved and walked away, and he didn't realize how shaken up he was until he reached Bennington Street. His head throbbed, and somewhere on his side, he felt a pain. He shivered too, but it wasn't from getting injured. It had been spring for two weeks and still felt as cold as January.

The city was coming back to life after the blackout. Although the shops wouldn't open until morning, he could see the headlights of cars, hear the bell of a trolley.

As he went up the hill, most of the houses on his street were still dark. He walked up to the porch and glanced up at Connie's bedroom on the second floor. Sometimes she would look out when he got home late, but tonight he didn't want her to see him.

He walked in, and a candle was lit in the parlor, his mother sleeping next to it on the recliner. He went over and reached for the glass on the side table, smelling to make sure it wasn't liquor. And it wasn't, just the last of some cream soda, the same thing his father used to drink after he gave up alcohol.

"Thomas?"

He looked over, and Abby was standing on the stairs in a nightgown, her feet bare.

"The test is over," he said.

"I know. Was there any trouble?"

He took off his coat, and as he walked over to hang it up, he turned his head.

"What do you think?"

Her face dropped, but she didn't panic. When he used to spar, he came home with welts and bruises all the time.

"What happened?!" she exclaimed.

"Is it bad?"

She reached out and touched his cheek.

"You've some blood under your nose."

"I caught some guys breaking into a meat warehouse."

"Did you get them?"

"I scared them off."

Their mother snorted, and they both looked over, but she was still asleep.

"I need a favor," Abby said.

"What?"

"One of my professors, he got detained..."

Thomas frowned in confusion.

"He's German," she added, and then he understood.

"What makes you wanna help him?"

"He helped me last semester. A lot. After..."

When she stopped short, Thomas knew why. They all had trouble talking about their father's death, and even their mother called it *that incident last summer*. Silence may have been a good way to stave off grief, but it was a terrible way to heal it.

"What's his name?" Thomas asked.

"Bauermeister. Martin Bauermeister."

"You expect me to remember that Kraut's name?" he snickered, removing his holster.

"Just remember Meister Brau."

Their eyes locked, and Thomas grinned, thinking back to the night when, at twelve years old, they stole four cans of beer from their father's cooler. It was in the summer, and they were at their cottage on Point Shirley in Winthrop. Walking through the dark streets, they guzzled them, and by the time they got to the beach to meet their friends, they were stone drunk.

"I'll see what I can do."

As much as they bickered, he never resented her like he did George.

"Thanks."

She skirted by and went toward the kitchen.

"How's the furnace?" he asked, and she spun around.

"I put on three shovels full an hour ago."

He nodded and walked up the stairs, his soreness increasing the more he warmed up. The attack had been so fast and so furious, it was like going five rounds in under a minute. After it happened, he pretended it didn't bother him, but as the adrenaline wore off, he started to get angry. His pride was hurt more than anything; even the most violent thugs wouldn't hit a cop in Boston because they knew they would regret it. So he was sure the assailants didn't know, but he knew who one of them was.

He went into the bedroom and put his gun in the case under his bed, locking it with a key. As he changed out of his uniform, he heard a car pull up. Moments later, the front door opened, and it was his brother. Thomas was about to go downstairs when George walked in wearing boots and a coverall.

"Looks like Aroostook out there," he said.

Thomas chuckled to himself, recalling how they used to visit their aunt and uncle in Maine as kids. Presque Isle was in Aroostook County, but George called it *Rooster* County, thanks to the speech impediment he still had traces of. Those were some of Thomas's best memories, lying on the hillside at night with his siblings, so dark they couldn't see each other.

"You had to work?" he asked.

George sat on the bed and undid his laces.

"We shut the dock lights down for twenty minutes. I think they knew when it was gonna start."

"I doubt it. They said even the governor didn't know."

"Was there any trouble?"

Thomas turned his head, but his brother still didn't notice the bruises. All his life, George had bad eyesight, and he wouldn't wear glasses because he said they gave him headaches.

"Nothing unexpected," Thomas said, sighing in sarcasm.

It was the second time he had been asked about the blackout, and he wasn't surprised. The city had never gone dark before, even during the

First World War, and everyone was concerned about robberies and looting.

"Who was the girl you met last summer?" Thomas asked.

"Angela?"

"Yeah. What was her brother's name?"

"Vin."

"Vin what?"

George stopped what he was doing and looked up.

"Labadini," he said. "Why?"

"No reason."

Thomas walked out, and as he went down the hallway, he felt a cold draft. The house was one of the oldest on the streets, built by his Irish great-grandfather after the Civil War. Like a lot of homes, it had no insulation except for shredded newspapers stuffed between the rafters and in the window casings. Their father had once tried to talk their mother into moving to the suburbs, but she had spent her entire life here and said she would never leave.

He opened the linen closet and got a blanket. When he went downstairs, his mother was still asleep, her arms crossed over her stomach, her head to one side, snoring. He watched her for a minute, touched by her innocence. After all that they had been through, he was thankful she was home. Approaching, he put the blanket over her, careful not to wake her. Then he leaned over and blew out the candle.

CHAPTER SIX

Abby stepped off the trolley at North Station and followed a line of passengers down the rickety stairwell of the elevated track. When she got to the street, there was a crowd in front of the Boston Garden, boys hawking tickets, and people waiting for the game between the New York Rovers and the Boston Olympics. She didn't know much about hockey, except her brothers used to play it in the marshes in Orient Heights. Back then, no one had the money for equipment, and the only reason her family survived the Depression was that her father was a union crane operator.

She crossed the street and cut through the West End, an immigrant neighborhood of narrow streets and alleys. All the shop signs were in Italian or Yiddish, and it felt like a European village. But there was no mistaking its allegiance because the American flag hung in every window and doorway.

When she came out the other side, she could see the Charles Street Jail at the bottom of the hill. With its barbed wire and granite clock tower, it looked like a fortress in the middle of the city. She had always been afraid of prisons, worrying that her brother George would end up in one. The Deer Island House of Correction was only a half mile from their cottage, and she remembered one summer when several prisoners escaped. All of Point Shirley was out looking for them, men walking the streets with rifles and baseball bats.

Abby walked through the arched entrance into the lobby, an open room with metal chairs and posters on the walls. A woman with her daughter was sitting in one corner, but otherwise, it was empty.

Abby went over to the counter, and an overweight guard looked up from his newspaper, his eyes fleshy and bloodshot.

"Yeah?" he asked bluntly, and she didn't expect him to be so rude.

"I'm here to see Martin Bauermeister."

The man reached for a ledger and flipped through it.

"You got an appointment?" he asked.

"I do not."

He looked up with a sarcastic grin.

"Just joshing, lady. There's no appointments. Visiting hours are two to five," he said, then he glanced at the wall clock. "Which leaves you about twenty minutes."

"I shan't need much longer."

"Good," he said, dropping a ledger on the counter. "'Cuz you won't get it."

She signed in, and the man made a phone call. Moments later, a younger guard came to escort her, and she was relieved when he even smiled. After checking through her bag, he took her down a hallway, and they turned into a stairwell.

"A family member?" he asked.

"Just a friend."

They went up two flights and came out into a long corridor.

"We don't keep goonies in the regular block."

"Goonies?" Abby asked.

"You know? Wops, Krauts…the foreigners."

She gave him a sour look but was in no position to huff. They stopped halfway down, and the guard reached for his keys. It was a normal door, nothing like the cage with iron bars that she had imagined. He knocked once before opening it, some indication that the professor was being treated more like a political prisoner than a common thug.

"Visitor," the man said.

Abby peered in, and Mr. Bauermeister was sitting at a small desk with a book. He looked over squinting, dressed in only slacks and a white undershirt.

"Abigail?" he said, finally.

"I'm sorry to disturb you."

He grunted, a muted laugh.

"Hardly."

Standing up, he reached for the only other chair in the room. She looked at the guard, who stood lingering in the doorway, and made a pointed smile.

"Ten minutes until visits are over," he said, then he walked away.

She sat down, close enough she could smell the professor's cigar smoke, hear him wheezing.

"How are you, dear girl?" he said, taking her hand and patting it.

"Fine, thank you."

"And classes? How are they?"

She looked down, embarrassed that he was more concerned with her than himself.

"Well," was all she said.

With his stout frame, gray hair, and handlebar mustache, he looked like a stuffy academic. But he had gentle eyes and a warm smile, and she always felt good around him.

"How did you find me?"

"I...I asked administration," she said, which was a lie.

"No great of admirers of foreigners at the moment."

Abby smiled sadly, but she couldn't disagree. With a football coach who was a Marine major and an Army recruitment assembly that had drawn over a thousand young men, Boston University was as patriotic as Fort Benning.

"I heard you didn't register as an alien enemy."

His expression changed.

"Someone told you that?"

"Just that you had been detained," she said, remembering Ms. Stetson hadn't said why. "I assumed—"

"That's untrue. I registered in February."

39

"Then why are you here?"

"I don't know. The officers wouldn't say, except that I was in violation of federal law."

"And you've done nothing wrong?"

He shrugged his shoulders, seeming more defeated than angry.

"There was a hearing. A court date has been set. I've not been issued an attorney."

"Couldn't you hire one?"

"I've contacted several. None have responded."

Hearing footsteps, she looked back, and it was the guard.

"Time's up," he said.

"Is there anything I can do?" she said to Bauermeister. "Perhaps your wife needs something?"

"She's already been in touch with a colleague of mine."

"Miss," the guard said, and Abby got flustered.

"I'll come back another day."

"Don't worry about me, dear. Focus on your studies."

"I will."

With a smile, she put her bag over her shoulder and headed for the door.

"Abigail?"

She turned around.

"Thank you."

......

A trip that should have been quick had taken almost an hour. Somewhere between Charles Street and the Boston Common, an air raid siren had sounded, and the conductor had to wait until they were cleared to go. They were underground when it happened, and as Abby sat in the darkness, she could sense the quiet panic of other passengers, the whispered conversations and nervous chatter. Her instincts told her it was only a test, but when they started to move again, she gasped out loud in relief. It had been the longest fifteen minutes of her life.

By the time they reached the station, it was almost six o'clock, and she hated being late for anything. So the moment the doors opened, she rushed out and up the stairwell, swerving around people in a flurry of *pardon me's* and *excuse me's*. Bursting out of the exit, she ran through Copley Square and crossed Boylston Street.

Soon the commercial bustle of the city gave way to the quiet of residential Back Bay. Once a muddy backwater, it was now one of the finest parts of the city, its streets lined with Victorian brownstones and other grand buildings. Her mother always said it was full of *muckety-mucks*, a term she used for anyone she thought was even slightly above her in social status. Abby knew it was out of envy, and maybe bitterness. Mrs. Nolan's father had worked on a road crew that filled the swamp and laid out the streets back in the late 19th century.

When she got to 238 Beacon Street, she was amazed to see an elegant townhouse with a stone façade and columns. Walking up the front steps, she waited to catch her breath before swinging the knocker.

Seconds later, a pudgy woman in a green uniform and cap opened the door.

"Name?" she asked coldly.

"Abigail Nolan."

The woman looked at her clipboard and then waved her in. They walked into a foyer that had gilded wallpaper and a chandelier, a wide staircase with an oriental runner. It looked more like a mansion than the headquarters of a military group. The rooms were crowded, and it wasn't just women because Abby heard men too.

"Ms. Nolan!"

She looked up and saw Ms. Stetson coming toward her, dressed in the same outfit as the lady who answered the door.

"Ms. Stetson," Abby said.

She never thought she would be so glad to see her.

"It's ten past six."

Abby froze.

"There was a siren...in the tunnel...the train was delayed."

However flustered she sounded, she was more offended than nervous. She had come there to volunteer, not to get berated.

"And in tennis shoes?" the professor said, glancing down.

"I thought you said—"

"I said *make sure you have* them. For training and drills. Tonight is registration only. Come, please. Major Dawson is about to speak."

Abby followed her down a corridor, smiling at people she passed. There were lots of girls her age, but none were familiar, and she always got more intimidated when she didn't know anyone.

"Lovely place," she said.

"It was a private home if that's not obvious. Graciously donated by Mrs. Pauline Fenno."

They turned into a large room that looked like it had once been a dining hall. But the furniture was gone, replaced by rows of folding chairs and filing cabinets in the corner. Along the far wall hung a large banner that said *Massachusetts Women's Defense Corps*.

Standing by a podium was a short woman, her hands clasped and expression stern. When she called for attention, everyone started to sit. Abby followed Ms. Stetson to some chairs near the front and took off her coat, put down her bag.

"Ladies," the woman said. "Welcome to the weekly recruitment drive of the MWDC. I'm Major Mary Ward, commander of the Boston company. Tonight Major Dawson will speak to you about the role of civil defense."

She turned with a smile, and a guy in a military dress suit stepped away from his two colleagues, the only other men in the room. He was tall and handsome, and when everyone got quiet, Abby knew it wasn't out of politeness because all the girls looked smitten.

"Good evening," he said. "First, the United States Army, as well as Governor Saltonstall, would like to thank you for your commitment to the war effort…"

He went on for twenty minutes, explaining the MWDC's history and purpose, and the more Abby heard, the more she was interested.

The organization had been controversial since it was established a year before, with many public officials saying women had no business in military matters. Newspapers wrote editorials against it; politicians threatened to revoke its charter. In the end, it survived and now had a lot of responsibilities, including assisting with evacuations and running canteens and first aid stations.

When the Major finished, he got a standing ovation. Mrs. Ward came back up, her face beaming, and thanked him.

"Enlistment forms are over there," she said. "Private McCarthy can help you fill them out..."

She looked toward a table at the back, and a young woman raised her hand with a timid smile.

"There will be light refreshments in the parlor. Our girls can answer any questions you may have."

The formalities ended, and everyone got up. When Ms. Stetson went to talk to someone she knew, Abby walked over to the registration table. The girl handed her a form, and she filled it out, and while it was mostly basic information, Abby got confused by a section with prices.

"Pardon?" she said, and the young woman looked up. "What's the $15.50 for?"

"Your uniform."

"We have to pay?"

"Yes. We do have donation funds we can apply if you can't afford it."

Abby shook her head. She had taken the scholarship for BU because she couldn't afford it. But when it came to any other charity, she was as proud and stubborn as her mother.

She handed back the form, and the girl stamped it and put it in a box.

"Schedules are by the window. All new recruits must do fifteen hours of training. Thereafter, you'll be required to participate at least two days per week to remain active with the company."

"Thank you," Abby said, and then she walked over to get a schedule.

The room was now full of chatter, and a lot of people seemed to know each other. It was starting to feel more like a social event than a meeting, and after a long day, Abby was tired. She grabbed her things, and slipped out down the hallway, stopping in the foyer to put on her coat.

"Ms. Nolan?"

Turning, she saw Ms. Stetson sitting in an alcove with some women.

Three of them were in MWDC uniforms, and the others had on casual clothes. One even wore pants.

"Won't you stay and mingle?" the professor asked.

She had her legs crossed, and there was a slight blush on her face, probably from the wine they were drinking. Either way, she looked relaxed, her smile much more endearing than her usual cold smirk. As Abby hesitated, they all watched, and something about their gazes made her uneasy.

"Thank you. I have to get home," she said.

And before Ms. Stetson could reply, she opened the door and went out into the night.

CHAPTER SEVEN

Thomas sat in the passenger seat while the patrolman drove, a detective named Cowing sitting in the back. As they went under the Sumner Tunnel, the officer hit the sirens, and Thomas realized it was the first time he had been in a police cruiser.

Like a lot of rookies, he had started out walking the beat, and all winter, he patrolled downtown, the North End, and Beacon Hill. It was cold but easy, and since the start of the war, crime had gone down in the city, something the newspapers had mentioned and the chief bragged about. Whether crooks were wary with all the soldiers around or they were feeling more patriotic wasn't clear, but no one expected it to last.

Soon they came out into the sunlight at Maverick Square, a busy intersection of mom-and-pop shops, diners, barrooms, and pool halls. When they passed the train station, Thomas got nostalgic, thinking about how he used to take the streetcar to work with his father each day. He had only been a guard at East Boston Works for a few months, but the things that happened had changed the course of his life. It was the place his father had died, and also where he met Connie, who was working at a small factory nearby.

They continued down Marginal Street along the waterfront. One side of the road was lined with tenements, the other with wharves. With the country at war, the shipyards were operating around the clock, their berths lined with ships and barges. Across the harbor in Charlestown, the Boston Navy Yard was the center of shipbuilding and repair, but it had annexes in East Boston. Areas that had been abandoned when Thomas was young were now docks, storage facilities, and refueling stations. He was glad it was vibrant again, remembering how during the depression work had slowed almost to a stop. The only reason his father survived the layoffs was that he had seniority.

"Turn here," Thomas said.

They pulled up a side street of attached rowhouses, all rundown and weathered. Their condition could have been blamed on the location; the salt air was harsh on wooden structures. But it was also one of the poorest parts of East Boston, with three-family homes full of first and second-generation Italians, the type of neighborhood Mrs. Nolan scorned. For a woman whose own ancestors had arrived penniless before the Civil War, it was as heartless as it was hypocritical. When it came to immigration, everyone looked down on the next group behind them.

They parked and got out, Thomas squinting to read the numbers. Once he found the address, he walked up to a front door where he saw the name *Labadini* taped to the mailbox. Nodding to his colleagues, he grabbed the knocker and swung it.

As they waited, he got tense. He had taken people into custody before, but it was mostly drunks or petty thieves. This was his first real arrest, and the fact that it was personal made him uneasy. He had learned from boxing never to act on rage or revenge.

He recognized Labadini that night because they had clashed before, and he never forgot someone he fought with. The previous summer, while they were staying at their cottage in Point Shirley, his brother met Labadini's sister Angela. George had always been wild, having been arrested twice as a youth, and Thomas could never recall a time when he wasn't in trouble. But after their father kicked him out and he ended up living with Angela on the beach, it seemed like a new low point. After some debate, Thomas went with his father and Abby to get him, only to discover that Angela's family had come for her too. Like any situation with two wayward lovers, an argument broke out between the families, and when Labadini attacked, Thomas knocked him to the ground.

"Yes?"

Startled, he looked up, and an older man was standing at the door. Dressed in a suitcoat and cap, he peered out with suspicious eyes. Thomas showed him his badge, which wasn't necessary because he already had on a police uniform.

"We're looking for Vincent Labadini."

"My son?" the man asked in a heavy accent.

"We need to talk to him."

"Vinnie at work."

Thomas looked at his watch.

"First shift ended a half hour ago," he said.

The old man leaned out, looking up and down the street. Then with a discouraged look, he waved them in.

"He home soon."

They entered a small front parlor with faded wallpaper, a plain couch, and a console radio in the corner. In the kitchen, something smelling of garlic and other spices was cooking.

Moments later, Thomas heard footsteps, and Angela came down the narrow staircase. With the low ceilings, she looked even taller, and she had put on some weight. The last time Thomas saw her, she was thin and ragged from living on the beach with his brother.

"Whadda you want?" she said coldly.

"We're here to see your brother."

"For what?"

Before Thomas could reply, her father went over and got his coat off the hook. Looking at her, he said something in Italian, and she nodded. Then he tipped his hat and walked out, leaving them all confused.

"He goes to evening Mass," Angela explained. "Every day."

"Nothing wrong with that."

"Since my mother died."

Thomas wanted to tell her he had lost his father too, but it was no time for sympathy.

"I'm sorry," he said.

"Now he can't work."

"Pardon?"

"The government took his fishing boat."

Thomas looked over at his colleagues.

"It might have been confiscated," Cowing explained.

"It was confiscated," Angela said, struggling to pronounce it.

"That's the FBI, Miss. Not the Boston Police. If he's not a citizen—"

"It's bullshit!"

"Calm down, Miss."

"Tell me why you wanna talk to my brother!"

"Please," Thomas said. "We just need to ask some questions."

He tried to calm her with a smile, and to his surprise, it worked.

"I gotta stir the pot," she said, and she went into the kitchen.

"When's he due back, Miss?" the patrolman asked.

"How the hell do I know? Sometimes he goes to Sonny's for drinks after work."

As she said it, a black Ford Coupe pulled up out front. Through the window, Thomas saw Labadini get out, dressed in his work smock from the shipyard. They all backed away from the door, and when he walked in, his face dropped.

"What the hell is this about?"

"Are you Vincent Labadini?"

"Yeah. Why?"

"Were you in the vicinity of Travaglini's Meats on Harmony Street the night of the 31st?"

"That was the blackout, right?"

"Just answer the question, sir."

Considering he was the witness, Thomas felt insulted that the detective was doing all the questioning.

"I was home. My sis will tell you."

"You sure about that?" Thomas asked.

Angela came back in, an apron around her waist, a wooden spoon in hand.

"He was helping papa fix the nets. I seen him."

"Nets?"

"My father fixes nets for the dockyard," Labadini said, "because he can't work. I help him."

Everyone turned to Thomas, who felt pressured to act. As he glanced around the small house, the cracked walls and simple furniture, he felt a sudden and overwhelming pity. He knew the rules were severe for alien enemies—he saw what had happened to the Ciarlones. Seizing radios, cameras, and guns was one thing, but taking a boat seemed unfair. He had only seen his father depressed a few times, and it was always when he couldn't work, either from shift reductions or the one time he broke his hand. There was nothing worse for a man than being deprived of his livelihood.

Finally, he looked over at Labadini, and their eyes met.

"It's not him. Wrong guy."

......

The drive back to headquarters took over an hour. They had used the sirens to get through the traffic, but an Army crane had gotten stuck at the tunnel entrance. Coming back into the city was a waste, and if Thomas didn't have to get his paycheck, he would have gone straight home. All his life, he straddled the two worlds of downtown and East Boston, and the distance often seemed wider than the harbor that separated them.

He ran into the locker room and quickly got changed. He was taking Connie to the movies, their first night out together in weeks, and just as important, he had to check on his mother. Since getting out of the hospital, she hadn't had a drink, but her moods wavered between sadness and despondency. She had refused to get out of bed that morning, and with George working overnight, Thomas had to wait until he got home before he could leave. As a result, he had been late for work, and it wasn't the first time. So he got worried when Lieutenant DiMarco walked in.

"Hi, Lieutenant," he said, bent over tying his shoes.

He should have stood to attention, but they had known each other long enough that formalities weren't necessary. Thomas met Nick DiMarco on the boxing team in high school, and while he was two grades behind, they were in the same weight class. The lieutenant was short but had movie-star looks, with a prominent nose and black hair that he always combed back. He was friendly with a touch of arrogance, and all the girls loved him.

"You get that beef burglar that cracked you?" he asked.

"We went by his house. It wasn't him."

The lieutenant's expression sharpened.

"You sure about that?"

Thomas hesitated. He wanted to let the robbery go, but he also felt guilty lying to DiMarco. During his first week on the job, the lieutenant had informed him his brother was on a list of suspects accused of stealing military supplies from the docks. At the time, Thomas had been reluctant to help George, and loyalty was no excuse to overlook a crime. But when DiMarco offered to remove George's name, he agreed, and his brother didn't get arrested.

"It wasn't Vin Labadini," he said, finally.

"Then who was it?"

"It was dark. I don't—"

"We can't let these guineas hoods think they can hit cops and get away with it."

Thomas chuckled. The slur was ironic coming from an Italian.

"I understand," Thomas said.

But he was more embarrassed than ashamed, his sore cheek a reminder of the assault. While Labadini was a thug, he was also a union steward at the shipyard, and Thomas knew it was too early in his career to be making enemies. He had let him go for the sake of his family, but he wouldn't do it again.

"The chief is forming a harbor unit," the lieutenant said, and Thomas was glad he had moved on. "We need volunteers."

"Harbor unit?"

"Yeah. Patrolling the docks, the shipyards. Should be an easy beat, but you might have to work some nights."

"Is that even our jurisdiction?"

"We're at war. There are no jurisdictions. We might work with the Coast Guard and State Police at times."

"Looking for saboteurs?"

DiMarco curled his lips down.

"More like thieves and trespassers. It's precaution mostly, a show of force."

Thomas liked his current assignment and already knew most of the shop owners. He was wary about working nights too, which was the only time he could see Connie.

"I need you," DiMarco added. "We're really short. Cullity and Brown leave for boot camp next week."

After what he had done for George, Thomas knew he couldn't say no. The department was down by a hundred men, the service flag over headquarters now covered with stars.

"Sure."

"Thanks. Go see Sergeant Flynn. He'll fill you in."

CHAPTER EIGHT

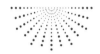

The snow had finally melted, leaving only scattered clumps of wet slush on the streets and sidewalks. All winter, the war had cast a gloom over an already dismal time of year, and the mild temperature was like a gift.

With only six weeks of classes left, Abby was starting to think about summer. But her anticipation this year contained as much fear as it did excitement. They hadn't been back to the cottage since her father died, and she knew it would never be the same. Still, she yearned to go there, her sanctuary by the shore, the source of her most cherished childhood memories.

She walked across the courtyard of Marsh Chapel, a wide plaza on Commonwealth Avenue. With its small gothic church and covered walkway, it had a historic grandeur and was the symbolic center of the campus. In the colder months, the wind off the Charles River was harsh enough to keep people away. But as spring approached, students would again start to gather there to study and socialize.

Frances was sitting on one of the benches, a cigarette in one hand, a sandwich in the other. She had on a red petticoat and gray scarf, her hair in pin curls. Even with her legs not crossed, she looked like a lady, and Abby always admired her grace.

Frances looked up and waved, wiping her mouth with a napkin.

"No lunch?"

"I had two donuts this morning."

"How do you keep that figure?"

Abby was blessed with her mother's build. Except for a few extra pounds her senior year, she never gained any weight.

"What's that you have?" Frances asked.

Abby sat down and reached into her bag, taking out the green jacket of her new uniform. With two chest pockets and brass buttons, it was plain, but soon it would have patches and other insignias.

"The Women's Defense Corps?" Frances said, surprised. "Did Stetson get you to join?"

"No. I joined on my own."

"But did she ask?"

Abby made a sour smile.

"Yes," she said.

"She's been asking all the girls. I've been considering it."

"Won't you? It's fun. Last night we studied maps in case of an evacuation."

"Darling, this is more what I prefer to study," she said.

Abby looked up and saw a young man in sunglasses swaggering across the courtyard. With his broad shoulders and close-cropped hair, he could have been a football player, but he was too boyish for her tastes.

"Our training lieutenant looks like a young Cary Grant," she said, and Frances turned to her.

"Like in *I'm No Angel* or *Blonde Venus*?"

Abby chuckled.

"Not sure. He had on a dress uniform."

"Which reminds me," Frances said, putting the last of her sandwich in tin foil, crumpling it up. "I talked to father about your German professor."

"What did he say?"

Frances looked around and leaned in.

"He was told the man's a special case."

"How do you mean *special case*?"

Frances got distracted again; she was the most skittish girl Abby knew. But this time it was Harold, walking toward them in a long coat, hat, and plaid scarf, a leather satchel over his shoulder. Even from a distance, Abby could tell something was wrong.

"Harold?"

"Glad you're still here," he said, his voice tense. "I've gotta go to New York for a few days."

"You'll miss Latin Night at the Grove," Frances moaned.

"Robert is headed off to the Army. He leaves for Georgia tomorrow evening."

It took Abby a moment to realize who he meant because he hardly ever mentioned his brother.

"You must be proud," Frances said.

He gave her a sharp look, and Abby understood why. With the country at war, everyone had to be patriotic, even if they had doubts.

"He and five of the boys from Cornell joined up. I'm sure it was nothing planned. Probably after a few too many Champagne cocktails."

Like anything serious, important, or urgent, he tried to downplay it. But when he put down his bag and undid the snap, Abby saw his hand shaking.

"If you don't mind," he said, giving her a folder. "For chemistry lab. Kinetics and equilibria, and all that blather."

"When are you back?" she asked.

"Not sure. Maybe Monday."

When he reached for his bag, they both got up.

"Don't be worried, dear," Frances said. "For all we know, Robert will end up doing traffic duty in Devon."

Usually, he had a clever comeback, but this time he was stumped.

"Let us hope."

"Be safe," Abby said, and they all hugged.

"Enjoy Latin Night. Find your Rudolph Valentino."

He backed away, blowing them kisses, and didn't turn around until he was halfway across the courtyard.

"And Happy Easter!" Frances called out.

He raised his arm, a reply that was polite but not enthusiastic.

Considering his mother was dead and his father lived outside the country, Abby knew holidays probably didn't have the same significance. Now his only sibling was going into the service, and he would have to live with that fear and worry. Harold never complained, and his optimism had helped Abby get through some tough times. But as she watched him walk away, she was overcome by a crushing sadness for him. Or was it for all of them? As much as they hid behind the routine of their day-to-day lives, the war loomed like a dark shadow. No one knew what the future would bring.

......

When Abby got off the streetcar, she saw a hazy light coming through the blackout curtains at Gittell's Tailor. With Easter just two days away, the city had made an exception to the curfew, and a lot of businesses were still open, including the barbershop and the butchers at the corner.

Standing at the curb, she waited until there was a clear stretch of no cars. The streets were darker under the dim-out order, and traffic deaths were up as a result. As she crossed over, a half dozen young men were standing in front of the pool hall. When one of them looked over and whistled, she just frowned.

She used to be afraid of the hoodlums on Bennington Street, but not anymore. She didn't know if it was that her brother was a cop or that she was older now and not intimidated by such things. They were always loud, waving at people they knew driving by, passing around cigarettes. While the youths would shoot marbles for nickels on the sidewalk, the older ones were into small-time rackets, running numbers and selling stolen liquor.

East Boston had always been a mix of the respectable and the criminal, and at some point, every child had to choose which path to take. Abby and Thomas had stayed out of trouble, but their brother George did not, and they all worried he would either end up dead or in jail. He had been better since their father died, some proof of the redemption their mother had prayed for. But it didn't change the fact of where they lived, and since starting college, Abby was torn. She would always love her home, but each time she came back, the area seemed a little seedier.

She walked into the small shop, a bell ringing overhead. The air was stuffy and smelled of fabric and cleaning solvents. At the counter, someone spoke with the owner, Mr. Gittell. With his back to her, she couldn't see the man's face, but the moment she heard his voice, she froze.

"May I help you?" Mr. Gittell asked, looking over.

Then the young man turned around.

"Abigail?"

"Hello, Arthur," she said.

When he smiled, she smiled back, more out of politeness because she was still angry that he left. She understood the world had changed since they last saw each other, but it didn't explain why he had never written.

"You're home," she said coldly.

"I arrived last night. Back for two weeks."

He leaned forward like he wanted to hug her, and she moved back just enough to avoid him. Then with a curt smile, she went around and over to the counter.

"I'll need this taken in," she said to the owner, taking her uniform out of the bag. "And this button is fraying."

Mr. Gittell laid the skirt out flat, examining it with his gnarled hands. She didn't know his age, but she was sure he looked older than it, and like a lot of immigrants, he had worked hard all his life. Considering he was so short and stout, she was always surprised Arthur was his son. But family traits were strange, and George and her father had never looked anything alike.

"How much?" he asked in a heavy accent.

"Maybe two inches?"

As they talked, she could almost feel Arthur behind her, and while she wasn't cruel, sometimes it felt good to get back at someone. She watched the owner put pins in the skirt, getting nervous knowing she would have to face Arthur again on her way out. She was saved when a woman walked in with her daughter, and he had to go help them.

"Enough?" Mr. Gittell asked.

"Yes, perfect."

"Ready Friday."

"And what time do you close?"

"Six," he said with a sigh.

No one liked to close early, but the dim-out regulations made it difficult to do business after dark.

He went out back to hang up the skirt, leaving her standing alone. She tried to wait, but hearing Arthur talking to the customer only increased her panic, and she felt ready to burst.

"Thank you," she called out.

Grabbing her things, she hurried toward the door, not looking over. When she got outside, she continued up the sidewalk, and by the time she reached the corner, she wanted to go back, but her pride wouldn't let her. Still, she regretted being so rude, and bitterness always seemed to hurt the embittered person more than the person it was intended for.

"Abigail?!"

Startled, she turned around, and Arthur was coming toward her. He was the only other person besides her mother who used her full name.

"You forgot your ticket," he said, holding it out.

She took it with a sincere smile, realizing she couldn't be angry forever.

"Thank you."

"I saw...the...uh...uniform," he said, sounding as anxious as she felt. "Are you with the WACs?"

"No. Massachusetts Women's Defense Corps."

"That's swell."

"I enlisted last week."

"We all have to do our part."

They stood facing each other in the shadows, and even with all the traffic, the space around them seemed quiet. There was something special about that spot, and they had stood there together on a crisp fall night six months earlier. He had just returned from basic training and was waiting for his assignment. At the time, she thought he looked dashing in his dress uniform and cap. But the luster of war had worn off, and she liked him more in casual clothes.

"I meant to write, you know," he said like he had read her mind. "After Pearl Harbor, they accelerated our training. I got swept up. I didn't even write my father until March."

"It was just a bad time all around."

It sounded like an excuse, but it was true. Her father had just died, and she was starting college.

"It's really good to see you," he said.

"Likewise."

After a short pause, he stepped closer.

"Say, could we go out before I leave?"

She hesitated. While she couldn't say no, she was afraid to say yes, remembering how she felt the last time he went away. But in wartime, there were no guarantees, only risks. Everyone had to wait and hope.

"Okay," she said, finally.

A gentle smile broke across his face, and he took a slight bow. She could tell he was pleased, but he never showed much emotion in public. In a place where a lot of people had no manners or self-restraint, it was a quality she very much admired.

"Can I call you?"

"Yes," she said, nodding.

"Happy Easter."

She looked up with a grin, although she knew he was serious. The fact that she was a Catholic and he was Jewish had always been a complication, but never an obstacle.

"Same to you."

CHAPTER NINE

Abby stood in her white coat, safety goggles on and a glass dropper in hand. The room looked more like a library than a chemistry lab, with arched windows and wood paneling, and she was told it had once been a chapel. The rows of tables were covered with things, beakers, Bunsen burners, and test tubes. Along the walls were jars of solutions, balances, and microscopes. She always liked science, but with the war causing shortages in everything from chlorine to ammonium hydroxide, they had to resort to experiments she did her senior year in high school.

As Abby held the potassium iodide over the hydrogen peroxide, Mrs. Sears stood watching, her expression stern, a pointer in her hand. At one time, she had taught chemistry, but she was now in administration, one of the few female deans at the university. She was filling in for Professor Nyers, who had left suddenly halfway through the semester. No one knew why, and the rumors ranged from that he was called by the Army to advise on chemical war production to that his Hungarian heritage made him an alien enemy.

"Just a few drops, Ms. Nolan."

When the professor walked up behind her, Abby got anxious, or maybe she was anxious already. Since seeing Arthur the day before, she couldn't stop thinking about him, which made it hard to focus. Her hand shook, and she poured too much. The mixture foamed out of control and went all over the table.

"Sorry," she said, reaching for a rag.

Mrs. Sears cleared her throat, some indication of her disapproval, and then continued down the aisle. It was a mild response, and Abby knew she had gotten off easy because she had seen her berate students for lesser mistakes.

Moments later, the corridor filled with activity, the sounds of footsteps and chatter.

"Class is over," the professor announced. "Enjoy your Easter. Please review chapters eleven and twelve before next week."

Everyone took their equipment over to the sinks by the wall, and no one had to wait. A lab that had started with fifteen people was down to eleven. One girl had changed her major after realizing she was allergic to latex, but three young men had left for the military.

As they filed out, Mrs. Sears stood by the door, giving them all cold nods as they left. Abby walked down the hallway and noticed Mrs. Stetson walking toward her. She didn't dislike the professor, but she found her to be awkward and always avoided her when she could. They passed each other with formal smiles, and Abby continued through the atrium where a few students lingered on the benches, smoking and talking.

When she walked into the cafeteria, Frances sat in the corner, and the table looked empty without Harold. She had on a blue crepe dress and matching felt hat, all ready for the Cocoanut Grove. Abby wished Harold was coming, as two women going to a club alone didn't seem right. As she thought about it, she remembered something and froze. She had forgotten to hand in his homework.

Holding up her finger, she spun around and ran back up the staircase, through the lobby, and down the corridor. With afternoon lectures over, the floor was quiet, and in the distance, she saw that the classroom door was closed. She slid to a stop and turned the knob, relieved it wasn't locked.

"Ms. Nolan?!" she heard as she stepped in. "How dare you enter without knocking!"

Abby gasped and looked away. When she glanced back up, Mrs. Sears and Ms. Stetson were standing apart, but the second before they had been embraced in a kiss.

"Sorry, Miss."

Mrs. Sears marched over, her face twisted in a scowl. She was never a pretty woman, but she looked almost evil.

"What's this all about?!"

Abby held out a folder.

"From Harold Merrill...He's in New York...His brother is going into the Army," she said, unable to look her in the eye.

The professor swiped it from her hand and looked through it.

"Very well then," she said, looking up.

Abby didn't know whether to thank her, apologize, or run away. Over at the desk, Ms. Stetson had her hand on her chin, the embarrassment of being caught. More than anything, Abby felt bad for them, and as much as she didn't understand it, she knew love was a mysterious thing. So instead of cowering, she arched her back and smiled.

"Happy Easter, Mrs. Sears, and to you Ms. Stetson."

The professor's expression softened, but only slightly. When she nodded, Abby flew out the door and down the hallway, still in shock but also amused. Growing up, she had been taught the world was a certain way, and it was only after coming to college that she realized all people were unique and everyone had their secrets. Sometimes it was troubling, but there was relief in seeing life for what it really was.

......

"Are you sure they were smooching?"

"It was plain as day," Abby said.

"Girls are more affectionate. Maybe she was consoling her."

Abby laughed, knowing Frances wasn't that naïve.

"Some consolation," she said.

"I'm not surprised by Stetson. She's a dyke if ever I saw one."

"Isn't Mrs. Sears married?"

Frances looked over, eyes raised.

"Maybe she is—"

Abby held out her arm and stopped her from walking into traffic.

"Oh, my," Frances said, putting her hand to her heart.

She was smart but ditzy and, like Harold, she was sophisticated enough to know the difference between roe and caviar, silk and satin. But when it came to the risks and dangers of the city, she was often oblivious, and Abby always wondered how she survived. Frances was independent enough to live away at college and yet still had her laundry sent out. And she never went longer than a week without a visit from her mother.

"So, tell me about this soldier," she said.

"We met last year."

"And you never told me?"

"He left for the Army in October."

"Is he Italian too?"

"Jewish, actually."

"That could get complicated."

Abby frowned, but she couldn't disagree. When it came to the list of petty grievances between groups, religion was near the top. Arthur never brought it up, so neither did she. Some things were better left ignored until they had to be faced. In high school, she knew a girl who dated a Protestant she had met at Hampton Beach. Even though he was still a Christian, it was enough of a difference that both families objected, and the couple ended up fleeing to Florida after graduation.

"Have you made it with him yet?"

"Fran," Abby said, rolling her eyes.

She was no prude, but the topic of sex always made her squirm.

"I'm serious, dear. You said he deploys in a couple weeks? If you want to keep a man, that's one sure way of doing it."

Abby didn't know if *doing it* was meant as a pun, but she appreciated the advice. And while she had always hoped to wait until marriage, the war added urgency to a lot of things that used to require time and caution.

They walked through Park Square, the weather so mild that some of the clubs had their doors open, the sounds of horns and basses blaring. People lingered on the sidewalks, young women dressed in the bright colors of spring, some not wearing coats. Taxis circled the plaza in the evening rush. After a long winter, everyone was out to have some fun.

The streets were busy, but they were also eerily dim because skyscrapers had to keep their lights off. In front of the Statler Building, a dozen sailors waited to get into a bar. In their dress whites, caps, and kerchiefs, they looked dashing, but they were drunk and rowdy, pushing each other, heckling women who passed by.

As they approached a light, Abby grabbed Frances' hand, worried she would walk into traffic again. They crossed and went into Bay Village, a hidden neighborhood of brick townhouses and gas lamps. Its quiet streets were like a sanctuary from the noise of the city. But it didn't last because the moment they turned the corner, there was a crowd in front of the Cocoanut Grove.

They got in line, and Frances checked her hair and makeup in the windows. Around them were people of all ages and backgrounds, from older married couples to college students and servicemen. As one of the most popular nightclubs in town, it was the place where everyone came to meet and mingle.

They had only been there a couple of minutes when Abby heard someone call. Looking over, she saw Sal waving from the door. She knew he had taken the night off because he wasn't in a tuxedo.

She looked at Frances, and they pushed to the front.

"Glad you made it," he said.

He glanced at the doorman, who nodded and moved aside to let them in.

"Why, thank you," Frances said, strutting through.

They walked into the lobby, and Sal took their coats and checked them in. When he came back, he looked at them both with a tight smile.

"Ready for some entertainment?"

"Indeed," Frances said, and it sounded pretentious.

They followed him into the ballroom where on the stage the band was getting ready, a long row of saxes, trumpets, and trombones, the drummer tightening his cymbals. Guests who had arrived early for dinner were finishing up, waiters rushing around to remove plates and utensils before the music started.

Sal took them over to a table in front of the dance floor.

"What can I get ya?" he asked, first looking at Frances.

As charming as he tried to be, he couldn't hide his Boston street slang.

"A Martini would be lovely. On the rocks."

"The same, please," Abby said.

Once he walked away, Frances reached for a cigarette. She hadn't had one for the whole way over, saying it was crass for a lady to smoke in public. She lit it, took a deep drag, and looked around.

"He's debonair, don't you think?" she asked.

"Sal's always been nice."

"I've never dated an Italian."

"He asked you to a show. It's not a marriage proposal."

"Well, at least he's a Catholic—"

Seeing him come down the ramp, Abby cleared her throat, and they stopped talking. He walked over with a waiter who held a tray with three drinks.

"I was wondering how you would carry everything," Frances joked.

Sal grinned and handed them the Martinis. When he sat down next to Frances, it was close enough to be significant, far enough to be proper. He lifted his glass, and as they toasted, the emcee walked out onto the stage, an older man in a tuxedo, his hair slicked back.

"Ladies and gentlemen," he said, adjusting the microphone as he spoke. "We'd like to welcome you to a night of sensuous Samba, raucous Rumba, and mesmerizing Merengue. For those who aren't familiar with the swings of Latin dance, our very own Grovettes will lead the way..."

With a drum roll, a line of chorus girls filed out in skimpy skirts and sparkling headbands.

"Now let's hear it for D'Arnez and his Cuban orchestra!"

Everyone clapped, and the lights dimmed. The band started to play, the horn section blaring. People started to get up, couples in evening attire walking to the dance floor hand in hand.

"Whaddya say?" Sal asked, and he stood up and held out his hand to Frances.

She looked over to Abby, who encouraged her with a smile.

"Delighted," she said with a curtsy.

After they walked off, Abby heard some soldiers drinking and shouting a few tables away. When she noticed one winking at her, she reached for her glass and sank into the chair. She wished Harold was with her, knowing obnoxious guys wouldn't usually bother a girl who was with someone.

For the next hour, Frances and Sal danced, coming back only for a cigarette or to sip their drinks. Abby was impressed by his moves, and she could tell Frances was too. Her mother always said Italians were too passionate, lacking the dignity and discipline of Northern Europeans. But Abby admired any man who could dance, and she wondered if Arthur could do the swing or foxtrot.

"Whew," Frances said, sweaty and out of breath.

Sal lowered her onto her chair, and she looked into her glass, now empty, the ice melted.

"Another?" he asked.

"Please."

He called over to a skinny waiter who was taking orders from the soldiers. As they cried out drink names, he wrote on a small pad, and it was obvious they were teasing him. By the time he finished and came over, he was flustered.

"Mr. Ciarlone," he said, wiping his forehead.

"Three more Martinis, all on the rocks."

"Yes, sir."

He scurried off, leaving Sal gazing over at the men. With the band on a short break, it was quiet enough to hear them, and they were getting rowdy.

"How long have you worked here?" Frances asked.

"Six years," he said, distracted. "I started as a busboy."

"A busboy?"

"Waitin' tables, gettin' booze from the cellar. All that jazz."

The moment she got a cigarette, he took out a gold lighter. As he held up the flame, she pursed her lips with a sensual smile.

"So you two live on the same street?" she asked, blowing out the smoke.

"Next door, actually."

"Then you must be thick as thieves."

"Naw, not really," he said, an awkward subject because their families didn't talk. "My mother ain't the friendliest sort…"

It almost sounded like an apology, but Abby never blamed him for his mother's coldness. He always waved, smiled, and said hello, and the only reason she didn't know him better was that he was always working.

"She struggles with English," he added.

"But you're still neighbors."

"Soon to be in-laws."

Abby froze. At first, she thought she misheard him until she peered up, and he was staring back.

"In-laws?" Frances asked, a flutter in her voice.

Abby wasn't shocked Sal knew, but she never expected him to bring it up there.

"My brother Thomas…and his cousin," she said. "They plan to wed."

Realizing she was stumbling, she looked at him to explain.

"He's engaged to my cousin Concetta," he said, pronouncing it as an Italian would. "She's been staying with us since last summer."

Frances' mouth dropped open.

"That's lovely," she said, turning to Abby. "You never told me."

"It's a bit of a secret."

"Well, the secret is out."

They were interrupted when the waiter returned with their drinks. By now, Frances had a glow on her face, either tipsy or enamored or some combination of both. When the band started to play, she put out her cigarette and got up.

"Whaddya say?" she said, looking at Sal with her hands on her hips.

"I'd say I'm game."

Frances waved her fingers at Abby, and they went back out to the dance floor. Abby was happy for her, knowing good men were rare, especially during war. Sal was gruff, but he seemed like a gentleman, and being kind meant more than money or refinement.

Suddenly, there was shouting.

She looked over, and the soldiers were all standing. At a table across the aisle, a dozen other guys faced them. She had been around enough tense situations to know the look of men before they brawled, and she hoped the waiters could get to them before it happened. But they didn't.

Both groups charged at each other, colliding in a flurry of kicks and punches. The band stopped, and employees ran over, even some guests, all trying to break it up. Abby jumped up from her seat, her heart pounding. Even though she hated violence, she always got some small thrill in seeing a fight.

"My goodness," Frances said, rushing over.

Through the chaos, Abby could see Sal throwing men back, and as they watched, Frances clutched her arm tighter.

It was over in less than a minute, but the damage was done, tables overturned, broken glass everywhere. With a basement bar and two separate lounges, the club was sprawling enough that a lot of patrons probably didn't even notice.

Cops rushed in from the lobby, people quickly moving out of their way. Sal came over, and while he looked agitated, Abby could tell he was trying to hide it.

"I'm sorry. I'm gonna have to straighten this out."

"No worries," Frances said. "I've got to be up early. I'm headed home for Easter."

She sounded calm, almost oblivious to what had just happened.

"Carlo will get you a cab," he said, calling to one of the waiters.

As they turned to go, Frances surprised everyone by leaning up and kissing him on the cheek.

"Thanks for a lovely night," she said.

Even in all the confusion, it was a poignant moment. With a bow, he looked into her eyes, and Abby got a twinge of jealousy.

"It was my pleasure."

CHAPTER TEN

St. Mary's Church was only two blocks away, but it took twenty minutes to get there. Thomas held his mother's arm as they went, and he never realized how mental distress could affect the body because she looked fine.

They passed a boarded-up house, water dripping off the gutters from melting snow. The only time he walked around was at night with Connie, and sometimes he forgot how rundown the streets looked during the day. There were even a few abandoned homes, something he never saw as a child. The depression had devastated cities everywhere, making people go bankrupt, forcing small shops to close.

Mrs. Nolan was unsteady, especially going over curbs, and each time Abby tried to help, she would wave her daughter away, saying she didn't want to *look like an invalid*. George followed behind them, hands in his pockets and dressed in the only suit he owned, a gray jacket and trousers, one of their father's silk ties. His shoes were from his Confirmation, now scuffed up and worn. Thomas grinned, thinking how they looked like a ragtag bunch. Considering he still had bruises on his face, Abby was the only normal one, wearing a long-sleeved dress and a pillbox hat.

George had offered to drive, but their mother insisted on walking, something she had done with her husband for over twenty years. When they were kids, Thomas and his siblings went with them every Sunday, dressed in their best outfits. They would giggle quietly in the pews, smiling at each other, mystified by the strange language of the priest. As they got older, they went less often, and after their father died, they stopped altogether. Out of everyone in the family, their mother had always been the most devout, but her husband's relationship with religion was more complicated. Raised in orphanages across Ireland, Mr. Nolan had plenty to begrudge about God and fate.

As they approached the church, there was a crowd out front, people waiting to go up the granite front steps. They got in line, smiling at friends and neighbors they had known all their lives. By Catholic standards, the building was never that big, but to Thomas, it seemed even smaller now.

For most of its history, St. Mary's was the Irish parish, but half the congregation was now Italian. Since the last time they'd been there, that number had grown, and Thomas could see in his mother's eyes the silent resentment of her people's fading significance. Her father had helped found the parish, raising the money and petitioning the Archdiocese. As a boy, Thomas heard stories about how the foundation stones were taken by horse cart from a quarry in Everett.

Once inside, they walked slowly up the aisle, the rows packed with families. Women were dressed in the bright colors of spring, men in conservative suits, and the scent of cologne and perfume was strong. People whispered, many in Italian, the solemn excitement of the holiday.

"Catherine?" someone said.

Thomas looked over and saw their neighbor Mrs. McNulty with her husband. Although his mother's age, she had married younger, and their children were already out of the house.

"Happy Easter, Nora," Mrs. Nolan said.

When Mrs. McNulty moved over, she bowed and slid into the pew, Thomas and his siblings following. He sat for a few minutes in uncomfortable anticipation, his collar tight and his neck raw from a bad shave. After the War Production Board announced that razor production would be reduced, all the shops sold out of blades, and he had been using the same one for two weeks. He never liked formal events, and the only thing he looked forward to was seeing Connie all dressed up.

Finally, Father Ward walked out, clearing his throat before asking everyone to rise. Thomas glanced over to Abby, and she grinned. George was at the end, slumped forward with his hands on the bench, a look of mild annoyance on his face. Thomas remembered how when they were young, his brother liked church, and they were both altar boys.

The organ sounded and the Mass began, and Thomas was surprised to find himself listening. The homily was about love and sacrifice in the face of suffering, and the implication was obvious. But the war didn't need to be emphasized, and throughout the rows, Thomas saw blue star pins on the lapels of women, indicating they had a son in the military. So far, the Nolans didn't know anyone who had died, but East Boston had already had casualties, including two killed at Pearl Harbor and one in the Philippines.

They all got up for Communion, Mrs. Nolan refusing Thomas' help, and after a closing salutation, the service was over. For the first time in Thomas' life, it felt quick and, just like the size of the church, the proportions of things seemed to have changed with age. Either way, he was glad he came because, as conflicted as he was about religion, he knew it was a bad time to abandon it.

As they stepped out of the pew, Connie was coming toward them with her aunt and cousins. Mrs. Ciarlone wore black in the tradition of a widow; Chickie had on a dress with ruffles, a flower in her hair. When their eyes met, Connie smiled, and by now their affair was like a private joke. They merged in the aisle, and Thomas walked beside her, imagining the day they would be going in the other direction, toward the altar.

Outside, the sun was strong, and people gathered on the sidewalk. Mrs. McNulty came over with her husband, a quiet man who always stood with his hands clasped.

"Lovely service," she said to Mrs. Nolan.

"T'was."

"I didn't see the O'Haras."

"I believe they go to their son's house in Haverhill. He's got three boys now."

"Then he's got his hands full."

"How is Paul?" Mrs. Nolan asked.

"He and his wife just moved to Bethesda, Maryland. He's still with the Department of State."

"Is Teresa still teaching in Watertown?"

Mrs. McNulty glanced at her husband, who responded with a tight grin.

"Actually, she's taken a leave of absence. She enlisted in the *Women's Army Auxiliary Corps*."

Mrs. Nolan raised her eyes, but none of them were surprised. The McNulty kids were always go-getters, staying out of trouble and never getting caught up in the mischief of East Boston.

"You must be so proud."

"As should you," Mrs. McNulty said, then she looked at Thomas. "I hear you're keeping the country safe on the home front?"

While he appreciated the praise, he didn't know what to say.

"Things are quiet at the moment, thank—"

He stopped before saying *God*, knowing how his mother's generation still considered the word blasphemy.

"These are trying times," Mrs. McNulty said, and everyone nodded grimly. "Katherine, there's a meeting with the *Catholic Women's Guild* on Tuesday night. We're considering ways to help with the war effort. Won't you come?"

Mrs. Nolan looked at her children, as if for permission. But it was mostly Thomas and Abby because George was never good for advice. Thomas smiled, knowing only she could make the decision. She had been sitting in the house all winter, and there was no better remedy for depression than the company of other people.

"Go on, Ma," George said, impressing everyone with his words of encouragement.

Finally, she looked up.

"Thank you. I'd love to."

......

By the time they finished eating, it was dark. In the past, Easter was a huge family celebration, and now it felt empty. Thomas didn't know if it was their father's absence or the war. When he was young, his aunt and uncle would come down from Maine, and all the neighbors stopped by for dessert, the men playing croquet in the yard while the women talked in the dining room. His mother only drank wine back then, a glass or two and no more, offsetting her husband's alcoholism by her example of moderation. Mr. Nolan gave it up when Thomas and Abby were in second grade, but his wife was close to taking his place before her doctor ordered her to quit. Of all her accomplishments as a mother and a wife, Thomas was the proudest of her for stopping, knowing it was hard to live without the comfort of alcohol.

After dinner, he went upstairs to change out of his suit, never feeling comfortable in formal clothes. When he came back down, George was in the parlor listening to the radio, and his sister was helping clean up. There were pies on the kitchen table, one their mother made and another that Abby had brought from work.

Grabbing a fork, Thomas scooped up some of the rhubarb and couldn't believe how sweet it was. With a sugar shortage, people were using corn syrup and even honey, which was twice the price.

"Use a plate like a civilized person!" Mrs. Nolan exclaimed.

She tried to smack him, but he laughed and dodged her.

"Is this from the bakery?" he asked.

"No. I made it."

"Tastes like real sugar."

"It is. Your brother got some for me."

His expression soured, and he stopped chewing. East Boston had always had a black market, but buying stolen goods in wartime was more than a crime, it was treachery, especially if they were scarce. If George hadn't learned his lesson, Thomas regretted getting him out of trouble before.

He got distracted when he saw Abby at the back door. He went over to open it, and she came in with the slop bucket.

"Your girl is out there," she whispered.

Seeing Connie in the yard, he walked out and went over, the ground wet and muddy. He tried to tiptoe, but he could never sneak up on her because she was as alert as a fox.

When he got to the fence, Connie strutted over, her arms crossed.

"Buona Pasqua," she said.

Thomas grinned; he loved it when she spoke Italian.

"Where's your aunt?"

"She went to her husband's grave."

"She didn't take you?"

"I didn't want to go," she said, always quick with a comeback. "I've had enough of death and dying."

Chickie came out in a baggy coat and rubber boots. She had a pile of things in her hands, and Thomas watched as she scurried over and dumped it all into a wooden crate.

"What's all that?" he said.

"For a scrap metal drive. My aunt gave her some old cans and biscuit tins."

"Can't build many tanks with that," Thomas joked.

Connie smiled, and they looked over to Chickie, who was squatting in the dirt, arranging the items. Whatever her limitations, she was always determined. Thomas remembered how when Sal built her a swing set, she practiced day and night until she finally got it.

"I have to take it to her school," Connie said. "Won't you come?"

"On Easter night?"

"I promised her. They weigh it every Monday."

"You really want me to go, or do you just need someone to carry the box?"

"Maybe both?" she said, expression both sensuous and sarcastic.

"I'll meet you at the end of the street?"

"Ten minutes. I have to get her bath ready."

When she called, Chickie came right over, waving to Thomas with a toothy grin. They went back inside, and he walked over to the shed, searching in the darkness for some of his father's tools to add to the collection.

Since the start of the war, the demand for iron and steel had been increasing, and the government called on all citizens to donate any unwanted metal. The first things to be salvaged were old automobiles and industrial junk, followed by household items like pots and pans, plumbing and light fixtures. What started as a small campaign had turned into a race for victory, with schools and civic organizations competing to collect the most. Even at police headquarters, they had a scrap heap in the parking lot.

Thomas grabbed a couple of old screwdrivers, a mallet, and the rusted hand drill he had been taught to use as a boy. While they could have been keepsakes, he wasn't sentimental, and his father always had more tools than he needed. Mr. Nolan spent hours in the shed, smoking his pipe while he built everything from a workbench to a cuckoo clock.

Thomas walked back into the house, and his mother was asleep in the recliner, the music on low. Upstairs, he could hear George moving around in the bedroom, and he knew Abby was in the bath because the water was running. Reaching for his coat and hat, he opened the door and slipped out.

As he came down the sidewalk, Connie was already at the corner, the crate on the ground beside her. He picked it up and was surprised at how heavy it was.

"You really think you could carry this the whole way?"

"With a strong man, I could," she said.

He laughed, and they started down Saratoga Street. He didn't know if it was due to the war or the holiday, but the neighborhood was dead quiet. Young men were leaving every day, and he knew at least a dozen families whose sons had enlisted. At times, he felt guilty not joining up, but as a police officer, his conscience was eased in knowing he was, like Mrs. McNulty said, *keeping the country safe on the home front.*

They turned onto the next street where, in the distance, he saw the brick building of the John Cheverus school. He and his siblings had gone there as kids, walking together every morning with their books and lunch boxes. In fifth grade, he had his first kiss with a girl named Louisa under a giant elm tree that had since been cut down. But it didn't ruin the memories, and one of the strange things about living in the place where he grew up was that everywhere he went he saw ghosts of himself.

"I didn't know Chickie went here," he said, as they approached.

Connie glanced over.

"Where do you think she goes each day?"

Thomas thought for a moment, but he had never considered it. Since moving in, the Ciarlones had been strangers, and he had never given them much thought until he met Connie.

He thought he heard someone and stopped.

"What's wrong?" she asked, but he didn't answer.

Putting down the box, he crept over to the schoolyard fence, and his instincts were good because he saw movement in the darkness. He grabbed the iron pickets and leaped over.

"Hey!" he shouted.

In the dim light, he watched three boys turn around, their arms full. And there behind them was a mound of scrap metal, radiators, sewing machines, sinks, and furnace grates.

"Get the hell out of there!"

For a moment, they hesitated, and he didn't know if it was out of fear or defiance. But when he darted towards them, they dropped everything and scattered, the clank of pipes and other things echoing in the night.

"Who was that?" Connie asked, rushing over.

"Kids."

"Kids?"

"Probably looking for copper or lead," he said, out of breath. "They can get good money for it now."

Wiping his hands, he turned and saw her holding the crate. She walked over to the pile and dumped everything out onto it.

"It seems so little," she said, staring into the darkness.

"Every bit helps."

"To make ships and tanks."

He never liked sarcastic women, but somehow it fit her.

"Leave that," he said, and she tossed the crate.

He took her hand, and they headed up the road that looped back to their street.

"Have you told your mother?"

Thomas glanced over, struck by a faint guilt. Every time they were out she asked, and he never had a good answer.

"Not yet," he said.

"When Thomas?"

With his mother sick, she had been patient, but he knew she wouldn't wait forever. They had been engaged for six months, and while men were never as eager as women, he wanted to be married too.

"Soon. I promise."

She responded with a quick smile that couldn't hide her disappointment.

They continued up the hill, and he could see the shapes of the massive oil tanks along the flats of Chelsea Creek. The Naval fuel depot was kept dark to protect it from enemy planes or saboteurs, and everyone in East Boston worried about what would happen if it ever exploded.

The route that seemed long when he was young only took a couple of minutes. As they got close to home, Thomas let go of Connie's hand, as much out of caution as to calm his libido. It was hard being alone with her without intimacy, but he loved her for more than just sex.

They parted with a kiss, and he waited for her to go inside first. Standing alone, he looked up and down the street. Compared to past Easters, it was almost deserted, and he missed those days when all the kids would come out to play after dinner. At one time, he had dozens of friends on their street, the McNultys and the Gallaghers, the Ianocconis and the Franchettes. Most of the guys his age were now gone, away in the service, working in the city, or living somewhere in the suburbs. And although he sometimes felt ashamed for still being at home, he would never leave his mother, or his sister, until he knew they were safe.

After a few minutes, he walked up the front steps and went in. His mother was still in the chair, her eyes closed, arms crossed like she was in prayer. Like everyone, she looked the most at peace when she was sleeping.

He hung his jacket on the hook and then went over and got the shawl off the couch, draping it over her and tucking it under her arms. Spring had arrived, but the nights were still chilly. He watched her for a moment, feeling a strange relief in realizing that, despite all their misfortunes, they were very lucky in many ways. Leaning over, he kissed her on the forehead, and she stirred but didn't wake. Then he blew out the candle and went upstairs to bed.

CHAPTER ELEVEN

Thomas stood at the bow of the small boat with the wind in his face. He had been on harbor patrol for two weeks, and the most exciting part was cruising around the waterfront, from Chelsea to Charlestown to South Boston. It was a token show of force for a port that was already heavily protected. Even the private shipyards were now all under contract with the Department of Defense, guarded by MPs.

Thomas always liked being out on the water, remembering how when he was young, a man from church used to take him and his brother fishing in Winthrop Bay. Around him were six other police officers, and two more in the cabin. As they left the Charlestown Navy Yard, they passed a Liberty Ship that had just been launched. Along the sides, men hung from ropes painting the hull. On the deck, welders were working on a hatchway, others on an air scoop. Aside from some finishing touches, the vessel looked ready to sail, with guns on the fore and aft decks. Soon it would be filled with young troops, making the dangerous trip across the Atlantic.

Thomas couldn't think too much about the war without feeling a subtle urgency that, while not quite guilt, wasn't contentment either. Everywhere he went, he was praised for his work, and with the whole country now under threat, people had a newfound love for law enforcement. He understood that someone had to defend the home front, but he felt like he wasn't doing enough, or worse, that he was missing out on some great adventure. He had considered enlisting, something he didn't even mention to his colleagues, and went so far as to talk with a major at the recruiting station at North Station. But in the end, he couldn't leave with his mother so unstable, and while he could always rush his marriage to Connie, he dreaded the thought of making her a widow for a second time.

As they pulled into the pier, the seawall had barbed wire, and signs were posted everywhere: TRESPASSING FORBIDDEN PER US ARMY. It was one of the few facilities that still allowed small craft, and while technically public, the war had blurred all distinctions between civilian and military property.

They got off and continued down the dock. Some lobstermen nodded as they passed, but with the harbor now consumed by wartime activity, most commercial fishing had moved north to Nahant and Gloucester.

When they came out to Border Street, they split up and went in opposite directions. It was an easy post, patrolling the waterfront for anything suspicious. One side of the street was lined with wooden tenements, the other with wharves and empty lots. Lieutenant DiMarco had done Thomas a favor by ending the shift in East Boston because it was closer to home. The area was nostalgic too, and as he approached the West Gate of East Boston Works, he remembered his time working there.

The guardhouse was still there, but with the expansion of the shipyard, they had built a warehouse beside it. Across the street was the building where he first saw Connie, who walked out one afternoon with a line of coworkers. Once a manufacturer of ladies' hosiery, the factory had gotten a contract to make military uniforms the summer before. She had worked there until Pearl Harbor when the owners said they could no longer employ non-citizens. Now she was at the General Electric plant, boxing light bulbs as they came off the assembly line. The work was cleaner than sewing, but it still left her hands dry and cracked.

A car horn honked, and Thomas flinched. He startled more than he used to, and the other cops seemed to notice because they chuckled. When it beeped again, he looked over and saw George stopped at the corner, his arm hanging out the car window, a cigarette between his teeth.

"Need a lift?"

Thomas looked at his watch—he still had a half hour left.

"Go on," the sergeant said.

"You sure?"

"Scram. We've got you covered."

"Will tell you if we find any Krauts," one of them joked.

When Thomas hesitated, it was more that he didn't want to accept a favor from his brother than fear of shirking his duty. But after a long day, a ride home was easier than taking the trolley. So he crossed the street and got in, taking off his hat and nodding to George. They drove away in silence, and Thomas could have gone the whole way without talking.

George lit a cigarette before offering Thomas one, some indication of his twisted sense of courtesy.

"No thanks."

"I heard you helped out Labadini?"

"Who?" Thomas said, looking over.

"Vin Labadini. You didn't snitch."

"Who told you that?"

"Just somebody."

Thomas frowned and stared out the window.

"We had the wrong guy, is all," he mumbled.

They had always kept their personal lives separate, and he wanted it that way. There was a time when they were friends, but it was so far back he could hardly remember it. Somewhere around middle school, George drifted towards a rougher crowd, and Thomas never forgave him for it. Either way, he had more reason now than ever not to gossip, knowing how local criminals were always trying to get in good with cops.

They went through Maverick Square which even in the spring sunlight looked dismal with the rundown buildings and nickel-and-dime shops. A lady with a shopping carriage darted into the street, and George hit the brakes.

"Damn gypsy," he said.

Hearing something rattle, Thomas glanced back and noticed a paper bag behind the seat. While he didn't say anything, he got a creepy feeling. Everything about his brother made him suspicious.

When they got to the house, Mrs. McNulty was taking out the trash, and a few doors down, the Braga twins were playing hopscotch on the sidewalk. Sometimes it was hard to believe there was even a war on, and Thomas loved the warm familiarity of the people and places he knew, if only because he knew it wouldn't last.

They got out, and Thomas stopped to wait for him.

"Go on," George said. "I gotta bring some stuff in."

Thomas gave him a cold look and continued up the steps. When he walked in, he smelled something cooking and went to the kitchen. A pot was simmering on the stove, but he didn't see his mother. Her life had become so predictable that anytime she wasn't where he expected her, he got worried.

"Hello, love."

He looked over, and she was at the dining room table, sheets of white cardboard spread across it. Her sleeves were rolled up, and there was a marker in her hand.

"What're you doing?" he asked.

"Making posters."

"Posters?"

"For War Bonds. I went to the Catholic Women's Guild meeting. We're starting a bond drive."

He gave her a sideways glance, almost like he didn't believe her. When he was young, she was active with many organizations, from the PTA to the East Boston Civic Association. Over the years, she had gotten less involved, and after her husband died, she stopped going out altogether.

"Need any help?"

"Could you check the stew?"

He walked over to the pot and dipped the wooden spoon inside. He stirred it and had a taste, the carrots and potatoes soft and delicious. Now that he was on the harbor patrol, he no longer passed by shops and diners that would feed him. It was something he was so used to that he kept forgetting to bring a lunch, and he was starving.

"Save some for the rest of us."

He looked up, and Abby was in the doorway, dressed in a military outfit, an olive-green skirt and jacket, white shirt and tie. He was so surprised he just stared.

"The Massachusetts Women's Defense Corps," she said before he could ask.

"Doesn't she look dazzling?"

"That's not the word I was thinking," he said.

Abby frowned and smoothed out her jacket, adjusting the gold pin on her lapel, an eagle with some letters.

"Do you even know what we do?" she asked.

"Get in the way of real work."

He smiled to let her know he was joking; he felt no personal scorn toward the group. But others did, and just that week he had heard a captain complain that they wanted to use headquarters for training. The MWDC had been around since before the war, started by an heiress and established by the state legislature. While some people didn't like the idea of women being in a military role, Thomas didn't care, and he supported anyone who helped the cause.

"Someone go tell your brother it's time for dinner."

"I gotta change," Thomas said.

When he got upstairs, he could hear George in the bathroom. He went into the bedroom and hung his uniform in the closet, locked up his pistol. He walked over to his brother's bed, which was a mess of magazines, clothes, beer bottles, and wrappers. There was an ashtray on the windowsill, but after an argument that almost turned into a fight, George agreed to only smoke when Thomas was out.

The room couldn't have been a better symbol of their different personalities. Thomas was disciplined, and as a boy, he lined up his toy cars, stacked his comic books, and folded his pants. George was a slob, and he would lose his shoes so often that, after many warnings, their father once made him walk to school in his socks. They had one desk between them, but only Thomas used it because George always did his homework on the floor.

As he looked around, he got a twinge of guilt. Despite their disagreements, he always respected his brother's area. But when he saw the paper bag from the car next to the radio, he picked it up. Peering inside, he saw a dozen crystal candle holders and was filled with a quiet rage.

"What the hell are you doing?"

He spun around, and George was in the doorway.

"What the hell am I doing?!" he snapped. "What the hell is this?"

George stormed over but didn't try to take it. The question of who was tougher had been settled long ago.

"It's for ma. For her birthday."

"For ma?"

"A British frigate came in today. We traded things with the crew. We always do. I gave some limey a box of cigarettes."

Their eyes locked, but it was a good explanation, and one Thomas hadn't anticipated. With a subtle frown, he rolled up the top of the bag and put it back.

Once George left, he got some clean trousers and a shirt, which both smelled of soap. While he appreciated Abby helping their mother with the laundry, she never rinsed it enough. He looked for some socks but didn't have any, so he went over to George's dresser, knowing their things sometimes got mixed up. When he opened the drawer, he found a pair and also noticed a manila envelope.

"Dinner," his mother called, and he knew they were all waiting.

"Be right down!"

As he stared at the envelope, he was torn. He had already been wrong about the sconces, and for his own pride, he didn't want to be wrong again. But his suspicions about his brother never ended, and he had to look.

Opening it up, he took out a document and unfolded it. At the top, he saw APPLICATION FOR ENLISTMENT and his heart sank. He stared at the form, reading the lines, so stunned his only thought was *my brother isn't 5'11"*.

"C'mon," he heard Abby yell. "We're starved."

He put it away and ran back downstairs. With his mother's poster project, space at the table was tight. Thomas was surprised to see George was in their father's chair with a Pabst Blue Ribbon, which, with metal scarce, now came in bottles. At one time, their mother would have been outraged. For months after her husband's death, she pretended as if nothing had changed, still buying the Sunday paper no one else read, the Quaker Oats oatmeal that only he ate.

Abby brought in the stew, still wearing her uniform skirt but not the jacket and tie. They filled their bowls, and for the first few minutes, no one spoke.

Dinners seemed like some kind of meditation on the seriousness of the times. In the past, the conversations were about the news, sports, and school. Now they couldn't even talk about local things without it somehow being about the war.

"I heard Mrs. Fazio's son signed up for the Navy," Mrs. Nolan said.

"*Enlisted*, they call it," Abby said.

"So now you're an expert?" Thomas snickered.

"The Women's Defense Corps is nothing to scoff at," their mother said.

Abby stuck out her tongue at Thomas.

"We get our posts at the end of the month," she said.

"What? Bake sales and tea parties?"

"Mind yourself, Thomas. We all have to do our part."

While her tone was firm, it wasn't scolding because they always teased each other.

"Which is why I patrol the harbor," Thomas said.

Abby just frowned.

"You get paid for that."

The whole time they talked, George was quiet, which wasn't unusual. As the black sheep of the family, he was never very sociable. If he wasn't out with his friends, he was alone in the bedroom, and the only time he came down was for dinner or to get a beer. Thomas realized that, in many ways, he didn't really know his brother. But this was a different kind of silence, one born of a deep doubt and uneasiness, and the only reason he recognized it was that he felt it too. It had only been twenty minutes since he learned that George had enlisted, and already he regretted they didn't talk more.

"You know, your father always wanted to join the American Army."

Thomas looked up at his mother.

"Then why didn't he?"

"Ha," Mrs. Nolan said. "How could he? He didn't have time. The war was over in nineteen months."

"He wouldn't have met you," Abby said.

Thomas smiled, but he was distracted. When he looked over, George finished his beer, putting down the bottle with just enough force to get everyone's attention. Thomas knew then what he was going to do and had to stop him. Their mother had had enough heartbreak for a lifetime and telling her that her oldest son was going off to war was going to require some planning and tact.

"Ma?" George said, and she turned. "I went to the recruit—"

"I've asked Concetta to marry me," Thomas blurted.

Confused, she looked back and forth between them.

"We're engaged to be married," Thomas said, and when her eyes landed on him, he knew he had avoided a catastrophe.

"Marry?"

He nodded, his nostrils flaring from emotion.

"She said yes."

Everyone sat stunned, and Thomas didn't look over, knowing his brother was probably fuming. George couldn't say anything, of course, because he didn't know Thomas had seen his enlistment papers. But it was still a snub, and all their lives Thomas had stolen his thunder, although it was never intentional. Whatever their old rivalries, he did it for their mother, and they would tell her another time.

"Darling," Mrs. Nolan said.

She stood up, came around the table, and wrapped her arms around him. For months, he had dreaded telling her, afraid of how she would react. She had always had her prejudices, and the fact that Mrs. Ciarlone was unfriendly only seemed to confirm them. But the world had changed, and he was glad to see she was changing with it. At a time when Americans of all types were dying, squabbles about ethnicity, religion, or even social class seemed petty.

As she hugged him, he patted her arms, and when he looked at Abby, she had tears in her eyes.

"So you're happy?"

"Why wouldn't I be? It's the best news in ages," she said. "She's a darling girl, I'm sure. Always says hello."

She started to collect the plates, no better sign of her joy, and he felt a tremendous relief. He had told his siblings after he gave Connie the engagement ring back in the fall. Abby was thrilled, and George just shrugged his shoulders and gave some halfhearted congratulations. But when Thomas glanced over, his brother held up his thumb with a tight smile. Considering all their years of hostility, his approval meant more than anyone's.

"Have you thought about a date?" Mrs. Nolan asked, walking into the kitchen.

"Maybe…early fall?"

They all got up to help with the dishes.

"*Maybe early fall*. You don't sound so sure, son."

"She'll have to see when she can get the time off."

"And what about the reception?"

Thomas hesitated, Abby watching with anticipation.

"I was thinking maybe Point Shirley."

Just the mention of it made them all stop. Standing at the sink, their mother put down her rag and turned around. With his new job, Thomas could have afforded a party at some downtown restaurant, or maybe the New Ocean House in Swampscott. But the summer cottage was a place they all loved, the source of their earliest memories together, and the one thing that never seemed to change. He had never considered having it anywhere else.

"That's a lovely idea."

CHAPTER TWELVE

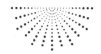

Abby knelt over the victim, who lay lifeless on the damp grass.

"Check the pulse!" the girl beside her said.

Abby's heart pounded, and she was shaking all over.

"Head wound, fractured tibia," she said, doing a quick assessment.

Fumbling with the bandages, she wrapped them around the wounds and secured them with safety pins.

"Faster!"

Abby peered up, frowning. They were supposed to be working together.

Seconds later, someone ran over with a stretcher, and they hoisted the victim onto it. Abby looked down at her, a young woman about her age, her lips red and her face dappled in mist.

"Ready?"

They each took a side and then counted to three. But when they lifted the stretcher, Abby's hand slipped, and the girl hit the ground.

"Ouch!" she said, jumping up.

Abby looked across at her partner, and they burst out laughing.

"Time's up!"

The whistle blew, and everyone stopped what they were doing. The instructor waved them over, and they stood in a circle. Considering the rain, the turnout was good; it was always hard to know how many people would show up for training and other exercises. Except for the college students, most women had children, and a few even had jobs. The MWDC leadership tried to be strict, Major Ward even threatening expulsion for members who had gone "AWOL." But like any volunteer group, they couldn't force them to do anything, an added humiliation for an organization that was still struggling to get respect.

After a short pep talk, they were all dismissed. As they walked off the field, the stadium was eerily empty, and the Boston Braves wouldn't be back for another week. On the sidelines, Ms. Stetson was standing with the Major and two other women, and Abby tried to avoid her.

"Ms. Nolan," the professor called.

Abby cringed but went towards them.

"Afternoon, Miss."

"This is Major Dunbar from the Quincy unit. And you know Major Ward."

They acknowledged Abby with polite smiles and then continued talking. The leaders of the MWDC were all the same, middle-aged ladies with traditional hair and plain makeup, more suited to Back Bay tea parties or Park Square luncheons than field training in the mud. A few were spinsters and no doubt queer, but most were the wives of bankers and stockbrokers. They were drawn from the city's social elite, and Mrs. Nolan had grumbled that *only Protestants have the time and money to raise their own armies.* Abby ignored her mother's hang-ups about status, knowing that just because someone was rich didn't make their efforts any less worthy.

"Let's not turn injuries into fatalities," Ms. Stetson joked.

Abby blushed, not realizing the professor had seen her drop the stretcher.

"They're slippery in the rain."

"German bombers fly in all weather."

When Ms. Stetson smiled, Abby smiled back.

"Yes, Miss."

"Carry on."

Abby walked away and went under the stands to get her bag. Leaving the gate, she passed two parked ambulances, *Massachusetts Women's Defense Corps* written across the front in white decals. While they looked impressive, their unit struggled to find drivers because so few of the girls had licenses.

As she came out to the street, someone called her name, and she turned to see Frances, dressed in a pink raincoat and holding up an umbrella that, while not the same color, was close enough to match.

"Don't you look sporting?" Frances said.

Abby looked down at her uniform, now decorated with two small MWDC patches, one on each lapel. The jacket was comfortable, but the leather belt wasn't, and her ribs were sore from stooping in it.

"I'd say you're the sporting one."

"A girl's gotta play the part to get the role."

Abby squinted. Sometimes Frances was more cryptic than she had to be.

"Sal is taking me to the Parker House tonight," she explained, and Abby raised her eyes.

"That's terrific."

"Come," she said, taking Abby by the arm. "I've got bigger news."

They stepped into the doorway of a building, and Frances got a cigarette from her purse, looking around before lighting it.

"I know you're still worried about your professor," she said, taking out an envelope too. "Which is why I got you this."

Abby stared but didn't take it.

"Go on," Frances said.

Opening it, Abby took out a sheet of paper, and she could tell it was a carbon copy. It had a government seal, and WARRANT FOR ARREST across the top. She had always been intimidated by legal forms and documents, which seemed written to keep ordinary people from understanding them.

Beneath the heading, she saw the name and address of her professor. She sometimes forgot he went by *Doctor* Bauermeister, a title that sounded too formal for such a gentle man.

"Violations of the Alien Registration Act," Abby said, looking up.

"Read on, dear," Frances said.

...It has been determined that Walter F. Bauermeister is the brother of Herman Bauermeister, Unterscharführer in the German SS. As such, the defendant's case has been remanded to the Alien Enemies Control Unit for further review..."

She tried to continue, but the lines were crossed out with a black marker.

"What's this mean?"

"Don't know," Frances said, taking a quick drag. Anytime she smoked in public, she acted like a spy in hiding. "My father got it from a friend at the Department of Justice."

Abby hesitated, looking at the document and then up to Frances. While she had no idea what she would do, she appreciated the help.

"Thank you," she said.

"Keep that safe. Technically, it's public information. But don't leave it on a streetcar or anything—"

"Speaking of. What's the time?"

Frances looked at her watch, diamond studded with a leather band.

"A quarter past six."

"I have to go. Arthur and I are seeing a film at seven."

"Oh, my. How will you ever make it home to get ready?"

"Actually, he's meeting me at the trolley stop."

"Isn't that romantic? So you'll go just like that?"

Abby glanced down at her uniform. While she could have felt insulted, she knew Frances was only being honest. But it didn't help when four soldiers walked by, and one said, "Evenin', General."

Frances frowned and looked back over her shoulder.

"Everyone's a general to a buck private," she snickered.

The young men all whooped and hooted, and even Abby had to laugh.

"Here," Frances said. She reached into her purse for a red lipstick case. "This should freshen you up."

Leaning forward, she applied some with the delicacy of an artist. Abby puckered her lips, and to her surprise, she did feel better.

"Thanks."

Frances dropped her cigarette and stamped it out. They walked together to the corner, the traffic busy on Commonwealth Avenue.

"Best of luck tonight."

"You as well," Abby said.

With a wave, Frances walked off in the direction of her dormitory on Bay State Road.

"Oh," she said, turning back. "Harold says we should all go to the Grove next week before finals."

Abby heard a bell and saw a trolley coming.

"I'd like that," she said, rushing to catch it.

"Toodle-oo!"

……

When Abby and Arthur walked out of the theater, the rain had stopped. The smell of spring was in the air, but that exhilarating feeling was missing. With a "dim out" order across the city, Bennington Street was dark and quiet. Shops that used to stay open later had to close by eight, a rule that somehow the bars and pool halls were exempt from. Businesses couldn't have lightbulbs over twenty-five watts, and neon signs were prohibited. Street lamps had all been fitted with special covers, giving off a weak and eerie glow, and Abby wondered how anyone could drive at night.

Such was life in wartime, something that, by now, she was used to. Despite the inconveniences, she knew they were lucky. Only a couple of days before, a young man from East Boston High had been killed, and another was missing in Guam. While she didn't know either of them, the conflict was getting closer to home.

Sometimes she wished she could forget all the bad news, but even the movies weren't a way to escape. They had just seen *This Above All* with Joan Fontaine, a romance about a soldier and upper-class woman in England.

"So strange to be back," Arthur said.

He looked around as they strolled down the sidewalk, dressed in his Army suit, his service pins shining, one from the 47th Fighter Squadron. Considering she had on her MWDC uniform too, she knew they were a striking pair, and people smiled as they passed.

"Not much has changed."

Even as she said it, she knew it wasn't true because life would never be the same after Pearl Harbor. The war was far away, but even in the safe familiarity of her neighborhood, she felt scared.

"It's funny to see it so dark."

"It's not dark down in Texas?"

He shook his head.

"There's no blackout. It's too far inland. My father didn't even know where Texas was. He had to look it up on a map."

"How is he?" she asked.

"He's good, business is not."

"No?"

"Dry cleaning chemicals are rationed now."

As they talked, he rubbed his hands together, and she didn't know if it was nerves or something else.

"I hear they may ration gasoline."

"We all have to sacrifice," he said, raising his eyes. "My father can't even get new sewing needles."

"We'll all be nude before long."

He smiled uneasily; he always shrank at anything suggestive. Whether it was from shyness or good manners, she didn't know, but she admired a man who wasn't just focused on sex.

"Have you flown much?"

"Yeah," he said, "mostly Bobcats. Once a Douglas A-33."

Abby knew nothing about airplanes and had never been on one. As a girl, she used to look up at the sky and dream, and now she just got scared, especially at night. No one expected a German attack by air, but the fact that it was even possible made it hard not to worry.

"Must be exhilarating," she said.

"Better once I get my wings. No more trainers, real fighters."

"When is that?"

"Six more weeks. Maybe sooner. They've already cut our flying hours by a third. They need pilots as fast as they can get them."

Finally, they got to the car, a black Buick with whitewall tires that his father let him borrow. They had parked across from the ice cream parlor, and Abby thought back to when they had gone there on their first date the previous September. It was closed until June, another victim of the Depression because, when Abby was younger, it was open year-round. The old Italian couple who owned it tried to sell coffee and pastries in the winter but couldn't compete with all the bakeries.

Arthur got the door for her, and she stepped in with a smile. As he started the engine, he glanced down at his watch.

"Still early. How's about a drive?"

"Sounds fabulous."

He pulled out, and they went north up Bennington Street. Rolling down the window, Abby stuck out her arm and waved her fingers in the air. It was a beautiful night, the streets calm and the temperature so mild it reminded her of summer.

They crossed the bridge into Winthrop, and she could smell the ocean. Coming to a stop sign, he hesitated a moment and pointed.

"I live just at the top of the street," he said.

"So close."

"Close to what is the question," he joked.

"East Boston."

"My father grew up on Saratoga Street."

"If he stayed, we could've been neighbors."

He turned with a smile, and she felt a warm tingle.

As they drove over the neck, she looked across the small bay. With so many homes shuttered, Point Shirley was always dark in the offseason. Now it was hidden, the shoreline a stretch of black indistinguishable from the water. She couldn't see the cottage, but she knew it was there. Of all the things in her life, it was the one place that never changed. Or at least that was what she wanted to believe.

"Will you and your family come out for the summer again?" Arthur asked.

"Of course. We always do."

She said it with confidence, but she really didn't know. Both of her brothers were working now, and even though she would be off school, she would have more hours at the bakery. After their mother's breakdown, they couldn't leave her alone, something none of them had considered, never mind discussed.

They drove by blocks of small cottages, Abby looking down the lanes toward the beach. At the end of Point Shirley, the road narrowed and continued toward Deer Island. Ms. Nolan said it used to have summer houses, but all Abby ever remembered was the prison, an ugly granite building surrounded by barbed wire. And while the coastline at the end of the peninsula was rocky, there were acres of paths to wander and explore.

Arthur slowed down, and Abby looked ahead to see flashlights. They got closer, and she realized it was soldiers, standing around a checkpoint made of sandbags, a wooden barricade across the road. She was sure it was for Fort Dawes, a small battery that had been on the backshore since the Great War. When she was a girl, it was abandoned, nothing but the foundation of barracks, remnants of a radio compass station. The summer before, there were rumors that the Army was rebuilding it, and Abby had seen trucks and other military vehicles go out there. She never expected them to close off the road, and it was a disappointment because there was a great place to park and watch the stars.

"Howdy," one of the soldiers said, walking up to the driver's window. "You don't look like you're with Coastal Artillery."

Arthur chuckled.

"I'm on leave. Just out for a drive with my girlfriend."

Abby tensed up, the word *girlfriend* giving her a slight thrill.

"You with the WAACs, Miss?"

Distracted, she didn't answer until the man pointed the flashlight.

"Massachusetts Women's Defense Corps," she said, squinting.

While he didn't grumble, his silence seemed scorn enough. Or maybe he wasn't aware of the organization, she thought. Soldiers were from everywhere, and the MWDC was hardly the French Foreign Legion.

"Sorry, this area is restricted now."

"I understand," Arthur said, and Abby was surprised when the man saluted.

"Have a good evenin', sir."

Arthur nodded and put the car in reverse. They turned around on the grass and headed back toward Point Shirley.

"At least we know they're keeping the shore safe," he said.

Abby smiled but didn't respond, watching him with a deep and curious gaze. He drove with one hand on the wheel, his shoulders back, and she noticed his hair was shorter than before, although it was hard to tell with his cap on. When they first met, he was lanky, and even a little awkward. Either time or the military, or both, had matured him.

"Shall I take you home?"

Abby hesitated.

"Could we...stop by the cottage?" she asked.

When he gave her a curious look, she got suddenly uneasy. But she knew he couldn't have known what she was thinking.

"Won't it be locked?"

"There's a key."

He curled his lips and looked straight ahead.

"Off Shirley Street, right?"

"Bay View Avenue."

When they finally turned down the road, it was so dark she thought they had taken the wrong one. Then she saw the reflection of the water, and moments later, they came around the bend. Across the harbor, she could see a few scattered lights in East Boston, but otherwise, the coast was black.

Arthur pulled in front of the cottage, and they sat parked with the engine running. Abby thought back to last summer when he came to drop off the pants her father had needed fixed. In an awful coincidence, Arthur's friends had clashed with George's the night before at the beach. So when he showed up, her brother tried to attack him on the lawn, uttering terrible slurs, and the only reason they didn't fight was that Thomas ran over and got between them. It was the day their father kicked George out of the house, and although Abby had felt bad for him, she had felt even worse for Arthur.

95

"Won't you come in?" she asked.

Their eyes locked.

"Yeah, sure."

They got out, closing the doors gently, and he followed her up the walkway. Next door, a light was on, but she wasn't concerned. Mr. Loughran was a retired cop who lived there with his wife, one of the few year-round residents on the block. He was a ham radio hobbyist, and all her life, Abby remembered hearing static and chatter late into the night.

When they got to the porch, she knelt and pulled one of the shingles just enough to let a key fall out. Mr. Nolan always had to be strict about the cottage, especially with two boys who, at different times, had snuck in during the winter to be alone with girls or get drunk with friends. But it wasn't all fun and adventure, and once, their father kicked George out for some crime or misdeed and sent him to live there in January with no heat.

Abby was the only other person who knew about the key, her father telling her it was in case of *calamity*, which she always assumed was the Irish version of *emergency*. Either way, it was some sign that he trusted her more than anyone else, and she got emotional just thinking about it.

As she went to put it in the lock, she saw something in the letterbox, which was unusual because they never got mail at the cottage. She took it out, and they read it together.

Massachusetts Committee on Public Safety

As a resident of Zone 1 (Coastal), you are required to maintain a permanent blackout state. During the period between one-half hour after sunset and one-half hour before sun-rise, all lights of every nature which are visible from the sea...

. . .

She folded it up and opened the door. Inside, the air was dank from dust and mildew. But she wasn't embarrassed or even disgusted, the smell reminding her of the summers of her childhood.

"Is there power?"

"Water too," she whispered.

She went over to the windows and pulled down the shades. While she did it out of caution, she was also feeling mischievous. It was the first time they had been alone together.

She turned on the lamp in the corner, knowing it was the dimmest one in the house.

"Lovely place," Arthur said, looking around.

"Cozy, isn't it?"

The home wasn't elegant, but it was solid, with wide-plank floors and exposed beams. None of the furniture matched, and it had everything from an antique walnut coffee table to a handmade rocking chair. The stone mantel was blackened with ash, but they didn't use the fireplace much because it was always too warm in the summer.

Her Irish great-grandfather had bought the land at the turn of the century when much of Point Shirley was still scrub grass and dunes. With his small salary from the shipyard, he built the cottage by himself on weekends and holidays, using scrap wood and metal from construction sites. Like Abby and her siblings, their mother had been going there since childhood, and it was the legacy of a family that had been in the country for a century but never strayed too far.

Abby wandered into the kitchen, making sure mice hadn't gotten into the pantry, and the ceiling above the stove hadn't started leaking again. Much of it was for show, however, because she hadn't come to the cottage to check on it.

"Your father was handsome in his youth."

She walked back out, where she found him staring at the framed pictures on the wall. In one, her father was standing with three men, some commendation they got for putting out a dock fire.

"That's at East Boston Works," she said.

"He had an accent, as I recall."

She was touched that he remembered, but she was embarrassed too.

The only time they met was when George confronted him on the front lawn and her father ran out to stop it.

"He was raised in Ireland," she said.

He turned with a smile, and they stood facing each other. There was a strange tension in the air, and whether it was around or just between them she couldn't tell. But her heart was in that cottage, and if she had to give it away, she would do it there. In all her juvenile flings and short-lived romances, she had done everything with boyfriends except sex. It was never out of honor, and always because she wasn't interested enough in them. Arthur was different, and knowing he was leaving, she wanted to give him something to remember her by. Or, as Frances had said, *If you want to keep a man, that's one sure way of doing it.*

Looking up, she stepped forward, enough to seem eager without being forward. And he took the bait, leaning down and bringing his lips to hers. At first, it was restrained, but then they burst into a frenzy of kissing and groping that made the floor creak.

"Let's go upstairs," she said.

"Upstairs?"

"To my bedroom."

He nodded quickly, his eyes beaming.

"Okay, upstairs..."

She took his hand, and they went up the small staircase, ducking at the turn. She led him to the end of the hallway and pushed open the flimsy door. The narrow space had once been a closet, but her father had made it into a bedroom after her mother complained that she was too old to sleep in the same room as her brothers.

They fumbled their way onto the small bed, which lay sheetless in the darkness with a coarse blanket and pillow. As they kissed, Abby undid her belt, and he took off his jacket, and soon they were down to their underwear.

"Are you sure?" he asked.

"I am—"

"Wait."

He reached into his pocket and took out a small tin. Something about the sight of condoms seemed to lessen the passion, demean the act. And she even got suspicious until he said, "I bought these for us."

"Thank you," she said with an awkward smile.

"It's safer."

While he put one on, she took off her bra and panties and leaned back on the mattress. He got on top of her, and they aligned their bodies, cheeks together and tightly embraced. She flinched when he entered her, but the pain didn't last, and as he rocked back and forth, she got a warm tingle that made her moan.

It was over in seconds, and he rolled beside her, leaving them both breathless and trembling. They lay facing each other, their faces just inches apart, and she giggled as she played with his bangs.

"It's so short."

He grinned.

"It's regulation."

"And lighter too."

"The Sun—"

Suddenly, there was a noise. Abby sat up and looked around.

"What was that?" he asked.

"I don't know."

She climbed off the bed and rushed to get dressed, pulling on her skirt, tucking her blouse into it. But when she heard the front door open, she didn't have time to put on her shoes. She flew out and down the hallway, stopping at the top of the stairs. Her panic was replaced by shame when she saw her brother and Connie walk in. For a moment, they all stood staring at each other like criminals that had stumbled onto the same target.

Thomas looked up squinting, and somehow she got the feeling that he knew.

"Are you alone?" he asked.

Abby looked at Connie and then back to him.

"No."

CHAPTER THIRTEEN

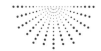

Thomas sat at the kitchen table having toast and coffee. It was a beautiful spring morning, the sky clear blue, and warm enough that his mother had opened all the windows. Next door, Mrs. Ciarlone was hanging the laundry, reaching for the line with her thick forearms. She had on a loose nightgown, and her hair was in a hairnet. Except for on Sundays when she went to church, she dressed like a spinster, which was unfortunate because, despite her weight and language trouble, she was still young enough to meet someone. Thomas thought the same about his mother, although he would never have dared mention it. A widow had to decide on her own when and if she would ever love again.

"Thomas?"

Startled, he turned to see his mother walk in.

"Did I scare you?" she asked.

"Would take more than that, Ma."

She stooped and glanced out the window.

"Spying on your soon-to-be aunt-in-law?"

Thomas smiled.

"When are you two gonna get together?"

"I haven't been invited," she said, walking into the dining room.

NIGHTTIME PASSES, MORNING COMES

She opened up the cabinet and took out his father's cigar box, which Thomas knew was empty. In a rare show of shared grief, he and his brother had smoked the last two on New Year's Eve. It was Mr. Nolan's favorite holiday, and Thomas was always amused by how he called it *New Year's Evening.*

"What's that?" Thomas asked.

She took out of a wad of money, mostly ones and fives but larger bills too.

"It's from bond sales."

"That's a lotta loot, Ma," he said, getting up to put the bowl in the sink.

She smiled and stuffed it into her pocketbook. As he followed her out to the foyer, George came down the stairs, his hair matted and eyes puffy. They had both slept in, something Thomas hadn't done in weeks because he usually worked Saturdays.

"Ready?" George asked.

"Where are you two going?"

"He's driving me to the bank," she said.

"What're you gonna do with all that money?"

"Get more bonds."

"How many more are you gonna sell?"

"As many as it takes."

Thomas looked at his brother, who just shrugged his shoulders. They were all impressed by her enthusiasm.

"Ma," he said, and she turned around. "I'll arrange something with Mrs. Ciarlone."

She leaned up and kissed him on the cheek.

"In good time, son."

As they walked out, Abby was coming up the front steps. With her sleeves rolled up and flour on her dress, Thomas knew she had worked the morning rush at the bakery. She walked in, and they acknowledged each other with quiet apprehension. They were each so busy they hadn't spoken since he found her at the cottage.

Realizing she was with her boyfriend that night, he was as irate as any brother would be. But he didn't explode, knowing it was an awkward situation all around. He liked Arthur, and they were both adults. He could hardly blame her for sneaking off when he was doing it himself. So he and Connie left, taking the shore most of the way back to East Boston. While it had done nothing to satisfy his libido, it gave them time to talk, and they even decided on a honeymoon destination, Monk Island, Maine.

Abby quickly hung up her coat and was halfway up the stairs when Thomas said, "You gotta minute?"

She stopped.

"Is this about the other night?"

He shook his head.

"Something else."

"What?"

"George joined the Army."

Her mouth dropped, and she came back down. He knew it was blunt, but there was no easier way to say it.

"I found his enlistment papers," he said.

She stood stunned, her eyes glassy, a reaction he had fully expected. But it was only a dress rehearsal for telling their mother, who he knew would take it the hardest.

"Why hasn't he said anything?" she asked, sounding more angry than upset.

"I don't know. I was waiting. I couldn't wait any longer."

"Thomas, we gotta tell Ma."

Their eyes locked, a feeling of mutual dread. Thomas knew their mother would be proud of George, but that didn't mean she wouldn't be devastated. With their father gone and her mental state, their family was only one tragedy away from collapse.

"I know."

......

NIGHTTIME PASSES, MORNING COMES

Thomas stood on the sidewalk with the rake in his hand, the sun in his eyes. It felt good to be clearing the dead leaves and twigs from winter, knowing his mother needed the help. But they really didn't have a front yard or a back yard for that matter. East Boston was as dense as a ghetto, with blocks of houses crammed together, only feet between them. If he hadn't grown up there, it probably would have felt claustrophobic.

It was hard to believe their small hill was once a farm, bought by his Irish great-grandfather before the Civil War. When Mrs. Nolan was little, there were still plots of open land, views of Chelsea Creek and beyond. She told them about the chicken coop at the end of the street where they used to buy eggs, and how the Franchette's house used to be a blacksmith.

Hearing a scraping sound, Thomas looked and saw Chickie coming up the sidewalk. She was dragging something behind her, and as she got closer, he realized it was part of a bed frame.

"Whatcha got there, Chickie?"

"Scrap metal," she said, sounding like *meh-dah*.

He dropped the rake and went to help.

"Where'd you find this?" he asked, taking the rusted end.

"Train tracks."

He winced in surprise; it was heavier than he thought. They pulled it together, but by the time he got it over the short wall and onto the grass, she had let go. He brought it down the side yard, where he saw a new pile of scrap, larger than before, everything from tin cans to tire irons. There was even a carburetor.

"That's quite a heap, Chickie."

She looked up with a wide grin that squished her cheeks and shut her eyes. Wiping his hands, Thomas smiled and walked away. When he got to the street, someone called, and he looked to see Mrs. McNulty waving from the door. He crossed over, and she held up the newspaper, *The East Boston Times*. Squinting, he could barely make out the headline, but when he did, a chill went up his back.

LOCAL WOMAN RAISES 10K IN WAR BONDS.

......

. . .

"You're a regular celebrity, Ma," George said.

"Hah," Mrs. Nolan scoffed. "It doesn't take a lot to give a little."

They cleared the table while Mrs. Nolan filled the sink. Over the months, they had each offered to do the dishes after dinner, but she always refused. Thomas knew it was better she did, and even Doctor Berman had warned them not to pamper her. Depriving someone of their responsibilities was no way to help them.

"Ain't she something else?" George said, nodding at their mother.

"We're very proud," Abby said, putting the casserole dish on the counter.

"If I get any more praise, I'll be drowning in it," Mrs. Nolan said.

"Speaking of drowning," George said.

He went into the pantry and came out with a beer. He used to keep them in the icebox, but there was no longer enough room. With rumors of meat shortages, their mother had bought as much as she could before prices went up.

"Think you'll make *The Globe*, Ma?" George asked.

"I'm not doing it for the fame, dear."

Thomas smiled and brought over the last of the plates. When George walked out, he knew he was going to listen to the Red Sox game in their bedroom.

"Can someone get the saltshaker?" his mother asked. "I need to refill it."

"I'll refill it, Ma," Abby said, giving Thomas a pointed look.

He left the kitchen and went upstairs. When he walked into the bedroom, George was laying on the mattress without shoes, his knobby feet hanging off the end. He had one hand around his beer and the other on the radio dial. The game was on, the staticky voice of Tom Hussey calling a catch by Dom DiMaggio. George glanced over, but he didn't seem to get distracted until Thomas shut the door.

"What's up?" he asked.

"Turn it down."

"What—"

"Now!"

George turned it down and then stood up. Staring at Thomas, he took a long swig of his beer like it was a show of defiance.

"Why haven't you told any of us?" Thomas asked.

His brother's expression changed, and he put down the bottle. In his eyes, Thomas saw that same look of sneaky evasion he used to get when, as a boy, he was asked about something bad he did. They faced each other for a tense minute, and while Thomas' teeth were clenched, he was more concerned than angry.

"I'm just waiting on a release from the doctor," George said, finally.

Thomas didn't have to ask why because he knew. Of all three siblings, George's health was the worst, and it was a surprise the Army even took him. Thomas always assumed it was the way he lived, the years of booze, cigarettes, and wild behavior. But he also knew that, when George was born, his father was drinking every day. Whether it was the alcohol or their mother's stress from living with it, he wondered if it had weakened his brother's constitution.

"I meant to tell you. I swear," George said.

"It's not about me. It's Ma."

"I'll tell her now if you want."

"Now?"

"Honest. I wasn't keeping it from anyone."

Thomas froze—it was like his brother had called his bluff. He had promised Abby he would confront George about enlisting, but he couldn't deny he had been dreading it.

"Then let's go," he said.

He opened the door, and they walked out together. When they got downstairs, their mother was in the rocker, classical music playing on the radio. The window was open to the mild night breeze, but she still had a shawl over her legs because she always got cold.

"Ma?" Thomas said.

She was startled in a way that told him she might have been dozing.

"Boys," she said, sitting up.

Abby ran in from the dining room where she had been studying.

"Ma, I've joined the service," George blurted.

At first, she looked more confused than shocked.

"The service?"

"The Army."

"What about your eyes?"

"Roosevelt lowered the requirements in March."

"And your flat feet."

"The recruiter said they were arched enough."

"But you've got asthma."

In his most dignified moment, she listed out his flaws like he was a horse on an auction block. But he didn't frown or otherwise get defensive.

"When?" she asked.

"I'm just waiting on medical clearance. The recruiter said two weeks."

"But your job?"

"I already gave the shipyard my notice."

She grasped for possibilities and alternatives, her voice shaking.

"Why?"

"Because I couldn't sit around and watch all these boys go off to war."

She put her hand to her mouth and turned away. It was a reason that none of them could argue with.

"Two weeks?" Mrs. Nolan asked.

"Maybe sooner."

A poignant tension filled the room, and she got up. With their father gone and George leaving for the service, the family would be down to three. Whatever their individual faults, the strength they got from each other always made up for them. Thomas looked over to Abby, who leaned against the wall, her arms crossed and tears rolling down her cheeks.

Thomas got choked up too, but he was also relieved. Considering their mother's fragile state, he had worried she would break down. But there was no great outburst, no explosion of grief, regret, or disappointment. She walked solemnly over to her son, and when she leaned forward to hug him, he was ready.

"I'm proud of you," she said, patting his back.

George responded with a twitching smile, and Thomas saw in him a humility he hadn't seen in years.

"Thanks, Ma."

When she finally pulled away, Thomas stepped over and extended his hand. He had meant to shake, but something came over either him or his brother or both of them, and they embraced instead. Abby ran to their side and joined them, and they stood huddled in a moment of brief intimacy that Thomas somehow knew they would never share again.

CHAPTER FOURTEEN

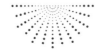

Abby got off at North Station and walked as fast as she could. At rush hour, the sidewalks were busy, and it was hard to hurry in her service uniform, which was still tight in places. As she went to cross the intersection, she heard a rumble, and everyone turned. Standing at the corner, she watched a line of Army vehicles come down Causeway Street. It was the largest she had ever seen, two dozen trucks loaded with young soldiers, their eyes peering out from under their helmets. They looked ready for battle, rifles at their sides, and she got a strange mix of pride and fear.

When someone started to clap, people joined in, and for a moment, it felt like a victory parade. Soon the convoy passed, heading towards the Northern Artery and most likely to the Charlestown Navy Yard where the troops would board a ship for Europe or Africa.

But Abby didn't know much about military logistics; everything she had been taught was about civilian defense. There was an Army base in South Boston and a Coast Guard station in Chelsea. The East Boston airport was used by every branch, and they were building barracks behind Wood Island Park. Other than that, the war was a mysterious conflict far away. Sometimes it felt like she was standing backstage while the actors prepared, never getting to see what was beyond the curtain.

With the trucks gone, she crossed over and cut through the West End. When she got to Cambridge Street, she ran towards the Charles Street Jail. She only had an hour until her MWDC meeting, but she also knew visiting hours were over soon.

As she approached the entrance, she slowed down to catch her breath, smooth out her jacket. She walked into the lobby and went over to the front desk, where a young guard with a mustache gave her a mock salute. His colleague beside the gate laughed, and Abby smirked. She could never go a day without being ridiculed for her uniform.

"I'm here for Martin Bauermeister?"

"You taking him to the brig?"

The other man chuckled again, but this time she ignored him. The guard picked up the phone, had a short conversation, and then hung up.

"Not here," he said.

"Not here?"

"That's what I said."

"Where is he?"

"Released."

Abby stood stumped. She was glad to know he wasn't at the prison, but she worried they might have taken him somewhere else. She had heard about what the government was doing to the Japanese in California.

She gave the man a formal nod and then turned around and left. With an hour until her meeting, she walked up Cambridge Street, stopping at each corner, looking in shop windows. Considering her hectic work and school schedule, it was the first time in months that she didn't feel rushed.

When she got back to North Station, she even let a couple of trains pass before getting on. But only ten minutes into the ride, she regretted dawdling. An air raid siren sounded as they were going under Boston Common, and the train had to stop for twenty minutes until it was over. The conductor assured passengers it was only a test, but as they waited, Abby could sense a quiet dread. After years of preparing for war, the country was finally in it, and people were afraid.

By the time she got to MWDC headquarters, it was past six o'clock.

She approached the door and could hear chatter within. As generous as the owner had been, the house wasn't big enough, and it always sounded like a party.

She knocked once, and a younger woman opened it, her cap pulled down over long ringlet curls. They smiled at each other, but Abby didn't recognize her. With over eighty members, it was hard to know everyone.

When she stepped in, the only thing stronger than the cigarette smoke was the smell of perfume, which she always found amusing. For an organization still trying to be taken seriously, some girls acted like it was a social event.

She continued down the hall, people rushing in every direction, the sound of typewriters clanging. It always had the manic rush of a control center, even if nothing they did involved military tactics or secrecy. But for all its amateur appearances, the MWDC operated like an army, and even if they didn't live in barracks and march in formation, rank was respected and everyone saluted.

Abby walked into the dining hall, which everyone called *central command*. The room was packed, dozens of women standing around, the new recruits obvious in their casual clothes. The leadership had tried to have special signup nights, but now people could join anytime.

"Miss Nolan?"

When she turned, Ms. Stetson was coming toward her. Her expression was stern; she always looked somewhere between annoyed and frustrated. But Abby was no longer intimidated by her, and she had reached an age where she realized that if people were grumpy or unsociable, they were the ones that had to suffer for it.

"You're late," the professor said.

"Sorry, Miss. There was an air raid siren. The train had to stop."

Ms. Stetson looked away, and considering what they were all there for, the excuse was poignant. She checked off something on the clipboard, her fingers as tense as her personality.

"Assignments are in," she said, nodding to a crowded table by the corner.

"Thanks."

Abby turned to go, and the professor added, "Some of the gals and I are going to Park Square for drinks after if you'd like to join us."

Abby hesitated like she was thinking, but she had no intention of going.

"I really have to get home and study for finals. But thank you."

Ms. Stetson pursed her lips with restrained disappointment. As a professor, it was an excuse she couldn't argue with.

"Very well. Carry on."

With a polite smile, Abby walked over to the table and had to get in line. After a couple of minutes, she reached the front, and a young private looked up.

"Name?" she asked before Abby could say anything.

"Abigail Nolan."

The girl ran her finger down the ledger.

"Air raid warden. East Boston."

Abby sighed, so relieved she smiled and clenched her fists. More than anything, she had wanted to be near home, but posts were never guaranteed.

Someone called for attention, and the room went quiet. Major Ward walked to the front, a staff member on either side of her. There used to be men at the meetings, officers from the Army or State Guard, but now that things were established, they no longer came, and the unit was on its own.

After welcoming new members, the major read from the weekly bulletin. Some of it was about the war abroad, but most was about defense at home. Two ships had been torpedoed in the St. Lawrence River, and the Army warned that U-boats might be coming down the coast. Training with the Boston Fire Department had been postponed until the end of the month, and they had new evacuation maps from the State Police. Any cars used by the MWDC were exempt from gasoline rationing, and they needed volunteers for the Gold Star Mothers banquet on Saturday. Finally, she congratulated the Red Sox on their win against the Browns, something that made everyone cheer.

With the meeting over, Abby turned to go. Feeling a tap on her shoulder, she spun around.

"Fran?!"

"I told you I'd consider it."

"You joined?"

Frances bit her lip and nodded. They were so excited they hugged, and when Abby pulled away, she noticed Ms. Stetson watching from across the room.

"Did you hear the sirens earlier?" Frances asked.

"Hear it? I was on the subway when it happened."

"I thought for sure we were goners."

"Believe me, if the Germans attack, it'll be at night."

"I'd probably sleep through it."

"Maybe it would get us out of finals."

While they quietly chuckled, the topic was too grim to joke about.

"Speaking of finals," Frances said. "I talked with Harold. We're going to the Grove Friday night to celebrate. Aren't you coming?"

Abby hesitated, tempted to say she had to work or study. The truth was, she didn't want to be reminded that the semester was ending. The busy days and weeks kept her distracted, and it was easier to forget your problems when you didn't have time to think about them. All her life, she'd looked forward to summer, and now she was almost dreading it. With her father gone, and George and Arthur leaving for the service, the world was like a tornado of grief, loss, and change. But she knew she couldn't let her friends down; everyone was suffering in their own way from the war.

"Sure," she said with a reluctant smile. "Friday sounds swell."

……

When Abby stepped off the trolley, the only lights on Bennington Street were from cars. It was late enough that all the shops were closed, their grates pulled down. Across the street, the pool hall was open, exempt from the curfew along with bars, restaurants, and pharmacies. Out front, she could see shadows and the flicker of cigarettes. The blackout regulations had changed a lot about the neighborhood, but they couldn't stop locals from hanging out.

She walked quickly, clutching her purse and looking around. After the air raid drill earlier, she was shaken up. In many ways, the war had brought the community together, especially the bond drives and scrap metal collection. A lady from their church had even started a fund for Italian orphans. But it also created suspicion, and now whenever Abby passed by someone, especially on a dark street, she got tense. It didn't help that Thomas was a cop because he told her about the briefings they got from the Department of Defense, the reports of German spies and saboteurs. Situated between the shipyards, which were stocked with ordnance and weapons, and the fuel tanks along the Chelsea River, East Boston seemed only one spark away from obliteration.

Hearing something, she glanced back, and a car rolled up. For a second, her heart pounded until she realized it was Arthur. He stopped and got out, facing her across the hood.

"Abigail," he said.

While she always found it cute when he used her full name, she could tell it was serious.

"You're leaving."

He gave her a slow, almost apologetic nod. The only reason she had blurted it out was to make it easier for him.

"I got my orders," he said.

"When?"

"Tuesday."

Inside, she got emotional, but she didn't show it. After everything she had been through in the past year, she no longer felt hostage to her feelings. Whether she was maturing or just getting cold, she wasn't sure, but she had no right to be bitter. She knew this day was coming. Their time together had been short—barely two weeks—and if she had accomplished anything, it was to give him a gift he couldn't forget.

"Good," she said, and he blinked in surprise. "Then you can come out to the Cocoanut Grove Saturday with me and my friends."

"So you're ready to have me meet them?"

She narrowed her eyes with a seductive smile.

"We're long past that point, I'm afraid."

He grinned and walked around, opening the passenger door.

"Let me drive you home."

CHAPTER FIFTEEN

Laying on the bed, Thomas stared at the watermark on the ceiling. The old house leaked from every corner and crevice, and he smiled in remembering how his father would patch one crack, only to have another appear somewhere else. The plaster walls were warped from age, the gumwood trim all nicked and dented. In winter, the draft was so bad the toilet would freeze. Mr. Nolan had once suggested moving to a newer home in the suburbs, Everett or even Saugus, but their mother wouldn't consider it. Her family had lived on the street for four generations, and as the last one, she was bound by a sense of honor or legacy not to leave. Thomas didn't agree, but he understood her devotion. In a neighborhood of immigrants and their children, people were fiercely territorial, and everyone had some stubborn and sentimental connection to where they lived. But he could never see himself raising a family in East Boston.

He got up, stretching with a yawn. He hadn't slept much the night before because George never came home. His brother was old enough to do what he wanted, but it still made Thomas anxious, some hang-up from their adolescence. In high school, George was at his worst, and it caused a lot of turmoil in the house. As a boy, Thomas had always put up with it. But by freshman year, he was no longer intimidated, something helped by the fact that he was twenty pounds heavier and had been boxing. The last time George tried to bully him, Thomas knocked him so hard over the kitchen table that he'd vomited.

As he buttoned his shirt, someone came up the stairs. He thought it was his brother until he heard a knock, and Abby looked in.

"Where's George?" she asked, looking at his bed.

"Not sure..."

Thomas stopped short of saying he didn't come home, knowing it would only worry her.

"Can I talk to you?"

He glanced over, fixing his tie in the mirror.

"I'm in a rush."

"It'll only be a minute."

When he nodded, she walked in and shut the door. He reached for his holster under the bed, and as he put it on, he could tell the pistol made her uncomfortable.

"Can you find out where someone lives?" she asked.

"Like who?"

"Just a friend."

"Is it that Meister Brau guy?"

He only said it as a joke, but she didn't smile.

"I need his address. Can you get it?"

At the sound of the front door opening, they both turned.

"Let me see what I can do," he said.

She walked out, and Thomas got his bag. When he got downstairs, George was in the kitchen. The burner was on, and he was stirring eggs for an omelet.

"Mornin'."

Thomas crouched by the icebox and reached in for his lunch, a ham sandwich and some leftover casserole.

"Have fun last night?" he asked.

"Some of the guys took me to Sonny's."

Thomas smiled, thinking about the dingy bar in Maverick Square. It was popular with all the shipyard workers, and he had gone there with his father when he was a guard.

"Yeah? Why?"

"Because I leave Monday."

Thomas was stunned. Closing the door, he slowly stood up.

"Monday?" he asked.

"From South Station."

While he had been expecting it, it didn't make it any easier, and for many reasons.

"Did you tell Ma?"

"Yep."

"I was wondering why you didn't come home," Thomas said, putting his food in a paper bag.

"I stayed at a friend's. Didn't wanna drive. You can't see squat at night."

Thomas just nodded, and if it were true, he was impressed because his brother had never been so responsible in the past. But he didn't snicker or make a sarcastic remark. They had been talking more now than ever before, and with George leaving, he didn't want to risk an argument.

He walked out to the foyer and got his coat. Reaching for the door, he was about to leave when he heard voices and stopped. He glanced out and saw his mother by the railing. She had a pot in hand, but she wasn't just watering the flowers because Mrs. Ciarlone was facing her on the opposite porch. It was the first time he had ever seen them speak, and although the conversation was a mix of repeated words and hand gestures, it was a start. Living next door to his future in-laws had always been awkward, especially when their parents didn't talk.

"Stop your snooping," Mrs. Nolan said, walking in.

"Don't you two seem fast friends?"

"I never said she was a bad woman. Besides, she said she'd buy some war bonds."

"I'm glad, Ma."

With a smile, he kissed her on the cheek and left.

......

. . .

The city looked like the center of a maritime apocalypse, with warships squeezed into every pier and dock, many others moored in the outer harbor. With so much military activity, fishing boats had been ordered to move to smaller ports up and down the coast; Salem and Gloucester in the north, Weymouth and Scituate in the south. Barges lined the wharves, and the Charlestown Navy Yard had more cranes than anyone could count. The sound of drills, torches, and riveters could be heard day and night.

All morning, they had patrolled the seaport of South Boston, past cargo lots, warehouses, and fisheries where the stench was awful. For security, the harbor units rotated, and out of five men, Thomas only knew Flynn from training. He was friendly for a sergeant, but he wasn't a pushover. At the Army base, he got into a shouting match with an MP who said they were on restricted property. Thomas and the others laughed it off, but things were tense in wartime where every organization wrestled over jurisdiction.

They walked along the seawall, the sky overcast and a light fog over the water. After a long day, everyone had run out of news, jokes, and grievances, so they were silent. When a Navy patrol boat passed by, it sounded its horn, and they all waved. Thomas smiled at the camaraderie, and even if he wasn't going off to fight, he got some pride from knowing he was guarding the home front.

"Sarge?"

Up ahead, two of the officers were standing over an abandoned tugboat that lay submerged in the shallows.

"What is it?" Flynn asked.

"Stowaways," one cop joked.

"Out!" another shouted.

Thomas and the others hurried over, and two homeless men crawled out of the wheelhouse. They were both middle-aged, with thick beards and dirty clothes, their faces chapped from the sun. One had on an old-fashioned sailor cap, the words *SMS Westfalen* written across the front in gold lettering.

"You with the Imperial German Navy?" the sergeant snickered, and he swiped it off the man's head.

"U.S. Army. I got it in Paris after the war."

The phrase sounded funny, if only because before *the war* had always meant one thing—the Great War.

"What the hell you two bums doing in this jalopy?"

While it sounded harsh, there was compassion in Flynn's voice.

"We were living in the South End. But you can't find a room for nuttin' now."

The cops looked at each other; it wasn't the first time they had heard the story. With the city flooded with workers for war industries, every flophouse and fleabag hotel was full.

"Have you tried Goodwill? Salvation Army? The Seavey House?"

As the sergeant listed off all the shelters from the West End to Dover Street, the men just nodded.

"Well, gentlemen," he said, finally. "I'm afraid you can't stay here."

They didn't argue or protest, instead reaching onto the deck for their bags. They mumbled goodbye and walked away, and there was no bitterness. For Thomas, it was sad to watch. All his life, he had seen the bums on Bennington Street. His mother said East Boston didn't have vagrants when she was young, but then she always romanticized the past. Either way, the Depression had made it worse, and even with the economy now booming, some people still hadn't recovered.

They continued down Atlantic Avenue past brick buildings, packing companies and manufacturers whose smokestacks blew black filth into the air. They crossed the bridge over the train yard and waited for the water taxi at the end of Fort Point Channel.

Soon Thomas saw it coming, a tiny boat cruising toward them between a Navy destroyer and an Army troop ship. Owned by the fire department, it had been loaned to the police. With equipment so scarce, departments everywhere were scrambling to borrow or share.

When it pulled up, the tide was so low they had to climb down a wet rope ladder to board. Thomas took off his hat and sat on the bench, wiping algae and other debris off his coat. The engine rumbled, and they turned around and went back across the harbor.

The trip took less than ten minutes, and on the way in, they passed East Boston Works. The shipyard where everyone in Thomas's family had, at one time, worked, had doubled in size, with four cranes and a half-dozen deep water berths. And while it had mostly been a cargo facility, it now did repairs and refitting. Not a week passed without some foreign ship arriving that had either been damaged by a U-boat or had blown its engines trying to outrun one.

To get to the pier, they had to go around a giant Red Cross ship. On the top deck, pretty nurses in white dresses stood smoking cigarettes, wisps of hair falling from their hats. When one of the cops whooped, Sergeant Flynn gave him a sharp look. With so many rowdy soldiers around, the chief had told staff that officers had to set a good example.

"I hear you're tying the knot," one of the guys said.

Leaning against the railing, Thomas looked over with a smirk.

"Maybe around my neck."

Everyone chuckled, including Flynn. As much as he meant it as a joke, Thomas didn't want anyone to know about his personal life. The gossip around headquarters was as bad as high school.

"Better do it quick," another said.

Thomas looked up to the pier where, to his surprise, he saw Connie, standing in a dark coat, her arms crossed.

The boat bumped against the dock, and the captain secured the lines. They always let the sergeant off first, but when Thomas turned to let him pass, Flynn said, "You go. You're dismissed."

Thomas looked at his watch. They still had an hour left.

"You sure, Sarge?"

"Never keep a woman waiting."

Thomas smiled and grabbed his bag. Stepping off, he climbed the gangplank and ran over to Connie, not wanting to give the other cops time to intrude.

"You're not working?" he asked.

He took her lightly by the arm, and they started to walk.

"I left early."

By the time they got to the street, any excitement he had at seeing her was replaced by a simmering dread. She was always hard to read, but he knew her well enough to realize when something was wrong.

They stopped at the corner, and she looked around before speaking.

"I was at the hospital," she said.

"Hospital?"

"Thomas, I'm pregnant."

CHAPTER SIXTEEN

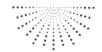

Abby leaned over the baking pan and tapped powdered sugar on the buns, careful not to get any on her skirt. With work in the morning and MWDC meetings after class, she spent most of her days in uniform, which was why she had bought a second one. She was proud to wear it, and even if some people still mocked the group, most probably assumed she was in the *Women's Army Auxiliary Corps* or an Army nurse. She never let them think otherwise, enjoying the smiles of admiration she got on the street and subway.

"I need those rolls, Ab."

Abby glanced over, and Eve was standing in the doorway.

"You could help, you know?" she said.

"I need to mind the front."

Abby frowned. They called Eve a manager, but all she ever did was gossip and order the counter girls around.

Abby finished the batch and put on mitts to lift the hot pan. While Eve stepped aside, she took the buns out and slid them into one of the cases. Mornings were the busiest time, and there was already a crowd. It was mostly women, pointing at bread, cakes, and pastries while employees rushed to get them.

Abby was about to go when someone called her name, and she turned to see her neighbor.

"Hello, Mrs. McNulty."

"Your mother is quite the patriot."

"She likes being part of the war effort."

"Well, we're all very impressed."

Abby didn't know if she meant the community was impressed or the *Catholic Women's Guild*. Either way, she appreciated the praise, especially coming from her. All her life, the McNulty's seemed like perfect neighbors, unlike her own crazy family. They never argued, and their kids didn't get into trouble. When Abby's father was drinking, his rampages sometimes spilled out onto the street, and she remembered the humiliation she felt seeing Mrs. McNulty watching from the window.

"A half dozen cranberry muffins, please."

Abby blinked, realizing she had daydreamed.

"Oh," she said, then she waved to one of the girls. "Lisa will help you. I do the glazing."

Mrs. McNulty smiled, and Abby returned to the kitchen. When she saw Loretta coming in the back, she knew it was almost time to go. But Carlo had taken two more pans out of the oven, so she refilled the shaker and got to work.

"Who're those men parked out there?" Loretta asked as she took off her coat.

Shrugging her shoulders, Abby finished the buns and gave her the mitts, the same handoff they did five days a week. Even if it was a couple of minutes early, Loretta didn't complain. Abby always covered for her if she was late.

She undid her apron and wiped the flour off her skirt. As she put on her service jacket, Carlo came out of the freezer with a box of butter, his hands speckled with dry dough. He bowed as he passed, and despite his bad English, he always acknowledged her service. Before she could smile back, the back door opened, and six men burst in.

"What the hell?!" she exclaimed.

At first, she thought it was a robbery until she noticed that some had on police uniforms. They flew by like a stampede of horses, and when they cornered Carlo, he dropped the butter and put up his hands. Eve came in from the front, and Loretta just watched stunned with her apron half on.

"Carlo Martignetti?" one of the men asked.

Carlo nodded.

"You're under arrest for failure to register as an alien enemy."

He squinted in confusion and looked at Eve.

"Tu sei sotto arresto," she said. "Non ti sei registrato come alieno."

Abby ran over and got between them.

"Why're you doing this?" she asked.

"Yeah. He ain't done nothing wrong," someone else said.

By now the whole staff was in the kitchen, even some customers. The officers tried to ignore them, but it was getting heated. One of the men in plain clothes pointed and circled the room.

"Ladies!" he barked. "I'm gonna have to ask you to step back and let us do our business."

"What business?"

"Government business. This doesn't concern you."

"He's our business!"

"Yeah, leave him alone!"

One woman raised a loaf of bread, and another yelled in Italian. Standing in the middle, Abby looked around in a panic. The situation was already tense, but when one of the officers grabbed Carlo, it became a riot.

The crowd charged, the men struggling to fend them off. A table got knocked over, and pans and utensils went flying. As Abby screamed for calm, an officer shoved her, and she stumbled back into the mixing machine and banged her head.

The melee ended when the cops all took out their badges and threatened to arrest everybody. It only lasted a few seconds, but the room was a cloud of flour dust, the floor covered in egg wash and raw pastries. Some girls were crying, but most were furious, shaking their heads and shouting insults as they slowly scattered.

Abby stood crouched in the corner, dizzy and out of breath.

"Collins! Get him in the wagon," one of the officers said.

She watched in horror as the cop who had pushed her handcuffed Carlo and led him out the back door.

......

Seeing the conductor come in, Abby reached into her purse. She hadn't been on a train that took tickets in years, the last time being when they visited her aunt and uncle in Maine during high school.

The man went down the aisle, squeezing to get by people, the car packed in the evening rush. When he got to her, she gave him the ticket, and he punched it.

"Army?" he asked, handing it back.

"Women's Defense Corps."

With a gentle smile, he continued down the rows. She sat quietly with her bag on her lap, glancing out the window. In the dusky light, she tried to see, but it was all unfamiliar anyway.

Everywhere outside Boston had always been a mystery to her, probably because her family didn't own a car. Even their cottage on Point Shirley, which was only five miles from their house, seemed far away. She never considered herself a city girl until she got to college, where most students were from the suburbs. Even Frances and Harold, with all their worldly charm, had both grown up in small towns.

The conductor called out *Belmont Center*, and the train slowed down. Abby grabbed her things and made her way to the door. She stepped off with a line of passengers, mostly businessmen and other professionals. The trip had taken longer than expected, and her unit was having a blood drive at the Red Cross at six. She knew she wouldn't make it on time, but she at least wanted to show up.

She walked down the steps and came out to the junction of two roads. On an island between was a headstone and two ornamental cannons, some monument to the Great War that now seemed insignificant. Reaching into her pocket, she took out a scrap of paper with the address and simple map she had sketched from an atlas in the library.

But she wasn't worried, and although she hadn't traveled much, she always had a good sense of direction.

She started to walk, clutching her purse only out of habit because the town was quiet, and she had never felt safer. She veered up a small hill where stately homes lay nestled behind hedgerows and stone walls. Turning at the next street, she read off the numbers until she found twenty-five, a stately brick home with casement windows and a slate roof.

The only light on was in the back, and she worried she would interrupt their dinner. But she walked up anyway, reaching for the knocker and tapping twice. Hearing footsteps, she got anxious, and, moments later, a woman opened the door. She was prettier than Abby had expected, with bobbed hair, blue eyes, and a long-sleeved dress.

"May I help you?" she asked with a heavy accent.

"Good evening. Sorry to bother you. Would it be possible to speak to Professor Bauermeister?"

Her expression changed, and she gave Abby a curious, almost suspicious look.

"Maybe I asked what this is in regard to?"

"I'm a student. He was my instructor. I wanted to talk to him," she said, knowing it didn't really answer the question.

"One moment."

The woman stepped away, abruptly enough that it seemed rude. Worrying she had made a mistake, Abby considered leaving until she heard the professor's voice.

"By all means. Let her in."

The woman came back and opened the door.

"Please," she said, waving Abby into the foyer.

The professor came down the hallway dressed in a suit and slippers. He had lost more weight, something that was often a sign of health in normal times, but not during war.

"Abigail?"

"Hi, Professor Bauermeister. I'm so sorry to bother you—"

"Have you joined the American military?" he asked.

He seemed more surprised by her uniform than by the fact that she was there.

"Massachusetts Women's Defense Corps."

He raised his eyes like he was impressed and then gestured to the woman.

"My wife, Theresa," he said.

Abby smiled and was relieved when Mrs. Bauermeister smiled back. After an awkward hesitation, she looked at the professor.

"I...I was concerned about...about your situation."

"Thank you, my dear."

"I wanted to make sure you were okay."

He smiled but didn't say whether he was or wasn't.

"Come," he said. "Let's sit."

Abby gave her coat to his wife and then followed him into the den, an elegant room with a long couch and oriental rug. The walls had built-in bookcases, and in the corner, a log was crackling on the fireplace.

"I hope I didn't disturb dinner," she said, noticing the faint smell of food.

"Not at all."

She sat on the couch, and he took the leather chair beside her, reaching for a half-finished cigar in the ashtray. As he lit it, he looked across and squinted.

"My dear, what did you do?"

She touched the side of her forehead, still red and swollen from the scuffle at the bakery.

"Walked into a door," she said, but somehow she knew he didn't believe her.

"We all seem to be stumbling into things these days."

Abby smiled; his remarks always had more than one meaning.

"I went to the jail," she said. "They told me you weren't there."

"Yes. My lawyer was finally able to obtain my release."

"Do you know what you did wrong?"

He took a puff, blowing the smoke out with a sigh.

"When I registered as an *alien enemy*," he said, and she could tell he didn't like the term, "they asked if I had relatives in any Axis military or government. I said no."

When he paused, Abby realized it wasn't true.

"My brother, it pains me to admit, is an officer in the SS. But we haven't talked in years. We're very different people. When all this madness began, he got swept up in it."

"The Nazis?"

"A damn plague. The reason my wife and I left. I wish I could say the same for my daughter, son-in-law, and granddaughter."

"They're in Germany?"

"They had been trying to get to America—"

Abby saw him get distracted, and when they looked over, his wife was in the foyer. She seemed anxious, standing with her arms crossed, almost squirming.

"Theresa?"

She said something in German, and he turned to Abby.

"Will you have tea?"

"No, thank you. I can't stay long. I have an event."

With a faint smile, Mrs. Bauermeister walked back to the kitchen. The professor lowered his voice and said, "She's been a wreck about our granddaughter. Little Kristina. She's just turned three."

"I'm sorry."

"Thank you. These are difficult times for all," he said, then his tone got more upbeat. "So, how are your courses?"

She was touched. Despite his own problems, he always asked about her life.

"Finals end this Wednesday."

"Another semester down," he said, raising his fist in triumph. "I knew you could do it."

"I signed up for German II next fall."

"And I wish I could be there to teach it."

"Pardon?"

He took a drag on his cigar and tapped it on the ashtray.

"The university found out about my detainment. Regardless of the circumstances, they say I'm in violation of their code of ethics..."

When he looked up, their eyes met, and Abby got a chill.

"They've revoked my tenure. I've been fired."

CHAPTER SEVENTEEN

For the past few nights, Thomas hadn't been able to sleep, something that had only happened twice before. The first was every Christmas as a boy when he and his brother would stay awake, thinking every creak or groan was Santa on the roof. The second time was in high school when he had to spar with Anthony Barletta, the toughest guy on the boxing team, during their annual homecoming event. In the end, he won the match, although it went a full three rounds, and he broke his pinky. He realized then that the fear of something was often worse than the thing itself.

The situation now was different, and while he was worried, he was also disappointed, and not just in himself. Connie had told him she had a diaphragm, and he was always careful. Mistakes happened, and he knew a girl in high school who had gotten pregnant. It was such a scandal the priest had even mentioned it at mass, although not directly when he cited Hosea 2:5: *"For their mother hath played the harlot; She that conceived them hath done shamefully."*

Thomas' parents had always wanted grandchildren, and under proper circumstances, his mother would have been thrilled. But having a child out of wedlock was a disgrace, and he only had two choices: leave town or get married.

"Ma?"

Mrs. Nolan stood at the stove frying bacon and potatoes. When she glanced back, he blurted, "We'd like to have the wedding next month."

She shut off the burner and turned around, wiping her hands on her apron.

"Next month?"

"It's the only time Connie could take off work."

She gave him a curious stare, but he kept a straight face, knowing she could always sense when her kids were being sly or sneaky.

"And who knows what the world will be like in the fall?" he added.

She pressed her lips together. It was a reason no one could disagree with. The war had added urgency to things that, in the past, would have required great time and consideration. With so many men leaving for the military, couples were marrying like crazy and often without the permission of their parents.

"I have a meeting at the church tonight," she said. "I'll talk to Father Ward."

Thomas smiled, feeling a big relief.

"Thanks."

"Tell your sister breakfast is ready."

He went back upstairs and down the hallway, tapping on Abby's door. When she answered, he opened it, and she was brushing her hair in the mirror. Something about her reminded him of their mother, and it must have been her posture because they had never looked much alike.

"What?" she asked.

"Breakfast is ready."

"Be right down."

As he turned to go, he noticed a welt on her face and stopped.

"What happened?"

"Pardon?"

He stepped forward to touch it, but she smacked his hand away.

"There was a raid at work. They arrested the baker."

"Arrested him?"

"He's Italian," she said, and he didn't need any further explanation.

"So how'd you get a bruise?"

When she hesitated, he gave her a sharp look. As twins, they could never lie to each other.

"I got pushed."

"Pushed? By who?"

"One of the cops," she said, and he surged with anger.

"Who was it?"

"It was an accident, honest."

"Who was it?" he repeated.

"I don't—"

"You can tell me now or I can find out."

"Collins or something…"

He grunted in anger and left the room.

"It really wasn't his fault," she said, pleading from the doorway.

"Like hell."

"Thomas, please!"

Ignoring her, he went into his bedroom and shut the door.

"What's wrong?" George asked, leaning up half asleep, his thin body tangled in the sheets.

Thomas saw some empty beer bottles on the sill, an ashtray on the floor, but he didn't say anything.

"Nothing. Go back to bed."

"As you wish, Corporal," he said, and he rolled back over.

Thomas chuckled and walked up to the mirror. As he put on his tie, he thought about how strange it was to have George home, his short time between quitting work and leaving for boot camp. It reminded him of when they were boys, those endless hours together on snow days, playing checkers or dominoes on the floor.

As much as they fought, they were forced to get along, a necessity that had been lost in adulthood. After dropping out of high school, George went out almost every night with his friends, coming home drunk or not at all, and their father had started calling him *the lodger*. Thomas' hatred of his brother had peaked during those years, something that, while he didn't regret, he was starting to reconsider.

For every father, son, or brother that went off to war, there was a chance they wouldn't come back. As Thomas reached under the bed for his holster, he glanced over at George, who lay sleeping like a child, his bare back heaving with each breath. Struck by a wave of emotion, he told himself any sadness he felt was for his mother and sister, not for himself.

......

Thomas sat at the back of the streetcar, staring out the window. Although the weather was mild, he had worn a coat because he didn't want any attention. The anxiety he always had about the day usually faded along the ride, but by the time they reached Maverick Station, he was still restless.

The trolley descended underground and came to a stop. When Thomas got off, most people went toward the platform to catch the train into the city. And while he should have followed them, he turned at the last minute and went up the stairs instead.

He burst into the light of morning, and the square was busy, with cars beeping and people rushing around. Shopkeepers were getting ready, and after a long winter, the fruit and vegetable stalls were finally out again. In front of a restaurant, Thomas saw a horse-drawn milk cart, a relic from a time when everything was delivered that way.

As he walked, he passed a group of Catholic school kids at a bus stop, and a little girl in a plaid uniform waved. He was in no mood to smile, but he did anyway and then crossed the street. He hated the feeling, that simmering fury, and while it wasn't unfamiliar, he used to be able to hold back his temper. It was strange to know he was taking a big risk and to do it anyway.

In the distance, he saw the yellow brick of the District 7 building. He had only been there once when, as a teenager, his brother got arrested for smashing the windows of a synagogue. It was an incident that horrified the community and humiliated their family, and the only reason his father took him along was to teach him a lesson.

He went through the front doors and came into a small lobby with a couple of chairs and pictures of past precinct captains on the wall. It still looked the same except they had changed the floor tiles and added some ceiling lights.

"Thomas Nolan?"

He looked over, and the cop at the desk was a guy from high school, although Thomas couldn't remember his name. When he joined the force, he worried he would get assigned to East Boston, and he was glad he didn't because it would have been hard working around people he knew.

"You got a *Collins* here?"

The officer crossed his arms, giving Thomas that sarcastic look of police bravado.

"We got a few."

"He raided a bakery on Bennington Street a couple of days ago."

"That's probably Jeremy Collins on special ops."

"Where is he?" Thomas asked coldly.

The officer leaned forward and looked over at the clock.

"If he's working, roll call is in fifteen minutes..." he said just as two cops walked in. "And there he is."

Thomas walked over so fast they were surprised.

"What's up, brother?"

"Which one of you is Collins?"

The men glanced at each other, and their expressions changed.

"I am," the bigger one said. "What's it to you?"

He had a square head and crooked teeth, and the fact that he looked like a thug made him easier to hate.

"You pushed my sister at Betty Ann Bakery."

"You're talkin' nonsense," he grumbled.

With a frown, he walked off, and his partner followed. Thomas stood with his fists clenched, but he had learned from boxing never to let your rage overcome your composure, something he could apply to his actions but not his words.

"You're lucky I don't break your goddamn neck!"

Collins stopped and slowly turned around. Shaking his head, he snickered and came back over.

"Don't tell me to—"

Thomas didn't know if the other man raised his arm to point or to strike, but he wasn't going to wait to find out. Lunging, he swung and hit the guy so hard that he stumbled backward, and the only reason he didn't fall was that his partner caught him.

The officer at the desk ran over, and three more patrolmen came out a side door. As everyone went to break it up, Collins held up one hand, his other holding his bleeding nose, and it was obvious he didn't want to fight. Thomas sneered at them all and stormed out of the building.

CHAPTER EIGHTEEN

With her bookbag over her shoulder, Abby walked to the front of the room and put her exam on the desk. The instructor looked up with a smile, a middle-aged woman who reminded Abby of her librarian in high school. She had been leading the class for a month, but Abby doubted she knew any German because she was a Latin professor. It wasn't their first substitute teacher, and all semester the administration had been struggling to fill the vacancy. Half the students had withdrawn, either out of frustration or boredom, and Abby got some small satisfaction in knowing they couldn't replace Professor Bauermeister.

When she left the room, Frances and Harold were waiting in the corridor. They had been there the whole time, and while it was distracting, the test was easy, and Abby was sure she got an A.

"Did you really have to stare?" she asked Harold.

He had on a pinstripe suit and vest with a lily boutonnière, his hair parted and combed back with Brylcreem.

"Darling, it was psychic encouragement."

Frances rolled her eyes.

"More like psychic impatience," she said. "And if he doesn't get a drink in him soon, we're all done for."

In her V-neck dress and hat, she looked as dashing as Harold. Abby had on her best skirt and blouse, the first time in weeks she hadn't worn her uniform to school, and she still felt underdressed. Beyond that, she was exhausted from months of work, school, and MWDC meetings. Along with her makeup, she had put on heavy blush that morning, as much to distract from the circles under her eyes as to hide the bruise on the side of her forehead.

"Did you pull it off?" Harold asked, and she could smell liquor on his breath.

"It was a breeze. With no instructor, I think they just want everyone to pass."

"That poor man," Frances said.

"A bloody injustice."

Abby smiled, but she knew they didn't understand her concern about the professor, and sometimes she didn't understand it herself. While she was glad he was out of jail, it was a hard time to be German. Even at BU, there was a petition to remove it from the language curriculum, and Goethe's *Faust*, which the drama club had put on each year for decades, had been canceled.

"So? Where's your Don Juan?" Harold asked.

"Arthur will meet us there."

He licked his lips and looked around. Abby could tell he was eager to leave and, like anyone, once he started drinking, he had to keep going.

"Shall we be off then?"

"Lead the way!" Frances said.

Harold held out his elbows, and they all locked arms, skipping down the hallway like a scene from the *Wizard of Oz*. With the semester over, the building was quiet, and many of the classrooms were dark. In the lobby, a few students lingered on the chairs and couches, but most of the people they saw now were soldiers. The Army had been on campus for so long that it no longer felt strange or intimidating, and all the girls seemed to like it. There had been a few incidents, but it was usually just drunken rowdiness, although there had been an allegation of rape in February that turned out to be a lovers' spat.

As they approached the doors, they passed a couple of officers, young men with buzzed cuts, pins gleaming on their shirts. Harold gave one of them a long look, and Abby nudged him.

"What?" he said, blushing.

"Really, dear," Frances whispered. "You're asking for trouble."

They had both warned him about making passes at men, something he only seemed to do when drunk. He once said *I've been queer since the day I came out of the womb*, which explained a lot for Abby because she had always wondered whether it was a choice or an instinct. Either way, he was clever enough to hide it which, for his sort, was critical. But when he drank, he got sloppy, and the semester before, he had gotten punched by a sailor for dancing too close to him.

They walked out to the sidewalk, and as Abby headed toward the trolley, Harold stopped her. Puckering his lips, he whistled loud enough that people turned. Across the street, Abby watched a cab make a wide U-turn and then pull up to the curb.

"This night is on me," he said, opening the back door.

Frances curtsied and got in.

"My books," Abby said, realizing she hadn't thought about what to do with them.

"We'll stop at my place. You can leave them there."

"Aren't you going home on Monday?"

"My dear," he said, giving her that tender but confident smile that always put her at ease. "You worry too much."

Abby squeezed in beside Frances, and he shut the door.

......

When they got to the Cocoanut Grove, it was nine o'clock, and there was a line out front. They had stopped by Harold's apartment to drop off Abby's bag and ended up staying for two hours. He made drinks, and they listened to jazz records. He had given the cabbie ten dollars to come back, but the man never did so he had to call another, and they were lucky to get a taxi on a Friday night.

They had only been waiting a couple of minutes when someone called out to them, and Abby saw Sal waving. Pushing through the crowd, they got to the front, and he took them through the revolving door.

"A savior," Harold said.

Frances stood on her tiptoes, and Abby was shocked that Sal kissed her on the lips, not the cheek. He checked in their coats and brought them through the club, staff bowing and nodding to him as they went by. Abby had always known Sal as the quiet boy next door, but she couldn't deny feeling some importance being with the head waiter.

They walked into the ballroom, and the dance floor was packed, the air thick with the smell of cigarettes and perfume. The band was playing a fast number, and as they went down the aisle, a twirling couple almost knocked them over.

They sat in the same section as before, and possibly the same table—Abby couldn't tell. With its dim lights and endless palm trees, the club was as murky as a jungle.

Sal pulled out chairs for Abby and Frances, and he invited Harold to sit.

"What can I get everybody?" he asked, looking first at Frances.

"Just the usual, darling."

Abby didn't know what *the usual* was, but she had the same. Harold asked for a Manhattan before changing to a Zombie, ironic considering he was already drunk. Sal gave the order to a waiter and then turned to Frances.

"How's about a warmup?"

She gave him a sexy sideways glance, raising her eyes.

"Why, sure."

Abby watched as he escorted her out to the dance floor, his hand on her lower back. She didn't know if they were in love, but they seemed well on the way to it.

"*How's about a warmup*," Harold said in a mocking voice.

Abby looked over with a frown.

"What's that supposed to mean?"

"The boy sounds like a bloody fishmonger."

"He's not a boy. And he's certainly not a *fishmonger*."

Harold struggled to light a cigarette with his hand shaking.

"Sometimes it's hard to tell with these guineas."

The waiter came back, and just in time because Abby was horrified. Harold could get mean when he was drunk. On their last night out of the semester, she didn't want to get into an argument, but the remark was harsh enough that the moment the man left, she said, "Maybe you're just jealous."

He took a deep drag and blew out the smoke.

"Maybe you're right," he said, reaching for his cocktail.

Abby was stunned. For all their long talks and shared secrets, he had never admitted any weakness.

"Is that so?"

She looked over, but he wouldn't look back.

"I'm lonely, Ab," he said.

"Surely you could…find somebody."

She wanted to help, but she couldn't give advice about things she didn't understand.

"Not here, I'm afraid."

"Then where?"

He chuckled and took a big sip of his drink.

"There's a place—"

"Abigail?"

She turned and saw Arthur coming through the crowd. While he was far from the only one in a military suit, he was striking enough that people stepped aside and smiled as he passed.

"Arthur," Abby said. "This is Harold."

They shook hands across the table.

"A pleasure."

"The pleasure is mine," Harold said, bowing. "Now what can I get you? We were about to get another round."

Abby looked at her glass, which was still full.

"Anything, really."

"Anything, really it is!" Harold said, and he called for a waiter.

Frances and Sal came off the dance floor, and Abby introduced everyone. Sitting among them, she got a warm exhilaration that almost made her cry. For the first time, all her closest friends were together, including the man she loved. Arthur was leaving Tuesday, but she wouldn't let it ruin the night. If the last five months had taught her anything, it was to take joy when it came and never expect it to last. The world could change in an instant.

"I've gotta take a powder," she said, getting up.

They were all too busy talking, and the only one to acknowledge her was Arthur, who raised his drink with a smile.

She grabbed her purse and walked away, making her way to the bathroom by the lobby. Inside, ladies stood chatting and fixing their makeup in a small foyer.

Abby went over to a row of gilded mirrors and inspected the bruise on her face. Even in the light, it wasn't too bad. The injury had hurt her pride more than anything.

"You little devil," she heard, and it was Frances. "Sneaking off?"

"When nature calls."

Frances leaned toward the glass to put on more lipstick.

"Sal's gonna take me home," she said, and Abby raised her eyes.

"Not like that," she added, "although anything's possible."

"I figured you'd wait until marriage."

"If that were the case, I'd have been married at seventeen."

Abby glanced over, and they burst out giggling. She admired Frances' honesty as much as her spunk, which was why she felt guilty not telling her about Arthur. No one knew they had slept together. At a time when everyone was looking for something to make life worth living, intimacy seemed too sacred to gossip about.

When they got back to the table, Sal took Frances out to dance again. Harold and Arthur were in a deep conversation, but Abby didn't feel ignored; she was happy they were talking. Sitting alone, she tapped her foot and looked around. Many people had on uniforms, including some women, and it was obvious a lot of them weren't from around there. The war had brought servicemen and government workers from all over, and every day in the streets, she heard Southern drawls and Midwestern accents. For a place that had always been so small and suspicious of outsiders, it felt like the entire country had descended on Boston.

Suddenly, a crash.

Abby looked over, and Harold was on the ground.

"Harold?!" she exclaimed, jumping up.

As Arthur went to help, a couple of waiters stopped, and Harold waved them away.

"My dear," he said, blinking in shock. "I dare say someone slipped a banana peel under my chair."

Although he tried to downplay it, Abby could tell he was embarrassed, and maybe even stunned. But it was so loud and busy that, except for two ladies at the next table, no one saw it.

He fixed his tie and smoothed out his jacket, whose lapels were now wet. He had spilled his cocktail but didn't drop the glass, a triumph for any good drinker. Abby picked up his boutonniere off the floor and propped up the petals.

"Here," she said, putting it in his pocket. "What happened?"

"I dropped my Chesterfield. As I reach down, kerplunk!"

"The floor is slippery," Arthur said.

Abby smiled, but it was more an excuse than an explanation. While Harold could handle his liquor, he sometimes reached levels of intoxication that all the charm and confidence in the world couldn't hide. She noticed it more in his eyes than in his actions, that vague and distant gaze.

His drinking had gotten worse since his brother left, and even though Abby didn't agree with the solution, she sympathized with the cause. Despite all the arguments and hostility between George and her over the years, she was terrified he was going off to war.

When she and Arthur sat back down, Harold remained standing.

"I must be going," he said.

"Going? But it's our last night."

"I find this place a bit stuffy. I think I'll go see some friends."

"Where?"

"Just a nearby joint."

Sal and Frances came off the dance floor, their faces flushed and out of breath.

"Oh...what...a...joy," Frances said, holding her hand to her chest. "I need water..."

Sal called for a waiter, who hurried over with a tray under his arm.

"Get us some water, Jimmy. Will ya?"

"You got it, boss—"

As the man went to go, Sal stopped him and turned.

"What can I get you all for drinks?"

Abby looked up at Harold, who was still in a daze, his body swaying. Considering his condition, she couldn't let him go alone.

"We're gonna leave," she blurted.

"So early?" Frances moaned.

"Harold wants to stop by another place."

There was a long pause, and everyone looked at each other.

"I'll take her home," Sal said, finally. "Go have fun."

He made it sound spontaneous, but Abby knew it was planned. She didn't feel bad about going, knowing Frances and Sal probably wanted to be alone. The only thing she regretted was that she and Arthur didn't have a chance to dance.

"Have a glorious summer, Darling," Frances said, leaning up to kiss Harold. "Do write from Bermuda."

"First chance I get."

Everyone hugged and the men shook hands, a warm farewell that got Abby emotional. The semester was over, and Arthur was going back to Texas. Even if they ever all got together again, she knew it wouldn't be for a long time.

She grabbed her purse, and they wound through the crowd, stopping in the lobby so Arthur could get her coat. He took her hand, and they went out into the mild evening air. As they walked, Harold was strangely quiet, but once they turned the corner, he perked up. Ahead, Abby saw a sign *Jacques* in glowing yellow neon. She had passed the building dozens of times but never noticed it before. Boston seemed to have a dive bar on every block.

They got to the entrance, a single black door, and Harold turned to them.

"Here, I shall bid my farewell," he said.

Abby frowned, almost insulted.

"Like hell. We're coming in."

He hesitated and then made a guilty grin.

"It's really not your scene, my dear."

"I'm no debutante," she said, and she reached for the door before he could stop her.

"Don't say you weren't warned…"

She walked in, and it was dark and crowded. Along the back wall was a bar, and in the corner, a small dance floor where a black trio was hammering out jazz numbers. It took her eyes a moment to adjust, but when they did, she saw women hanging on other women, men flirting with other men.

"Can I get some drinks?" Harold asked.

"Yep," she said, nodding quickly.

"A gin and tonic, please," Arthur said.

When Harold walked away, Abby looked around, still in shock.

"Not what I imagined."

"Nice to see people enjoying themselves," Arthur said.

She smiled; she always admired his tolerance.

Harold came back, handing Abby a dry Martini, and she realized she hadn't said what she wanted. They stood together sipping their drinks, and the music was loud enough that it didn't feel strange not to talk. Harold took out a cigarette and offered one to Arthur, who declined with a polite smile.

"Dammit," he said, patting all his pockets. "My lighter must have fallen out."

He turned to two women beside them and asked for a light. As one of them went into her purse, her friend looked up, and Abby froze. Standing in the shadows was Ms. Stetson, dressed in a gray suit and slacks. They were close enough that Abby couldn't pretend not to recognize her, and she knew it would be one of the most awkward greetings of her life. But she didn't have time to make it because the door burst open.

"Don't move!"

A dozen police officers ran in. The band stopped playing, the lights went on, and patrons looked around panicked. The cops didn't have their guns drawn, but their billy clubs were just as threatening. They went up to groups of people, inspecting their clothing and asking questions. When one young man tried to resist, they handcuffed him and dragged him out.

Abby looked at Arthur.

"Stay calm," he whispered, and when two cops came over, he said, "What seems to be the trouble, officers?"

"You got any ID?" one of them barked.

Arthur went into his jacket pocket and took out a small booklet, the words *Army Corps – United States Army* with an eagle stamped across the front.

"Army?" the officer asked, and his tone was more respectful.

"47th Fighter Squadron."

"May I ask your business here?"

"Just out for drinks. I'm on leave until Tuesday."

"And who's in your party?"

As he asked, Abby watched Ms. Stetson's expression get tense. All around, people were getting taken out of the bar, the sounds of shouting, arguments, and nervous pleas.

"The five of us," Abby said, pointing to everyone including the professor and her friend.

The cop looked over at the two women.

"Miss, do you know there's an ordnance against girls wearing guy's clothes, and vice versa?"

The professor stood up straight, humiliated but proud.

"I wasn't aware, officer," she said coldly.

With a sigh, the man closed Arthur's ID and handed it back.

"Just so you know, this is a fag joint."

"What a crime," Arthur replied.

He said it in a way where his sarcasm wasn't entirely obvious, and even the cops looked confused.

"Healy," the man yelled, calling over to his sergeant. "These ones are okay."

CHAPTER NINETEEN

The streetcar began to slow down, its metal wheels screeching as it crept around the bend. Thomas glanced over at Abby, who sat nestled between him and their mother, her arms crossed and yawning. George was across from them with his duffel bag between his knees. There was something significant about their positions, the three of them together and George not, but Thomas never gave much thought to symbolism.

They came to a stop, and some passengers got up. At 6 am, Thomas had expected it to be quiet, but the trolley was packed. They walked down the stairwell and to the street where newsboys shouted out the headlines. The RAF had obliterated Cologne, and three Japanese subs had been sunk off the coast of Australia. Thomas read the paper most days, and based on the reports, it sounded like the Allies were crushing their enemies on every front. But it wasn't just the Germans who used propaganda, and he was sure they weren't always getting the full story.

As they waited at the curb, a cop directing traffic saw Thomas' uniform and waved them across. They walked through the large granite archways of South Station, and inside, people rushed in every direction, schedule boards flickering on the walls. For some reason, Thomas thought there would be a ceremony, or at least a reception, a lieutenant or corporal to greet recruits with a salute, maybe a table of coffee and donuts. But he realized then that George was on his own, slipping off to war like a commuter going to work.

"I think it's track one, Ma," George said.

They watched him as he looked at his ticket and then up to the timetable, but no one had any thoughts or advice. Trains and travel were intimidating for a family that had never gone farther than Maine.

"This way," he said, finally.

They followed him out to the platforms where a dozen trains sat waiting, their engines rumbling. Thomas saw signs for Providence, Stanford, and Newark, places he had heard about but had never been to. A part of him was even jealous that George would get to see things and go places that he might not.

When they walked up to the first car, a conductor with a mustache and blue hat smiled.

"New York?" he asked.

"Washington D.C.," George said.

"That's right. You'll change at Penn Station."

As they waited, there was a somber silence, and George's departure was more real than it had ever been. In the distance, Thomas saw a mother and father hugging their adult son. He didn't know if the young man was leaving for the military, but it was some poignant reflection of their own situation.

"All aboard," the conductor called out.

With the time so close, they all got anxious. Glancing over to Abby, Thomas saw her lip quivering, and it got him choked up. As a family, they had never been emotional like Italians. Their father had probably cried more than all of them combined, unusual for a man who was tough as steel. But the moment George grabbed his bag and tossed it over his shoulder, Mrs. Nolan threw her arms around him and burst into tears.

"Ma, it's okay," he said.

"Be careful, be careful," she said, the agony in her voice sending a chill up Thomas' back.

"I will, Ma. I promise."

He gently took her arms off him and then hugged Abby. Whether she was too upset to speak, Thomas couldn't tell, but when they pulled apart, all she could say was, "Write."

"First chance I get."

Finally, he turned to Thomas who, for a second, thought he saw that mischievous smirk from their youth. It was the same look George had right before he smacked him or pulled their sister's hair. And if it was, Thomas didn't mind. Sarcasm was always easier to handle than sadness.

"Brother," he said.

Thomas smiled, and he thought they would shake. But instead, George reached into his pocket, took out his keys, and dangled them.

"What's this?" Thomas asked.

"The Chevy. It's yours. Take care of her."

Thomas swallowed.

"Thanks."

"There's some gas rations in my dresser. Top drawer."

When the whistle sounded, George hugged Abby and their mother again. He went toward the door, looking back every few steps. He got on, and the train began to roll, slow enough that the conductor was still yelling for latecomers to hurry.

While his mother and sister waved, Thomas just watched with a blank stare. Then he quietly turned around and started back down the platform.

"Thomas?" Abby said, but he didn't look back.

"Thomas!" his mother exclaimed.

"Wait..."

Hearing them trying to catch up only made him walk faster. And when he walked into the station, he went straight for the bathrooms because he didn't want them to see him sobbing.

······

For a place that had once been as dull as a government office, headquarters was now busy all the time. Whenever Thomas came to work, he would see officials from the Army, State Guard, and Office of Civilian Defense, as well as people from the endless civilian volunteer groups that had formed since Pearl Harbor. There were members from the Women's Defense Corp too, society ladies in big hats and long coats, marching through the hallways like they were on a mission. Somedays it felt like the country was running the entire war out of the building.

Once roll call was over, Thomas headed for the stairwell. Before each shift, men with the harbor patrol had to get their assignments from the captain. While the routes didn't vary, the units did, and it was a clumsy attempt at secrecy because no one believed there were spies or saboteurs among them. The coordination was even worse, the water taxis always showing up late and sometimes not at all.

"Thomas?"

He stopped and looked back to see DiMarco in the doorway.

"Lieutenant," he said.

"Have a minute?"

Thomas hesitated, if only because he didn't want to be late. Of all the responsibilities of the job, roll call and assignments were the most important because once they left the building and started their shifts, they were on their own.

"I've gotta—"

"Don't worry. I'll put you down."

Thomas relented with a nod and went into the office, and the lieutenant shut the door.

"Have a seat," DiMarco said.

Thomas took the rickety swivel chair across from the desk. The small room looked more suited to a clerk or typist, with a cabinet and a single window that looked out to a fire escape. Everything about headquarters was shabby, from the furniture to the walls and ceilings. Like any public organization, the department struggled for funding, and now with the war, money was even tighter.

"So, George is off to boot camp?" DiMarco said, sitting down.

"Who told you that?"

"A little birdie."

Thomas made a sour grin.

"We saw him off this morning, actually."

Their eyes locked.

"I know it ain't easy. I got two cousins overseas."

Thomas appreciated the sympathy, but as someone with just two sisters, DiMarco would never have to worry about losing a brother in combat.

"One is on the *USS Yorktown*," he went on. "They got hit pretty bad last week in the Pacific."

"I read about it."

"The other is with the 1st Armored Division in Ireland—"

"You didn't call me in to talk about war, did you?" Thomas asked, and he knew DiMarco well enough that he could interrupt.

"No, I didn't. We've got a problem."

"What's the problem?"

"Officer Collins," he said, and Thomas cringed. "He's filed a complaint."

"What's that mean?"

"It ain't good. And you've only been on the job six months. Things are different now, Thomas. With the country at war, the chief ain't letting anything slip."

Thomas knew it was a risk to confront Collins, but he had never expected to get turned in. Even as a rookie, he understood that, in the code of police honor, disputes between officers were always kept private.

"A reprimand?"

"It might be more than that, unfortunately. It's gotta go before the disciplinary board."

"Shit."

"There might be a way out of it," DiMarco said, and Thomas looked up.

"Yeah?"

DiMarco paused, tapping his fingers on the desk.

"The feds need help monitoring the shipyards," he said.

"Don't we have that covered?"

"It's not just about German sabotage. Theft too. And there's talk of another strike at Bethlehem Steele, possibly the Chelsea Shipyard. They want someone on the inside who can keep an eye on things."

"A mole?"

DiMarco smirked.

"You've been reading too many dime novels. They just want a contact. I know you worked there."

"I was a guard."

DiMarco tilted his head as if to disagree.

"Your pops wasn't, your brother neither," he said, and the mention of his father made Thomas uneasy. "You put us in touch with someone, and I'll talk to the chief. Maybe we can get this situation with Collins squashed."

Thomas sat thinking. He didn't like background deals, and he didn't like feeling pressured to set one up. He had always prided himself on being honest, and all his life he had been around cons, scams, and deceit. On the scrappy streets of East Boston, everyone seemed to have an angle, from shop owners running numbers to church ladies cheating at bingo. But he believed in loyalty and, considering DiMarco had gotten his brother out of trouble, Thomas owed him a favor.

"Yeah," he said, finally. "I might know somebody."

CHAPTER TWENTY

Abby sat next to Arthur on the bench as cars sped by in the early morning rush. Despite all the congestion, the narrow streets and endless buildings, East Boston was prettier in the spring when the trees were in bloom.

They held hands the whole time, shoulder to shoulder, and he even told her he loved her, although that much she knew. When she made him promise he would come back, he did, but she realized it was foolish, the girlish demands of young romance.

She had always imagined this day to be more dramatic, a teary farewell at some dock or airfield. But his father was giving him a ride to South Station where he would get the train to New York and then a plane back to Randolph Field in Texas. It was sad to think his family had no farewell party, but his mother had died five years before, and his brother lived in California. Aside from some cousins in Chelsea, Arthur only had his father. Growing up, Abby had always resented her family, but after losing her father, she realized that nothing was more important.

"Avraham?"

They both turned, and it was his father. He was locking up the shop, unable to leave it open because he had no help. His last employee had joined the Navy a week before Arthur came back, and with the economy booming, he was having trouble finding someone else.

"Avraham?" Abby said with a curious frown.

"Yiddish. It's my birth name. Only he uses it."

They got up, and he threw his duffle bag over his shoulder. As they walked over, she could still see the faint marks of the graffiti Mr. Gittell had removed, ethnic slurs scribbled on the wall. Prejudice against Jews had gotten bad before the war, ironic for a neighborhood that had once been half-Jewish. Like everything, Mrs. Nolan blamed it on the Italians, but Abby knew the Irish were no better. As a girl, she heard *Kike* and *Hymie* in the schoolyard as much as *Wop* and *Dago*.

"Miss Abigail," his father said, lifting his hat with a smile.

When he tried to take the bag, Arthur swatted him away, and they both laughed. They all walked over to the Buick, the same car she had watched him drive away in six months earlier when he left the first time. She had worried about him then, of course, but it was more the selfish angst of a love affair cut short. The country wasn't at war, and they had only gone out a few times together. This visit had changed everything, and any doubts or reluctance she had before were gone. She knew he was the one.

"Pa, what if I told you we're gonna get married when I get back?"

Abby was stunned; it was like he had read her mind. But she also felt a little insulted because, while he always liked to tease his father, it wasn't something to joke about.

"I would be most happy," Mr. Gittell said as he got into the car.

Even with his heavy accent, it sounded sincere. If they ever did marry, getting the approval of even one parent would be a hurdle, especially with their religious differences.

She gave Arthur a cute smirk, and he walked over, glancing at all the trash barrels that had been left on the sidewalk for collection.

"I wish this could be more dignified," he said.

"There's only one way to do it."

"Which is?"

"Get in the car and go."

He leaned forward, and they embraced. It was the tightest he had ever hugged her, and she didn't want him to let go. When some guys in a work truck whistled, she wasn't embarrassed because she didn't care what people thought anymore.

Finally, they pulled apart.

"You take care of your mother," he said.

"I will."

"And yourself."

She looked up, her lips pressed together.

"I will. Please be safe."

They kissed, and he walked over and got in the car. Mr. Gittell revved the engine and squinted into traffic. Inside, she felt like she was going to burst, and she impressed even herself by staying so calm. Whatever happened, she didn't want his last memory to be of her standing on the curb in a fit of tears.

As they pulled out, she waved, and Arthur smiled, a smile that, however tender, couldn't hide some underlying dread. For all his talk about coming back, they both knew there was a chance he might not.

Soon the car disappeared down Bennington Street, leaving her with the same hollow feeling she had the last time she watched him drive away.

"Abby?" someone called, but it sounded more like *uh-buh*.

When she turned, Chickie was walking toward her. She had on a sack dress, dirty shoes, and a paper boy's bag over her shoulder. Sometimes she looked like an urchin, which made Abby mad because the Ciarlones weren't poor like families in Maverick Square.

"Morning, Chickie."

"You cry."

Abby smiled, wiping her eyes with her fingers.

"I know. It's okay," she said. "Whaddya got there?"

She looked in the bag and saw pieces of wire, tobacco tins, a rusted electrical outlet, and more.

"Collecting scrap?"

Chickie nodded.

"With your help, we're gonna win this war!"

Chickie's face brightened, and Abby knew how it felt to be praised.

She continued down the sidewalk, lifting the lid on every barrel and looking inside. As Abby watched, she was touched by Chickie's kindness and determination, and it somehow made Arthur's departure a little easier.

Abby headed home, hoping the two blocks would give her enough time to compose herself. But when she walked in the front door, her mother put down her mop and rushed over.

"What's wrong?"

"Arthur," Abby said, her voice cracking. "He left. Just now."

Mrs. Nolan stepped forward and hugged her, more affection than she had shown in months.

"Oh dear, I'm sorry. I was wondering why you left so early."

"He had to be at South Station by eight."

Abby wiped her eyes again, forcing a smile.

"I saw Chickie on Bennington Street digging through barrels," she said.

"She goes down before school on trash days to find scrap metal and rubber and such."

Thomas came down the stairs in his uniform, his badge shining, gun on his hip. Abby had almost expected George to be behind him, and realizing he was gone gave her that same hollow feeling she used to get in the weeks and months after her father died.

"Come," her mother said. "Let me make you breakfast."

"No, thanks. I'm not hungry. I gotta go into school."

"Thomas, give your sister a ride to BU."

Looking in the mirror, he ran his fingers through his hair, and then put on his cap.

"Aren't you done for the year?" he asked.

"I've gotta take care of a couple of things."

"Sure then. Let's go."

......

It was funny to see Thomas behind the wheel, his hands tense and staring ahead. For years, George had been the only one with a license, but Thomas got his that winter after one of his colleagues said he would need it if he ever wanted to make sergeant. Still, he looked uneasy, and Abby didn't think it was just the normal nerves of being a new driver. He had been irritable lately, his temper short, something that was more obvious because he had always been the most stable one in the family. Now he was always distracted, snapping if he burned toast or stomping back into the house after forgetting his wallet. Abby could have attributed it to his upcoming wedding—everyone got anxious—or because George had left. But she knew Thomas well enough to realize it was something else.

For weeks, she had wanted to ask him, but she knew he wouldn't tell her. And she could hardly blame him. As close as they all were, everyone in the family hid their deepest fears, their most private insecurities. Abby was sure they had gotten it from their mother, who was always more concerned with appearances, because their father would talk about anything.

They pulled over on Commonwealth Avenue, and she reached for the door.

"Thanks for the lift," she said, glancing over.

"Anytime."

"Is everything okay?"

He frowned.

"Of course."

She waited until he looked at her, and when their eyes met, she smiled.

"See you later," he said with a faint grin.

"Yeah. See you later."

She got out and waved, watching as the black Chevy sputtered away. When George first bought it, they were all so impressed they didn't care that it was ten years old and rusty.

She went up the steps of the Charles Hayden Memorial Building whose grand façade always made her proud to be in college. When she walked in, the corridors were quiet, and everyone she passed looked like they were either teaching staff or in administration. Most of the students were gone, and while summer courses didn't start until mid-June, professors stayed on for another week to finish grading and make the fall curriculum.

She turned into the stairwell and went down to the basement, following a long hallway until she saw the plaque: *Janet Stetson, English Literature*. Through the crack of the door, she could see light, and she heard classical music playing. Knowing the professor was in gave Abby a mix of relief and dread, but she knew she had to see her.

She knocked once and waited. Moments later, the door opened, and Ms. Stetson stood in a flowered dress. With her makeup and hoop earrings, she looked more feminine than the night Abby saw her at the bar.

"Ms. Nolan?" she said, her tone somewhere between haughty and confused.

"May I speak with you?"

The professor paused so long that Abby thought she would say no, and she wouldn't have been surprised because Ms. Stetson was that type of person.

"Come in," she said, finally.

Abby stepped into the small room, which had a desk, bookcase, and not much else. Without windows, it felt claustrophobic. Female teachers always seemed to get the worst offices.

"Now," the professor said, not offering Abby a chair. "What can I do for you?"

"I went to see Professor Bauermeister. He told me he was fired."

"I'm sorry. I don't deal with personnel issues."

"But you must have been aware of it?"

"We were informed he had been terminated for violating the ethics of the university."

"He didn't do anything wrong. He was arrested because his brother is a Nazi."

"We're at war. Precautions must be taken."

"But he hasn't seen his brother in twenty years."

"I'm sure that was taken into account."

"How can they fire him? Even the police let him go."

"Ms. Nolan," she said, getting flustered, "I don't really have time to—"

"Could you at least talk to the administration?"

"It's beyond my purview, I'm afraid."

"What about Mrs. Sears? She's a dean."

Ms. Stetson stopped, and her expression went flat. After seeing them kiss in Chemistry class, Abby had suspected they were involved, and now she knew.

"This conversation is over," the professor said coldly.

Since coming to BU, Abby had tried to be proper and polite like her mother asked. But she was tired of being meek, and she knew that to get anywhere in life, she would have to be tough.

"You can help the man!" she said, and as the professor urged her toward the door, Abby turned to her. "You know what it's like to be an outsider!"

Ms. Stetson stamped her foot.

"How dare you!"

Their eyes locked, and the professor stood fuming. Abby knew it sounded like blackmail, but she didn't mean it that way. After a minute of tense silence, the professor sighed, and in some way, she even looked relieved.

"Okay, okay," she said, nodding. "I'll see what I can do."

CHAPTER TWENTY-ONE

When Thomas stepped off the boat in East Boston, it was almost dark. They had been delayed in Charlestown for an hour after two oil tankers got to port early and had to wait for Navy tugs to take them up the Chelsea River. The ships had arrived with a military convoy, but with the risk of sabotage, they couldn't go a mile through the harbor without an escort.

They hadn't finished their patrol, but the sergeant let them go anyway. It had been a long day, and busier than usual. At noon, an air raid siren went off, creating panic in the streets, and they ran to their post by the Customs House only to find out it was a false alarm. Later, when they caught some kids stealing scrap metal in the North End, Thomas chased one of them and cut his hand jumping a fence.

When he got to the end of the pier, he always felt a slight relief to see that the Chevy was still there. Growing up, anything that wasn't locked up, nailed down, or hidden was vulnerable. At eight, his first bike was stolen in front of the penny candy shop; at twelve, someone took his boots while he was playing hockey on the marsh behind Saratoga Street. But any worry was only paranoia because, since the war started, petty crimes like auto theft and pickpocketing were down. And with the military all over the waterfront, even the most brazen criminals stayed away.

He got in the car, and it took three tries to start, the engine spewing black smoke. As he pulled out, he looked over to East Boston Works. He could never drive by without thinking of his father. With its new cranes and warehouses, it looked nothing like when he worked there, which somehow made it easier. Not only was it twice the size, but it was surrounded by barbed wire fencing, the entrances guarded by MPs.

As he waited in traffic at Maverick Square, three men walked by, and he realized one of them was Vin Labadini. The light turned, and he quickly pulled over and parked in front of a pharmacy. He got out and followed them up the sidewalk, watching as they turned into Sonny's bar. In their work clothes and boots, he could tell they had just come from the shipyard, and it seemed late for the day shift.

When he walked in, everyone turned, and he sometimes forgot he was in his police uniform. In the back, men were crowded around the pool tables, and bebop was playing on the jukebox. He went over to the bar, and the bartender looked up from pouring a beer. At first, he gave Thomas a cold look, but then his face brightened.

"Barry Nolan's son?" he asked.

Thomas smiled. He had never been so happy to hear his father's name.

"I am."

"Welcome. What can I getcha?"

"Just lemonade, please."

As the bartender filled the glass, Thomas looked around the dark room and saw Labadini and his friends in the corner.

"On the house," the bartender said, sliding the glass over to him.

"Thanks."

"Anytime."

Thomas walked over to the table, and when Labadini saw him, he stopped talking.

"Nolan," he said with a nod.

His two friends turned, their faces red and smudged from work.

"I was hoping we could talk," Thomas said.

"Talk?"

"Just a couple of minutes."

"Guys, go take a powder."

They gave Thomas a hard stare and then looked back at their friend.

"What?"

"Go. Beat it!"

Without another word, they took their drinks, got up, and left. Thomas sat down, trying to hide an amused grin.

"I didn't think first shift ended so late," he said.

"We had a union meeting."

"Yeah," Thomas said, sipping his drink. "How'd it go?"

Labadini ignored the question.

"What can I do for you?"

"We need your help."

"Who's we?"

"BPD for starters."

"Who else?"

Thomas hesitated, tapping his fingers on the table before looking up.

"The feds."

Labadini's face dropped.

"You asking me to be a rat fink?"

"Nothing like that," Thomas said, trying to downplay it even though he really didn't know. "They just need a contact. Someone on the inside. They know I worked there—"

"As a screw."

Thomas frowned. It was the worst insult for a security guard.

"Look," he said. "I'm gonna be straight with you. I'm in a jam. I cracked another cop."

"How's that my problem?"

Their eyes locked. Pleading with a thug was humiliating and seemed like punishment enough for punching out Collins.

"I can't lose my job. I'm getting married."

While the two things seemed unrelated, it was the truth, and Thomas wasn't just looking for sympathy.

"Married?"

"An Italian girl," Thomas said, hoping it might soften him.

"Italian-American, you mean?"

Thomas shook his head.

"From Italy."

Labadini leaned back, arms crossed and chewing his gums. Thomas could tell he was considering it.

"Okay," he said, finally. "You helped me out. I know how to return a favor…"

Thomas nodded, but his decision not to arrest Labadini had been more for his family than for him.

"But I need a favor too. Get my father's boat back. The old man can't work. He's miserable."

The seizure of boats and other property from Italians, Germans, and other foreigners was done by order of the Attorney General. Thomas didn't know if the feds would agree, but he had to try.

"Deal."

……

Thomas sat at the table, slurping the beef stew with the same restrained disgust as when his mother used to make him and his brother eat porridge as kids. It didn't taste the same without pepper which, for some reason, was now in short supply. No one knew what and when something would be hard to get. There was plenty of sugar again, but hardware stores were out of paintbrushes because the pig bristles came from China. Rumors of an oil crisis were making many people switch back to coal, and to conserve wool, the city passed an ordinance that said men no longer had to wear tops on the beach.

However strange and unpredictable life was now, they didn't have to be reminded of the war because they looked at George's empty chair each night. And while they were proud of his service, his absence made them think of everything they had lost and might lose. Since their father's death, dinners had become quiet, somber events. Now with George gone, the silence was almost unbearable.

"I talked with Father Ward," Mrs. Nolan said, and Thomas and his sister looked up. "He's set the wedding for the Fourth of July."

"Fourth of July?" Abby moaned.

"Ma, that seems—"

"It was the only date available."

"The funnest day of the year," Abby said.

Thomas gave her a sharp look.

"I'm sorry," their mother said. "But with all the weddings…and funerals."

The remark was grim enough that they all stopped chewing. Just the week before, the brother of a girl Thomas and Abby had gone to grade school with was killed in the Solomon Islands. While neither of them knew Patrick Donegan well enough to grieve, it was always shocking to hear that a local boy died. Their mother pointed out that, of the dozen casualties from East Boston so far, he was the first Irish one.

With the country at war, churches were busier than ever, and people always seemed to seek religion in bad times, never in good ones. Thomas had wanted the wedding in late July, but he knew the earlier the better. With Connie pregnant, they had to marry as soon as possible to avoid any scandal. He didn't care what people thought, but he knew she did, and the shame of having a child out of wedlock was no way to start a life together.

They finished eating, and everyone got up. As Thomas reached for the casserole dish, Abby asked, "What happened to your hand?"

He looked at the gash on his palm, which was small but swollen.

"I cut it shaving."

"Liar," she said, and he smirked.

Their mother filled the sink, and they brought everything in. The kitchen seemed emptier now without George, and Thomas even missed the nights when they all had to jostle for space.

Once the table was cleared, Thomas turned to go upstairs.

"Would you do me a favor?" his mother asked, wiping off her hands.

He nodded and followed her into the dining room. She opened the drawer of the china cabinet where she kept her war bonds and money in a lockbox. He didn't like her having so much cash around, but they had never been robbed, which was lucky because they were always away in the summer. The closest they came was when their father said his wheelbarrow had been stolen, only to remember that he lent it to Mr. Ianocconi.

"This is for Mrs. Ciarlone," she said, taking out an envelope and checking inside. "Won't you take it over?"

"Sure, Ma."

"Everything's in there. Tell her to keep it somewhere safe."

"I'll try, but I don't think she'll understand."

With a frown, she handed it to him.

He walked out, and it was warm enough that he didn't need a coat. When he got to the Ciarlones' porch, he didn't have to knock because someone had seen him coming. The door opened, and it was Chickie.

"Hi, *Tomma*," she said.

Her pronunciation was still off, but it was getting better. Thomas attributed it to Connie, who had been helping her to speak and act right, the skills only one young lady could teach to another.

"Is Connie here?"

"Connie here. Yes."

There was an awkward pause, Chickie squirming with a wide grin.

"Would you mind getting her?"

Connie came rushing over to the door.

"You can't be here!" she said with a forceful whisper.

"What?"

She nudged Chickie inside and shut the door. Then she took his hand and led him down the steps.

"It's gotta be planned."

"Planned?"

"Now that we're betrothed."

It sounded like a word from a Shakespeare play, and although Thomas wanted to laugh, he didn't.

"You mean engaged?"

She ignored the question, and they headed up the sidewalk.

"My aunt likes the old ways," she said, lighting a cigarette. "That's how they do it back home."

Considering they had been sleeping together for months, the formalities of courtship seemed silly. But he couldn't argue, and Mrs. Ciarlone was the closest thing she had to a mother. He didn't know much about Connie's family except that her father had died in a mining accident when she was young. And while she never talked about her mother, she had mentioned him enough that Thomas knew his name: *Antonio*. The mystery of her past life was something that both tormented and fascinated him.

They got to the top of the street and stopped at the fence where a small cliff looked over the roadway below. The sky was clear, the air rich with the smell of flowers and grass. In the distance, the tank farm was a stretch of black, but beyond it, the city glowed like it always had, although it was only half as bright. Thomas never understood the reason for a *dim-out*, and it seemed that darkness could only help with defense if it was total.

"These are for your aunt," he said, giving her the envelope. "War bonds."

"They will be needed."

The reply was cute but vague.

"How do you mean?"

She stared at the horizon, her hair blowing in the breeze. Her eyes were narrow, her face tense. Even if she was a master at hiding her feelings, he could always tell when something was wrong. But he didn't mind. As warped as it seemed, he always got some quiet thrill from her distress. She was prettier when she was anxious and devastating when she was upset.

"We were told G.E. will no longer make light bulbs. They will make things for the American army."

The news was no surprise. Factories everywhere were changing their production over to war supplies and materiel.

"Who needs lightbulbs?" he joked.

"But they can only use American workers. Citizens. Everyone else must go."

"Don't worry. By then you'll be my wife."

She turned suddenly, her expression sharp but hopeful.

"My mother set the date," he explained. "Fourth of July."

"Fourth of July?"

"For the wedding."

She closed her eyes, and he thought he heard her sigh. Whether it was from relief or joy, he didn't know, but she looked like she would cry. He leaned forward to hug her, and she was at first stiff. Then he pressed his lips to her, and she collapsed into his arms.

CHAPTER TWENTY-TWO

As they crossed the neck to Point Shirley, the sky was cloudy, the sea a haze of gray. But the air was warm, and with the window down, the smell of the shore reminded Abby of summers past. In the distance, she saw a Navy patrol boat, but she wasn't startled or even curious because the military was everywhere. With Fort Dawes at the end of the peninsula, Army convoys passed through East Boston and Winthrop almost every day. A sight that had once inspired in people feelings of awe and patriotism was now ordinary.

They drove in silence, their mother in the front seat wearing a felt hat and short-sleeved dress, her hands around her pocketbook. After two weeks with the car, Thomas still looked nervous behind the wheel, leaning forward and squinting.

There was always something dramatic about going to open up the cottage, a tradition so old it was like a sacred family ritual. For years, their uncle Walter used to drive them, and after he died, they would all pile into a taxi. As a girl, Abby got that same feeling she had at Christmas, bursting with anticipation and unable to sleep the night before. All that had changed, however, and whether it was from the war or getting older, that giddy excitement was gone, replaced by the dull sadness of having lost it.

They turned onto Bay View Avenue, a narrow lane of modest summer homes, most of which were still shuttered for winter. Abby wondered who would be back this summer; over the years, the community of Point Shirley had been dwindling. Lots of families had sold during the Depression, and many left once their kids were grown. Even for those who stayed, it was hard to vacation in wartime when restrictions were harsh. Coastal areas were under a permanent blackout order, and any house showing even a sliver of light would be fined. While the beaches were open during the day, they were forbidden at night, and throughout the town, signs were posted warning of German U-boats.

But they weren't just there for fun and relaxation. Thomas was getting married, and with only two weeks until the wedding, they had to get things ready.

They came around the bend, and Abby could see the small cottage that looked out to Winthrop Harbor. It seemed different in the daylight, its cracked shingles and uneven porch, more like a modified shack than a summer home. But despite its modesty, it held some of her most precious childhood memories and recent ones too, including her night with Arthur.

On one side was the large yard where they would have the reception; on the other was a rotted picket fence that their father had built years before with the help of their neighbor Mr. Loughran. In the back, a large elm tree hung over the picnic table where they ate dinner each night.

They parked and got out, and the first thing everyone did was stretch their legs. Even if it was just three of them, the ride over felt cramped with all their things.

Thomas walked to the trunk and, using a penknife, he cut the twine holding it down and opened it. Inside, there were three large suitcases, none of which were full. Now that he and Abby were working and their mother was busy with her civic activities, they would all split their time between Point Shirley and East Boston. It was a big change from previous summers when once they arrived, they never left. By August, their life in the city would feel as vague and distant as a dream.

As Thomas reached in for their bags, Abby walked over to help.

"No!" he said, and she stepped back. "Take Ma inside."

While she could have been insulted, she smiled instead, knowing that bringing the luggage in was something he always did with George. Then she tried to take her mother's arm, but Mrs. Nolan shooed her away, which wasn't a surprise. The stubbornness that ran through their family was intense, and they all refused help when they most needed it.

Abby followed her mother up to the porch where a few scattered leaves lay stuck to the floorboards. As Mrs. Nolan put in the key, Abby noticed her hand shaking, but it was probably more from excitement than mental anguish because she had been doing great.

They stepped inside, and the air was stale. The first thing her mother did was drop her pocketbook and open some windows. Thomas walked in behind them, the suitcases light enough that he was able to carry all three.

"Don't forget the linens," their mother said.

"And the food," Abby added.

With a sigh, he turned around and went back out to the car.

"I think this is where we'll have the buffet," Mrs. Nolan said, pointing at the couch.

"Why not outside?"

"It depends on the mosquitoes," she said, hands on her hips and out of breath. "Make sure the icebox is clean. We'll have to call down to Pulsifer's for ice."

"Are they even open?"

Her mother ignored her, instead going over to the mantel to wind the clock. Abby went into the kitchen, and she didn't have to run her fingers along the cabinets to know everything was covered in dust. On the window behind the sink, some flowers lay slumped and withered in a ceramic vase. Glancing out to the backyard, she saw the picnic table and remembered how her mother and father would sit there talking long after she and her brothers had gone to the beach to meet friends.

"You forgot the biscuit tins."

Abby spun around to see Thomas in the doorway. In his arms were the two bags of dry goods they had brought from home, flour, sugar, oatmeal, and baking soda.

"I don't eat biscuits," she said with a smirk.

He put everything down on the counter and looked around.

"Not much has changed."

She couldn't tell if he was being naïve or sarcastic, but something about the remark got her emotional. She didn't have time to react because he smacked the wall and then held out his hand to reveal a flattened ant.

"Repulsive," she said.

She went back out to the parlor and saw her mother standing on a step stool by the window.

"Ma?"

"I've gotta wash these curtains," she said, struggling to unhook the rod. "They're filthy."

"Can I help?"

"No. See if there's any soap. And tell your brother to ask Mr. Loughran if he has any folding tables we could borrow."

They had only been there ten minutes, and already she was frantic.

"Ma, I can hear you," Thomas said.

He looked over at Abby, and they both grinned. When he left to go next door, she went into the pantry which, except for some cans of fruit and vegetables, was empty. They always took everything home at the end of the summer.

She knelt in the darkness and reached under the bottom shelf where they kept the cleaning supplies. The moment she felt a box of soap, her hand hit something else too, and she froze. She didn't have to see it to know it was one of her father's pipes. Holding it to her nose, she breathed in, and the faint smell of tobacco filled her with nostalgia. She could have cried, but she was more amused than sad, thinking how her mother scorned his smoking so much he had to hide it.

"Abby!"

She shoved the pipe in her dress pocket and ran back out, holding up the soap.

"Good," her mother said as she gathered the curtains in a pile. "Fill up the sink. I'll see if there're any linens upstairs that need washing."

Abby went back into the kitchen and turned on the faucet, the water sputtering a few seconds before a smooth stream came out. Taking a sponge, she wiped the sides of the sink and then plugged the drain. She shook the soap, which was caked from sitting, and was about to pour it when she heard a terrifying scream.

"Ma?!" she shouted.

She got to the parlor just as Thomas was coming in the front door, and they flew upstairs. At the end of the hallway, their mother was leaning against the wall, her hand over her eyes.

"Ma, what's wrong?"

"In there," she said, nodding.

They both peered into the tiny bathroom. It took Abby a moment to see it, but once she did, she cringed. There on the floor beside the tub was a wrinkled rubber condom, and she knew it was from her night with Arthur.

"This is…unconscionable," their mother said. Anytime she was upset or overwhelmed, she used big words.

Thomas took his penknife and picked it up, tossing it in the toilet and pulling the flush chain.

"Ma," he said, and when he tried to put his arm around her, she flinched.

"Is it gone?"

"It's gone."

When he glanced over to Abby, she shrank in shame and humiliation. He knew she had been alone with Arthur because he had shown up that night with Connie. But they never spoke about it, and sometimes avoidance was as good as secrecy.

"Ma," Thomas said, but she still wouldn't look up. "I'm sorry. It's mine."

……

Abby ran up the front steps, fumbling through her purse for the key. They once kept a spare under the mat, but after kicking George out, their father removed it so his son couldn't sneak back in. There was a time when no one on the street locked their doors, but it was so long ago that only their mother remembered it.

"Abby!"

She turned and saw Chickie on the porch next door.

"Hi, Chickie. Getting ready for the blackout?"

"Abby!"

"Sorry, I'm in a rush—"

"Connie," she said, and when Abby glanced over, she rubbed her belly with both hands.

As much as she was in a rush, Abby stopped, and she was curious enough that she walked over to the railing.

"Pardon?"

"Connie," Chickie said again, and this time she mimicked rocking a baby.

Abby smiled, but inside she got a nervous, almost horrifying feeling. She knew she could have misread the gesture, and after what happened at the cottage, she was sensitive about issues of sex and procreation. But she didn't have time to find out because the moment she went to ask more, Mrs. Ciarlone burst out, grabbed Chickie by the wrist, and took her inside.

Abby went into the house and up to her bedroom, pulling her dress over her head and taking her MWDC uniform off the hanger. She put on her skirt, blouse, and blazer, and tied her necktie. Finally, she adjusted her cap in the mirror, pausing to admire herself. Then she looked at her watch and, realizing she only had twenty minutes until roll call, she grabbed her purse and ran out the door.

She got off the streetcar in Day Square, and already the streets were dark. While the dates of backouts were announced, the times were always kept secret, something everyone complained about. Despite community meetings and public hearings, the authorities wouldn't budge, saying that surprise was a test of preparedness. So most shop owners just closed early, and people stayed home if they could. The bars were still open, but the crowd that frequented them never obeyed rules anyway, something Abby worried about as an air raid warden.

Walking down Neptune Road, she passed rundown apartment buildings and triple-deckers. In the alleyways, she saw overflowing garbage cans and clothing lines strung between the buildings. Only five blocks from her house, the neighborhood was a slum, and it was hard to believe it was the same part of the city.

When she reached the end, she could see Wood Island Park, the 70-acre expanse on the bay between the mainland and the airport. With a bathhouse, beach, and walking paths, it was a hidden escape from the congestion of the city. Every winter, the football field was flooded, and kids from all over East Boston would come down to skate or play hockey.

But those days of happy recreation were over, and the war had changed everything. The Army was taking half the land for a new runway, and they had already started clearing trees to build barracks. People could still walk during the day, but it was closed at night and patrolled by soldiers.

Abby crossed the tracks and followed the road along a stretch of saltwater flats where, in the distance, she could see movement. As she approached the park entrance, someone stepped out from the shadows.

"Identify yourself!"

Abby stopped.

"Abigail Nolan."

After a short, but tense pause, the woman said, "Carry on, Private."

Abby walked over to the group standing nearby, two dozen girls in brown uniforms talking quietly.

"Abby?"

Even in a whisper, she knew the voice, but she didn't believe it until Frances walked over.

"What the hell are you doing here?!" she exclaimed, and the leader looked over.

"I'm assigned to *Eastie*."

"Eastie, huh?"

"Isn't that the affectionate term?"

"All the way from Duxbury?"

"I requested it. I'm staying on campus this summer…"

Abby frowned, as surprised as she was confused. After hearing

Frances brag about two months of tennis, boating, and lobster bakes, she couldn't imagine why she would remain in the city.

"Father and I had a dreadful spat, I'm afraid."

"I'm sorry."

"Don't be. He's a lout. My mother found out he's been carrying on with some WAAC in his office."

Abby was stumped, not sure what to say. Frances was always so cheery that it was strange to hear the bitterness in her voice. Just as Abby went to comfort her, the lieutenant called out *Ladies!* And all the chatter stopped.

"I'm Lieutenant Hastings, your unit commander. We'll break into groups of four. Each unit will be assigned a patrol. Our job is to ensure compliance with the blackout order. Nothing more. If anyone gives you any grief, you're to ring the nearest police box. Understand?"

"Yes," everyone said in a low mumble.

"Good. Now, this is Sergeant DiMarco. She'll give you your assignments. Flashlights are in the crate over there."

A short line formed, and when Abby got to the front, she realized it was *Giannina* DiMarco from high school.

"Hi, Nina," she said, the nickname everyone called her by.

"Abigail Nolan? How's Thomas?"

Abby made a sour smile. All her life her girls always asked about Thomas and never about George.

"He's good. He works with your brother."

"Oh, I know," she said, flipping through a notepad. "You're with Private Campanella, Private Joyce, Private—"

"Can I be with them?" Frances blurted. "Frances Farrington."

Nina looked up, her expression sharp. The request was bold, but when Abby gave her a pleading smile, she nodded. A favor between old friends always meant more than protocol.

"Sure, I guess."

"Marvelous!" Frances said.

Nina took out a pen, and Abby could see her smirking. At BU, Frances' elegance was impressive, but in East Boston, it was plain pretentious.

"Done," Nina said. "Day Square to Addison Street. West Side of Bennington."

Abby had to think which side was west, but once she knew, she was relieved. As the area around her neighborhood, it couldn't have been more convenient.

"Thanks."

When they walked over to get flashlights, some girls were struggling to find the switches and others were pointing them at the trees. The box was marked *US Army*, but it was obviously a spare because it also said *K Rations*.

The lieutenant called for attention, and they were all so anxious, she had to ask three times for quiet. After a short talk about safety, duty, and honor, she ordered them to get into columns. Clapping her hands, she waved, and they began to march.

"Is *Eastie* dangerous?" Frances asked, clutching Abby's arm.

"Some parts."

"Are there thieves and ruffians?"

Abby frowned, although she knew her friend was only half-serious.

"Only where we're going," she said.

"Oh, good. Murderers too?"

"If we're lucky."

"Will you protect me—"

Suddenly, a siren blared, startling everyone enough that the procession stopped, but only for a moment. Across the harbor, the city went black, and in the distance, the lights of East Boston flickered off block by block. Immersed in darkness and with only the stars to guide them, they marched back across the salt marsh toward the streets in silence.

CHAPTER TWENTY-THREE

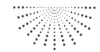

Squinting in the morning sun, Thomas leaned under the hood, careful not to get his uniform dirty. With a screwdriver, he tightened the clamp he had put around the radiator hose to stop it from leaking. George bought the old Chevy from a friend who owned a junkyard in Chelsea, and it was no surprise because it looked like it had been pieced together from parts. It was clunky to drive, the steering loose and the suspension stiff. Thomas couldn't replace the bald tires because there was a rubber shortage. But he already had a sentimental connection to the car, even leaving the cigarette butts in the ashtray because the smell reminded him of his brother.

More than ever before, he needed transportation because getting to and from Point Shirley wasn't easy. In high school, he worked at the theater in East Boston and often got out so late he had to walk back to the cottage. The summer before, he would take the bus and streetcar every day to his job at the shipyard. And while the commute was long, he missed those rides each morning with his father.

"Is it working?"

He glanced over and Abby was on the lawn in a summer dress, her pocketbook dangling from her arm. Even with Arthur gone, she had a twinkle in her eye, a skip in her step. The thrill of love lingered long after a separation, something Thomas experienced when he didn't see Connie for a couple of days.

"It never wasn't working," he said, reaching in the window to start the engine.

"Then why are you fixing it?"

He smirked and walked back to check the leak. When he was sure it had stopped, he slammed the hood shut.

"You ready?"

She smiled and scurried over to get in.

As they pulled away, their mother walked out onto the porch with a porcelain jug. Thomas always liked it when she watered the flowers, seeing it as a sign of her hope and optimism about the future. He tapped the horn, and she waved but didn't startle. After six months without a drink, she was calmer than she had been in years, and he could see it on her face. She still had the bottle of barbiturates Doctor Berman had given her for when she was feeling *particularly morose*. But she never took them, and Thomas was glad. He always believed in the body's ability to heal itself from grief and despair.

"How'd it last night go?" he asked.

"Good, I suppose. The jeweler on Bennington Street forgot to turn his lights off. An old lady on Chaucer Street left a lamp burning. How'd it look from out here?"

"Dark."

He smiled, and not just at his own sarcasm. The night before, he had picked up Connie at work, and they walked the pebbly beach across from the cottage. When the blackout started, they snuggled behind the seawall. It was warm enough that they made love under the moonlight, and he no longer had to be careful because she was already pregnant, a bittersweet benefit.

"Thomas?" Abby said, and when he looked ahead, he saw two soldiers in the street.

He slowed to a stop, and one of them walked over.

"Morning, sir. Can I ask you to hang there for just a bit?"

"Sure."

As they waited, Thomas listened to the engine, always worried that idling for too long would aggravate the leak.

"You hear about Midway?" the young man asked.

"We sank four Jap carriers," Thomas said.

"A hell of a clobbering."

Suddenly, there was a roar, and an Army convoy came around the bend. At the center was a long flatbed truck, and although the tarp over the back was camouflage, it was obvious what was underneath it.

"Artillery?" Thomas asked, and the second soldier grinned.

"Two 90 millimeters. That'll keep the Germans on their toes."

Thomas smiled back, but inside he got an eerie feeling. He didn't like being reminded that they were, in some ways, on the front line.

Once the trucks passed, the men thanked him and got in their jeep, speeding off toward Fort Dawes. Thomas turned onto Shirley Street, and it was dead quiet. It was still early in the season, but in the past, people would have already been arriving for the beach. As they drove down the shore, most of the houses were still closed, and Thomas had yet to see anyone he knew. He didn't know if the desolation was a result of the war or the natural course of time, but it was getting harder to distinguish between the two.

"Seems different, doesn't it?" Abby mumbled.

He nodded but didn't look over.

"Yeah. Seems different."

They were silent for the rest of the ride. When he finally pulled over at the bakery, she just got out and waved.

Thomas continued toward Maverick Square and went down into Sumner Tunnel where traffic was backed up because an Army bus had hit a barrier. It was impossible to go anywhere now without being disrupted by the military, and the only reason he wasn't late for work was that he knew a shortcut through Scollay Square, which he remembered from his days walking the beat. But it didn't matter anyway because by the time he found a parking spot and got into headquarters, it was past seven-thirty and officers were still coming in.

Discipline had gotten sloppy since he had joined the department, more a consequence of the war than poor leadership. Every week, they were losing men to the armed services, and with so many special patrols, it was hard to keep order. At roll call, he realized his tie was loose, but the sergeant didn't notice or care, something that never would have happened in the past.

The moment they were dismissed, someone called, and Thomas looked over to see DiMarco in the doorway.

"Lieutenant?"

When he waved, Thomas didn't hesitate, following him down to his office.

"You hear what happened in the South Pacific?"

"Quite a rout."

"That'll teach the Yamamoto. That bloodthirsty bastard."

The Battle of Midway was two weeks before, but everyone was just talking about it now, mainly because the front page of the *Boston Globe* had a wide photo of U.S. warships repelling Japanese dive bombers. With fighting all across the world, news got delayed, trickling in from different sources. The only reason Thomas wasn't surprised was that his neighbor Mr. Loughran had been getting information over his ham radio, which was always faster.

"Good job with Labadini," DiMarco said, and they both sat. "You sure he wasn't the guinea who whacked you?"

Thomas chuckled.

"It was dark. I gave him the benefit of the doubt."

DiMarco accepted the answer with a long nod.

"The feds are happy. He's been helpful."

Thomas smiled, but that was about as much as he wanted to know. He didn't like intrigue or backroom deals and had only met with Labadini to save his job.

"I'm glad."

"You're off the hook with Collins," the lieutenant said, and Thomas was relieved. "I've got some other good news. We're gonna make you sergeant."

"Sergeant?"

"It's already been cleared with the chief."

"I didn't take the exam."

"Tsk," he scoffed. "You're gonna get an override. We have to make room for the rookies. These ain't normal times…"

Thomas blinked, stunned beyond belief.

"Just one change. You're gonna be in District 7 now."

"East Boston?"

"You're gonna be transferred."

Getting assigned to the station where he had caused a scene was ironic, but that wasn't the only reason he was uneasy. He liked being downtown where he didn't have to see anybody he knew. Working in his own neighborhood, he would now have to deal with people he grew up with, all expecting favors or leniency, the curse of familiarity. Either way, the promotion was a blessing, and with Connie pregnant, he needed the money more than ever.

"Thank you," he said, his voice shaky.

Hearing some officers pass by in the hallway, he glanced over at the clock.

"I won't keep you," the lieutenant said, and they both got up.

When they shook, Thomas could feel the bump from the knuckle DiMarco broke in their match with English High School. He had always considered the lieutenant more of an acquaintance, even though they had trained and sparred together for two years. He never had a wide social circle like his brother George, but in a time of so much fear and uncertainty, he knew friendship was a precious thing.

"I'm getting married," he said.

A smile broke across the lieutenant's face.

"Married?"

"Next week. Fourth of July."

DiMarco patted him on the shoulder.

"Congrats, pal. A local girl?"

"Italian, actually."

"Oh, you poor bastard."

They both laughed.

"I'd like you to come. St. Mary's Star of the Sea. Reception afterward at our place in Point Shirley."

They shook hands again.

"I'd be honored."

......

When Thomas pulled up to the cottage, he immediately shut off the engine. The tank was close to empty, and there was nowhere to get gas on Point Shirley. Rationing didn't start for another few weeks, but already it had caused a run on fuel. On his way home, he had stopped by three service stations, and they were all out. He knew he could always take the bus and train, something he had been doing his whole life. But he was used to driving now, and it was hard to give up the freedom of a car.

He got out and stretched his legs, which were stiff and sore. One thing he wouldn't miss with his new assignment was walking all day. He had been with the harbor unit for almost three months, and it was always the same routine. Other than kicking kids and vagrants out of restricted areas, the most exciting thing that happened was finding the buoy from a ship that had been sunk by a U-boat off of Provincetown. With the fighting three thousand miles away, all the patrolling and preparation seemed pointless, or maybe, for America, the war just hadn't started yet.

Leaning against the car, he looked out at the water, the gentle breeze in his face. He always loved the silence of summer nights, and as a boy, he would go down to the shore by himself and stare at the stars. His mother called him a dreamer while his father said he was a *slacker,* which always sounded funny with his Irish accent.

Over at the airport, Thomas could hear activity, but he couldn't see the planes or hangars. Across the bay, East Boston was nearly as dark with only a few flickers of light from shops and headlamps. He wondered if Connie was home, but he couldn't have called her even if they had a phone at the cottage. The closer they got to the wedding, the less they saw each other, and she wanted it that way. Mrs. Ciarlone's ideas about courtship were almost medieval. Connie had been married once before, but considering she had no children, Thomas wouldn't have been surprised if her aunt thought she was still a virgin.

As he came up the front steps, the lights in the hallway and parlor were off. But it wasn't unusual because, aside from the Loughrans next door, all the homes along the shore were dark.

He walked in and thought no one was home until he heard a creak and went toward the kitchen.

"Ma?"

She was sitting at the table in a dirty nightgown, her hair in a bun. With a mop and bucket in the corner, it was obvious she had been cleaning, and sometimes he felt guilty leaving her all day.

"Thomas," she said, but she didn't look up.

"Where's Abby?"

"Out with her friends."

"What's wrong?"

She shook her head, rubbing her chin, her hands jittery. In her face, he saw that same blank look she had after his father died, and it gave him a chill. Since getting out of the hospital, she had improved, and he dreaded thinking her depression was coming back. Noticing a glass beside her, he quickly grabbed it.

"What're you doing?!" she exclaimed.

When he smelled inside it, he was both relieved and embarrassed to realize it was only iced tea.

"Ma, I'm sorry."

"You think I would—?"

"You looked...*morose*," he said, the term Doctor Berman had used.

"Well, I am morose! I went to all the markets today. There's no beef to be found anywhere."

"Spinelli's?"

"None."

"Lombardo's? Dillon's? The Porter? Grants?"

He listed off every shop and butcher from Maverick Square to Winthrop, and she shook her head. People had been complaining about beef for weeks, and while the government said there was no shortage, it was getting harder to find. Prices had been capped since March, but that did nothing to ease demand. At headquarters, they had all been warned about a black market, and that week police in Cambridge had broken up an illegal beef ring.

"Just Salisbury steak," his mother said. "But it's mostly lamb and breadcrumbs."

"It's fine, Ma. We'll have pork. Or chicken even."

She gagged in disgust.

"Chicken for a wedding? That's for peasants."

Thomas laughed, but he was more dismayed than amused. At a time when everyone was suffering, she was still concerned about impressions. He knew she was only trying to make the day special, and in some ways, she wanted it more than him. Marriage was important, but with the country at war, it didn't seem urgent. He and Connie had already said and done everything a devoted couple would, and they were mostly doing it for the child.

Crouching down, he put his hand on her back.

"I'll see if I can find some steak," he said.

She peered up, her eyes red.

"You will?"

He nodded. And while he knew it was a big promise, it was one he had to make.

CHAPTER TWENTY-FOUR

Abby sat on the bench to rest, her sleeves rolled up and a rag in her hand. The tables they borrowed from Mr. Loughran had cleaned up fine, but the picnic table was covered in dried berries from the holly tree, and she had chipped a fingernail trying to scrape them off.

Sipping her lemonade, she looked around the property, a corner plot four times the size of their yard back home. She had raked all morning, and it still looked ragged. All the white linens, glass vases, and serving trays in the world wouldn't hide the crabgrass and bald spots.

She had always imagined the first wedding in the family to be an elegant ceremony followed by a party at Lombardo's or the Winthrop Yacht Club. But Thomas' was going to be modest, even by East Boston standards. To save money, their mother had asked her friends from the Catholic Women's Guild to help cook so they wouldn't have to hire a caterer. The arrangement seemed to fit her brother, who never liked attention or formalities, and if Abby felt bad about anything, it was his reason for getting married.

She knew Connie was pregnant, and not just because Chickie had tried to tell her. Her mother always said women had some special insight that men did not. At the time, it sounded old-fashioned, almost superstitious, but the older Abby got, the more she realized it was true.

"Abigail?"

When Abby looked over, her mother was kneeling in the dirt, a trowel in her hand. The garden she had been tending every summer for years she now called a *Victory Garden*, although Abby didn't know what the difference was.

"Yes, Ma?"

"I need the squash seeds. Can you see if they're in the pantry?"

Abby put down her drink and went inside. As she passed the kitchen table, she shooed away some flies hovering around the oak cakes she'd made the day before. She didn't even like to bake, but with Thomas at work, and her mother off selling war bonds, she needed something to do. While she still worked part-time at the bakery, her days off were long stretches of empty time.

The cottage was quieter than ever before, and it wasn't just that her father was deceased and her brother was away because all of Point Shirley felt deserted. So she had invited Frances to visit for a few days, and it was as much to attend the wedding as to keep her company. Otherwise, she would have gone crazy from boredom.

She found the seeds in a jar, and if they hadn't been marked, she would have mistaken them for roasted pumpkin seeds. When she went back out, she heard voices and saw someone talking to her mother.

"Sarah?!" she exclaimed.

"Hi, Abigail."

Abby ran down the steps and across the yard. After they hugged, they stood facing each other with giddy smiles, almost too excited to speak.

They had met as young girls at a time when Point Shirley swarmed with children, and every street was like an extension of their backyard. Sarah only lived in Quincy, but anywhere south of the city was like another universe at eight years old. So they only saw each other in the summer, which was hard when it ended but made the friendship more significant.

Abby looked at Sarah's hair, a heap of curls pinned to the top of her head.

"I love it," she said.

"Do you really? They're called victory rolls."

"Victory rolls? Like my mother's *victory garden*?"

On her hands and knees, Mrs. Nolan glanced back.

"You can never have too much victory anything," she said, and they all laughed.

"How are things?" Abby asked.

"My father stayed home this year. He's working at Bethlehem Shipyard. It's just me and mum."

"And Frank?"

Abby asked in a gentle, cautious tone, knowing her brother was in the Army.

"We haven't heard from him in four months. His last letter just said he was going to the South Pacific."

For a brief moment, she looked sad, but it didn't last. Her face brightened, and she looked around at the tables.

"So, Thomas is tying the knot?" she asked.

"Can you believe it?"

"It's gonna break a lot of hearts."

"It's gonna break the bank," Mrs. Nolan chimed in.

"Won't you come?" Abby asked.

"I've nothing to wear."

"Just a long dress. It's casual."

Sarah nodded, smiling.

"Yes. I sure will."

"Oh, good."

"I'm going to the beach. Wanna go?"

"I have a friend visiting from Boston—"

"I need those squash seeds," Mrs. Nolan said, and Abby was starting to get annoyed.

"I have to get her at the bus stop."

"Let's go!"

......

. . .

Abby sat on the towel between Sarah and Frances, and it was intentional. She never knew how people from different parts of her life would get along. As a teen, she was afraid to bring her friends from home to the cottage. It wasn't that girls on Point Shirley looked down on girls from East Boston, although some of them did. Everyone at that age was petty and critical, and she didn't want to break up arguments or, even worse, fistfights.

"Delightful, delightful," Frances said, leaning up on her elbows and gazing out at the water.

Her large sunglasses consumed her face; her red checkered bathing suit was snug in all the right places. Although she was short, she was slender enough that she could have been mistaken for a pinup model if she didn't always have a cigarette between her fingers. She smoked twice as much as Harold, but for some reason, the smell reminded Abby more of him.

"Tell me," Frances asked, pointing. "What's that?"

"Nahant," Sarah said.

"There's a club on Nahant, I think. Father has played there."

Abby glanced over, and Sarah was already smirking. Neither of them knew anything about golf or country clubs. But the remark wasn't meant to be some sign of status, and as flighty as Frances was, she wasn't a snob.

Once the clouds passed, the sun was warm, and it finally felt like summer. But even for a weekday in late June, the beach was quiet, with a few scattered groups, mostly housewives with children. Abby tried to lay back and close her eyes, but she was too anxious. While she blamed it on the wedding, the truth was she could never sit still for too long without thinking about her father or Arthur. She had considered getting more hours at the bakery; staying busy was a good remedy for grief. But even if she got a lift with Thomas every morning, she would have to take the streetcar and bus back. After getting used to the fresh air and calm nights, it was hard to leave Point Shirley for the city.

"Is that who I think it is?" Sarah said.

Abby looked over and saw Hal Francis walking toward them with a football. At East Boston High, he was a star athlete and as one of the few guys with blonde hair, all the girls liked him.

"Ladies," he said.

"Long time, no see," Sarah said.

"This is Frances," Abby said, and Frances waved.

He responded with a faint smile, making circles in the sand with his foot. Considering he was always so friendly and outgoing, it was clear something was wrong.

"Who's here this summer?" Sarah asked.

He shrugged his shoulders.

"Are you on Pebble Ave. again?" Abby asked, knowing his family rented and didn't own.

He nodded.

"Are you—"

"Ray Lanier was killed," he said.

Abby and Sarah turned to each other, mouths open, that look of sudden shock. She knew Ray Lanier, but more as a distant acquaintance, one of the dozen if not hundreds of boys who came out to Point Shirley each summer. He kept his hair long on the sides to cover a disfigured ear; he snorted when he laughed. Just thinking about him got her choked up, and she wondered why it was always the small things that stuck out after people died.

"How?" Sarah asked.

"The Japs. Wake Island."

"God, Hal, that's awful."

"Yep," he said.

They sat under a gloomy silence, and even Frances looked upset, although she didn't know him.

"See ya around," Hal said.

Without another word, he walked away, and they watched as he continued down the beach, spinning the football in the air and then catching it. Something about his swagger reminded Abby of George, or maybe Ray's death made her worry about her brother.

"Poor thing," Frances said, craning her neck. "And so handsome."

"You already have a boy."

Frances spun around to Abby.

"Sal is a man, honey," she said.

"At this point, I'd take either," Sarah said, rubbing baby oil on her shoulders.

"Maybe you'll meet someone at the wedding."

Sarah stopped and looked over.

"You really think?"

"One never knows," Abby said.

But it was a lie. She knew everyone on the guest list, and none of them would have been a good match. Thomas always had a lot of companions, but only a few close friends, most of which were now overseas. He had asked for a small wedding, saying anything more would have been an extravagance in wartime, and their mother didn't argue. While it sounded patriotic, Abby knew the real reason. The longer they waited and the more people they had, the bigger the risk that someone would find out Connie was expecting.

"How's about a dip?"

Abby came out of the daydream, and Frances was standing in front of her.

"Maybe in a little while," she said.

Frances looked over to Sarah, who shook her head.

"No way. Too cold."

"I thought you city gals had thick skin?"

When she headed down to the shore, Abby looked at Sarah, and they both grinned. Everyone on Point Shirley knew the water was freezing in June, especially on the ocean side. But Abby didn't try to discourage her, knowing it would have been a hard thing to explain to a girl with a heated pool.

CHAPTER TWENTY-FIVE

Thomas stood beside Connie, glancing over every few seconds. In her long white dress, she looked stunning, her dark hair in curls, her lashes long. In the harsh light of the altar, he noticed some faint blemish or scar on her cheek that the makeup couldn't hide. He had stared at that face a thousand times and always saw something new.

The back of his shirt was damp, and not just from nerves because Father Ward was sweating, too. In summer, the old stone church got hot, and Thomas remembered long masses as a boy when even knickers and shirtsleeves weren't enough to keep cool. While he could always handle a little discomfort, his brother George could not, one time getting so restless their mother dragged him out of the church by the collar.

Once the priest finished the homily, he turned to Thomas and Connie, and they turned to each other. Up until that moment, the wedding had seemed more like a dream than real. And even though he was happy beyond belief, some part of him was ashamed that she was pregnant. He would have married her anyway, but this would fix things, and if there was ever any suspicion or questions, the worst they would have to do was lie about the timeline.

"Do you, Thomas Michael Nolan, take Concetta Ferrara to be your lawfully wedded wife?"

The priest startled them both by pronouncing *Concetta* with a soft "c," an unusual mistake for a man who led a parish that was half-Italian. Thomas wondered too about *Ferrara*, whether it was her maiden name or her dead husband's, something they never talked about. But it was no time for jealousy, and if he hesitated at all, it was only because he was lost in the moment.

"I do," he said.

Father Ward then looked at her.

"And do you, Concetta Ferrara take Thomas Michael Nolan to be your lawfully wedded husband?"

She peered up, and Thomas felt a shiver. There was a glow in her eyes, but she had none of the weepy sentiment of other brides. He always loved her quiet composure.

"I do," she said, and they both smiled.

"You have declared your consent before the Church. May the Lord in his goodness strengthen your consent and fill you both with his blessings. I now pronounce you man and wife..."

Everyone clapped, and for the first time that day, Thomas got emotional, although he didn't show it. When they turned around, he saw a sea of beaming faces. The music started, and they walked down the aisle. With the regular organist away in the Army Nurses' Corp, they had to hire a woman from the Lutheran Church, something Mrs. Nolan had, at first, objected to.

As they came out the front doors, they were showered with rice, and Thomas blinked. The crowd poured onto the lawn which now looked bare without a fence. Like a lot of institutions, the parish had donated it to the local salvage committee so it could be melted down and turned into bullets, cannons, and tanks.

A small greeting line formed, friends and neighbors Thomas had known forever. He saw Mr. & Mrs. Braga, the Costellos from Saratoga Street, and even Carl Seymour, a childhood friend who had moved to Swampscott when they were ten. Mr. McNulty was there, but his wife was at the cottage setting up. Chickie looked adorable in her purple dress and bonnet, and Mrs. Ciarlone, like always, was dressed in black.

As people called to him, Thomas spun around, waving, smiling and shaking hands, and it was so hectic, he became dizzy. He could have spent a week talking, but they couldn't stop because Mr. Loughran was holding open the door of his Cadillac Lasalle convertible, red with white-wall tires and gleaming chrome. He bought it after he retired from the police department and seemed to spend more time washing than driving it. As kids, Thomas and his brother would sneak into the garage just to catch a glimpse, and once, George had even suggested stealing it.

"Congratulations, Thomas," Mr. Loughran said, looking dignified in his three-piece suit and fedora.

"Thank you."

Thomas held Connie's hand as she slid across the vinyl seat. He sat beside her, and Mr. Loughlin walked around and got in. As they pulled away, everyone cheered, and Thomas got a little self-conscious. Over by the steps, he could see Lieutenant DiMarco standing in his service uniform. Thomas had thought of wearing his too, but he didn't want the attention, especially now that he was stationed in East Boston.

As they cruised down Bennington Street, people looked up. It was probably more the curiosity of seeing a Cadillac because, aside from the way Thomas and Connie were dressed, it wasn't obvious they had just gotten married. Mrs. Nolan had wanted a sign and streamers, some grand display of the event, but Mr. Loughran had talked her out of it. While he said it was too flashy, Thomas knew he was more worried about his car and the damage that tape could cause.

Thomas was silent the whole ride, so Connie was too. Ever since they met, he was always the first one to talk. He liked her reserve, but he was sometimes tormented by the mysteries it concealed. He knew enough about her to love her, which eased his guilt about getting her pregnant. When his hand bumped against her stomach, they both looked at each other, and she giggled. After weeks of quiet panic, he could finally think about being a father.

They drove across the neck to Point Shirley with the windows down. Clutching her bouquet, Connie stared out at the horizon, her hair fluttering in the breeze. Even with a Navy patrol boat offshore, it didn't feel like the Fourth of July. The beach was empty, with no stacks of wood in preparation for the bonfires. In years past, the streets would have already been lined with cars, the smell of barbecues in the air. It was strange that, at a time when people most needed to honor their country, they were forbidden from doing it.

They pulled up to the cottage and weren't the first ones there. An automobile was parked on the lawn, and two more were across the street. All morning, the ladies from Mrs. Nolan's church group had been getting things ready. There was American flag bunting on the front porch, and in the yard, Thomas could see tables with white ribbons on the chairs, a long buffet table with chafing dishes.

Mr. Loughran got out and opened the back door, extending his hand to Connie with the poise of a chauffeur. Thomas had always liked him, and all his life the Loughrans were more like close friends than neighbors. Back when Mr. Nolan used to drink, he would get into vicious fights with their mother, and while he never hit any of them, his rage had all the force of violence. During those times, Mr. Loughran would take Thomas and his brother to his house and make them hot chocolate, show them his ham radio.

As they walked up the path, Thomas held the train of Connie's dress, which she had gotten from her aunt. He was glad Mrs. Ciarlone was overweight because it gave Connie an excuse to get it altered, asking Mr. Gittell to leave some room around the waist. While it would have been suspicious to most tailors, Thomas knew Jews didn't have the same hang-ups about sex before marriage. Either way, all their fretting was just paranoia because she was too early to show.

The moment they got to the porch, the door burst open, and two women greeted them with big smiles. Just as Connie went in, the McNultys pulled up, and Thomas ran over to help his mother.

"Did the ice arrive?" she asked, stepping out.

"We just got here," Thomas said, taking her by the arm.

In her long blue dress, she looked beautiful, but she was frantic enough that she had already smudged her lipstick. Dangling from her ears were her grandmother's diamond earrings, which, although too ornate for the times, held some symbolic family significance.

When they were young, Thomas and his siblings had been told that their great-grandmother Margaret was the daughter of a protestant landlord in Ireland. At sixteen, she had run off with the stable hand, their great-grandfather, taking with her only her jewelry and dreams of a new life in America. It was a romantic story, the stuff of fairytales. But considering their mother's tendency to embellish the past, they weren't sure it was true.

"The napkins," Mrs. Nolan said, breathless. "Pulsifer's was supposed to deliver them."

"I'm sure they did."

She stopped on the walkway.

"And the beef?"

When she peered up, Thomas got a twinge of guilt. More than anything, she had wanted steak, which, in a time of shortages, was some sign of status or prestige. To Thomas, it seemed petty, and he never cared what people thought. But the day was as much about her as it was about him and Connie, and he had decided that whatever the cost, he wouldn't let her down. Throughout the ceremony, he worried whether it would arrive, but when he saw a black car approaching, he knew it had.

"It's here, Ma. Now go inside," he said, and Mr. Loughran led her up to the house.

He walked out to the street, and the car stopped in front of him. Vin Labadini and another guy got out, both wearing shirtsleeves with hats, the look of lowbrow chic.

"Congrats," Labadini said with a stiff grin.

Thomas forced a smile but didn't answer. He followed them to the back of the car, and when Labadini opened the trunk, Thomas looked around, feeling exposed. But there weren't many places on Point Shirley for secrecy, and what he feared most was DiMarco showing up.

"Forty sirloins," Labadini said, as proud as a gourmet butcher.

"Are they fresh?"

He laughed and looked over at his partner, who stood with a frozen smirk.

"Fresh as daisies, my friend."

He took out the crate with exaggerated strain and turned to Thomas.

"Want me to take 'em inside?"

Not sure if he was being sarcastic, Thomas ignored the question.

"What's the bill?"

"Bill?" Labadini said with a slight snicker. "No bill. Consider it a wedding gift."

As generous as it was, Thomas felt uneasy, almost defensive. He had only approached Labadini because good beef was hard to find, and he knew he could get it. He never meant it as a favor; he didn't want to owe Labadini anything. But when he heard a car, he knew he didn't have time to argue.

"Right, okay, thanks," he said quickly.

Labadini nodded to his partner, and they got back in and drove off. Thomas stood in the road, relieved they were gone because, seconds later, George's Chevy pulled up. Abby got out from the passenger's side, her friend from school behind the wheel. Frances had shown him her license, but Thomas only let her take the car to the ceremony after Abby begged.

"Who was that?" Abby asked, holding up her dress as she scurried over.

"Steak delivery."

"In a Ford Coupe?"

"Should the groom really be moving boxes?" Frances asked.

Thomas was glad about the interruption; he could tell Abby was suspicious.

"How'd it drive?" he asked Frances.

She peered up, struggling to light a cigarette with her long white gloves.

"A little bouncy."

She had been staying with them since Wednesday and was the first guest they ever had who called the parlor *the den*. Despite her upper-class airs, Thomas liked her, and she was different from any of Abby's other friends. She was pretty in a glamour girl way, petite and spunky, smiling even when unnecessary. He guessed she was short, but it was hard to tell because she always wore heels. When Abby told him she had been seeing Sal, Thomas was surprised. He wouldn't have expected someone like her to date an Italian from East Boston.

"You know our mother detests smoking?" Thomas joked, trying to rush her because the steaks were getting heavy.

"Which is why I'm doing it out here, darling."

Taking a final drag, she stamped it out on the ground, and they headed into the cottage.

......

Thomas sat beside Connie at the head of the table, which was covered with plates, silverware, and glasses. While some guests hadn't finished their roasted potatoes and coleslaw, there wasn't a scrap of steak left. The four-tier wedding cake Mrs. Ciarlone had baked was now half-eaten and attracting flies. Insects were always a problem on Point Shirley, and even if it was too early for greenheads, everyone dreaded the mosquitos.

In the distance, the sun was setting, casting a yellow haze across Winthrop Bay. Soon the lights of the city would be off, the coast immersed in darkness. Over by the fence, the Braga twins were playing hide and seek with Chickie, reminding Thomas of when he and his siblings were young. At the next table, Sal and Frances sat close together, sipping champagne and talking. Abby's friend Sarah had gotten along well enough with Nick DiMarco that they went for a walk down the beach. Whether the blackout order barred loud music, no one knew, but Mr. Loughran had set up his Zenith console radio, and couples were dancing on the lawn.

Thomas yawned and looked around, overcome by a feeling of deep gratitude and contentment. Even the people he didn't know felt like family. Three of his father's coworkers from the shipyard had shown up, but they couldn't stay long. After a slow start, Mrs. Ciarlone had warmed up, and she was inside talking with some ladies from the Catholic

Women's Guild. Many guests had left, including Sal, who had to go to work, but enough remained that it still felt like a party.

"Stay awake," Connie said, leaning over.

When she put her hand on his, he smiled; when she rubbed his thigh, he got aroused. Along with her aunt and Chickie, she was staying over, which, now that they were married, was proper. But the walls were too thin for intimacy, the floors too creaky, and as horny as he was, he would never risk the embarrassment of being overheard.

"I've got news!"

Everyone turned, and Mrs. Nolan came down the back steps with Abby and Frances. Thomas had worried about his sister, knowing that weddings were hard for anyone whose loved one was far away.

"What news, Ma?" he asked.

As she approached the table, she slowed down, giving them both an eager look. It was the first time Thomas had ever seen her not drinking at a social event, and she was no less cheerful.

"A letter," she said, holding up an envelope.

"Letter?"

"From George."

Thomas sat up.

"Really?" was all he said.

His mother called everyone over and then unfolded the note.

Dear family,

I hope you are all good. We finished boot camp on the 10th of June. After a couple days' leave, we were put on a train to Fort Bragg in California. I don't know why we didn't fly, but the quartermaster said that planes were in short supply.

The journey took four days, and we broke down outside Reno. But we made it. The weather here is rainy and gray. My bunkmate got trench foot after a ten-mile hike. I met Mark Simmons from East Boston. He's with the 14th Signal Corp. Thomas will remember him from high school. Also, I met a guy from Chelsea, but I can't remember his name.

By the time you get this, we will already probably be gone. Deployments are confidential, but everyone is pretty sure we're going to the Aleutian Islands. I will try to write again when I can. Say hello to everyone for me.

Love,
   George

The crowd went silent, people looking around at each other in the shadowy light. As his mother read, Thomas could hear his brother's voice, which gave him a chill. He was sure she had ignored some misspellings; George was never a good writer. But the sentiment was clear, and he couldn't believe his brother was going to war.

"Aleutian Islands?" someone said, finally.

"Aren't they in Scotland?"

"I think the South Pacific," Mr. McNulty said.

"Sounds more like the Mediterranean."

"No, that's the Azores," another person said.

As they all went back and forth, Thomas just stared ahead, feeling helpless. He wished he'd paid more attention in geography class so he could at least know where his brother was.

"They're off of Alaska," Abby said, so confidently no one questioned her.

"Why on earth would we be in Alaska?"

"The scenery is meant to be spectacular," Frances said.

"Maybe Eisenhower thinks the Japs will invade?"

"But Alaska is next to Russia. And they're our allies."

"Whatever the reason, he's protecting democracy," Mr. Loughran said, walking over to the cooler.

He was the only one drinking beer, which Mrs. Nolan had bought special because she knew he liked it.

"God bless him and keep him safe," he said.

He raised the bottle, and anyone with a glass or cup did the same. As they toasted, Thomas got the same mix of sadness and envy he had been experiencing since he found out George joined the Army.

"Is all okay?" Connie asked in her cute, clumsy English.

"Everything's perfect."

But it wasn't. The guilt of not enlisting was always there, and he could have dwelled on it all night. He got distracted by two figures creeping across the street, and when they came into the yard, he realized it was DiMarco and Sarah. Her dress was wrinkled, her hair a mess, and he had beach burrs all over his uniform. While everyone else was too drunk to notice, Thomas was sure they had just had sex, and it made him smile. In a time of upheaval, that irrepressible human need for love and affection seemed like a small triumph.

CHAPTER TWENTY-SIX

Abby woke up Monday morning on the floor. The party that had started on Saturday continued all weekend, some last hurrah for a summer that everyone knew would be difficult. Mrs. Ciarlone and Chickie had gone home early, but some people who hadn't planned on sleeping over had stayed, including two women from church and a neighbor named Muriel who was somehow related to them.

With all the rooms taken, Abby and Frances had to stay in her bedroom, which was no more than a closet with a window. So she offered up the bed to Frances who acted like she expected it. Abby didn't mind, and she could handle a little discomfort. When she was a girl, she used to go camping with her cousins in Maine, and it made her tough.

As she got ready for their MWDC meeting, her head pounded, and her neck was stiff. She hadn't drunk so much in months, but she was more worried about her appearance than her health. She could tell she had put on weight because her skirt was tight.

"Are there mites in the house?" Frances asked, looking in the mirror.
"There's a lot of bugs."
Frances dabbed on makeup, rubbing it in to cover some small welts.
"It's like the frontier out here."
While she sounded appalled, Abby knew she got a thrill out of it.

"C'mon, Calamity Jane," she said.

They went downstairs, and no one was home. The rooms were clean, everything had been dusted and mopped. Walking into the kitchen, Abby looked out and saw that the tables and chairs were gone too. Aside from Thomas' tennis shoes by the door, the only sign that someone was living there was a plate of teacakes her mother had left out for breakfast.

Mrs. Nolan had gone back to East Boston to sell war bonds, and Thomas was at work. Now that he was married, they all wondered what he and Connie would do. With their houses beside each other, it was already like they were living together, and Abby could never imagine Thomas leaving her and their mother alone. He hadn't even planned a honeymoon, and when someone asked, all he said was *maybe a few days in Niagara Falls in September.*

Abby grabbed her purse, and they left, Frances dragging her suitcase like it was some form of punishment. The streets were quiet, and as they approached the bus stop, Abby saw someone waiting. They got closer, and she cringed when she realized it was Angela Labadini. She was even more surprised that she had on a *Massachusetts Women's Defense Corps* uniform.

Abby smiled, but Angela looked away, which, considering it was only the three of them, was awkward. Abby knew the girl was troubled, from the kind of family her mother used to warn her about. But she never hated her, and the fact that Angela had dated George the summer before gave Abby a special sympathy, if only because she missed her brother.

"You joined the MWDC?" she asked, although it was obvious.

Angela just nodded.

"This is Frances."

Angela glanced over with a hesitant smile.

"Nice to meet you," she said.

"Same."

Any conversation was cut short when the bus came around the corner. They all got on, the driver complimenting them on their service, and Angela even sat near them, which was strange because there was no one else on board.

As they continued over the neck, they passed a column of Army vehicles. By now it was a common sight, and the only reason Abby noticed was one of them was blowing black smoke.

"Are you here all summer?" she asked, looking back at Angela.

"Weren't supposed to be. But my father got his boat back."

"Back?"

"Boat?" Frances interrupted. "A sailboat or cruiser?"

Angela looked like she wanted to frown but didn't out of politeness.

"A fishing boat," she said.

"You're going to headquarters?" Abby asked.

"Yes. 238 Beacon Street."

"I hear there might be another blackout this week."

"With all these drills, how will we ever know when there's a real attack?" Frances said.

"Your brother got married," Angela blurted, and Abby couldn't tell if it was a question or a statement.

"Word gets around."

"My brother Vincent got the steaks."

Abby got a tense, almost sickening feeling, and she wasn't about to show thanks for something she knew was probably illegal.

"Is that so?" was all she said.

"How's George?"

"He's in the Army."

"My younger brother just signed up."

With a smile, Abby turned away, her neck getting sore from craning. For the rest of the trip, they were quiet, the only exception being when Frances asked Abby to point out the bakery she worked at.

At Maverick Station, they separated. While Angela continued to the train, Abby followed Frances out to the street so she could buy more cigarettes. Standing on the sidewalk, she heard a beep, and her brother rolled up. She still couldn't get used to seeing him in a uniform, never mind a police car.

"Need a lift?" he asked.

She wanted to confront him about the steaks, but it wasn't the right time.

"We're going to Back Bay."

"Get in."

Frances came out of the shop, a cigarette in her mouth. She had a coffee too, which seemed rude because she hadn't asked Abby if she wanted one.

"Oh, my. Am I under arrest?"

"Do you wanna be?" Thomas said as he got out.

As quiet as he was, he had always been a flirt. But Abby never doubted his devotion to Connie, and something about being in love let her see it in others.

Thomas put Frances' suitcase in the trunk, and they got into the backseat. The vinyl was torn and stained, but Frances didn't seem to mind, looking over at Abby with an eager smile. They pulled into traffic and headed toward the tunnel.

......

The meeting at MWDC headquarters lasted all afternoon. They had over three dozen recruits, mostly young women, so many that the supply company they used ran out of uniforms. The surge could have been due to the summer, but people everywhere were on edge and wanted to help.

The Germans had reached the Ukraine, and they were deep into Egypt, spreading their tentacles of tyranny across the world. The FBI announced they arrested eight Nazi saboteurs who had been dropped off by U-boats. Another cargo ship had been torpedoed off the New England coast, killing eighty-eight men, eighteen of them soldiers. Abby never read the news because she didn't want to know, especially since she still hadn't heard from Arthur. But it was hard to deny that things were getting worse.

Their battalion had gotten new maps from the *Office of Civilian Defense*, which seemed to change the evacuation plans every couple of weeks. They had two training sessions, *How to Spot a Spy* and *How to Evade the Enemy*, which, as Frances pointed out, seemed like the same advice in reverse. At the end of the day, there was a small ceremony for a member who was going to be the first black officer in the WAACs. Then finally they got to meet Mrs. Pauline Fenno, the heiress who had donated the building.

Once the business was over, the food and drinks came out, and any gathering of women turned into a social event if given enough time. Everyone broke up into groups, which were based as much on rank as they were on the neighborhood. In the hallway, Angela was standing around with some girls from East Boston.

Abby walked through the rooms, Frances clutching her arm. The oriental rugs had been taken up, and most of the finer furniture removed, replaced by plain office chairs and desks. But even in the summer with the windows open, the old mansion felt stuffy.

They turned into the library where people were sipping tea, eating pastries and sandwiches. A couple of ladies were even bold enough to have wine at five o'clock.

They had only just stepped in when Abby stopped. Through the crowd, she could see Ms. Stetson talking to Major Ward and some other higher-ups.

"C'mon," she said.

"Wha—?"

She grabbed Frances' hand and would have left her there if she resisted. They hurried through the parlor, into the foyer, and went out the front door.

"What is it, darling?" Frances said.

"Stetson."

"Stetson?"

"The professor."

"She doesn't bite," Frances said, lighting a cigarette. "Although I'm sure she'd be delighted to if you asked."

Abby grinned, but she was in no mood to joke.

"I blackmailed her, sort of."

"Blackmail?" Frances said, taking a sensuous drag. "Do tell."

Abby hesitated when some girls walked out, and more came up the sidewalk. MWDC Headquarters was always busy, with people coming and going, and it made her uneasy.

"Not here."

"My place then?"

"I've got work in the morning."

"C'mon. It's just a few blocks. I'll get you a taxi home."

Abby thought for a moment.

"Okay. Sure."

......

Abby sat next to Frances, two sofa chairs with a small table between them. Sipping her drink, she winced. She hated the sour taste of wine. After Thomas's wedding, she never thought she would drink again, and the hangovers only seemed to get worse with age. But a glass or two always took away the edge, relieving her headache along with her worries, filling her with a warm tingle. Alcohol never seemed to affect her the way it did her parents, and as a girl, she swore she wouldn't drink after seeing her father's outbursts. But she couldn't deny it had its uses.

As Frances poured another glass, Abby looked around. The apartment was small, with a kitchenette, bathroom, and parlor whose only window looked out to the back alley. With its gold wallpaper and dentil molding, it was hardly the *hovel* Frances called it and was impressive for any student. Like a lot of dormitories, the elegant brick townhouse had been carved up from a former home, either bought by the university or a donation from some rich elderly widow.

"Considering the times," Frances said, her shoes off and legs tucked beneath her. "I can't see anyone stretching their neck out for a Kraut. Still, it's a noble thing you did for the man."

Abby made a sour smile. France's opinions were always such a mix of criticism and flattery that Abby could never tell when she was being nasty.

"He was good to me, that's all."

"You got him out of jail. Isn't that enough?"

Abby pressed her lips together, restraining any annoyance. She didn't expect Frances or anyone else to understand. After the death of her father, Professor Bauermeister had been the only man in her life to show her any encouragement.

"They had no right to fire him," she said.

"He's a foreigner."

"He's been here over ten years."

"He's still a foreigner."

She sounded like Eve from the bakery. With the real war far away, people seemed to draw their own battle lines of who to trust and who not to.

"Is that Duxbury?" Abby asked, changing the subject.

Frances looked over at a painting on the wall, an empty beach with dunes and seagrass.

"Ha, no. Most of the stuff here was provided."

"Was that provided?" Abby asked, pointing to a picture.

Putting down her glass, Frances got it off the table and brought it over.

"Richard Parker," she said, kneeling beside Abby. "My high school prom date. You met him at my party last year."

Abby remembered him, tall with wavy hair and a shy smile. At the time, he was stationed in Texas at the same base as Arthur, and she always wondered if they ever met.

"Isn't he a doll?" Frances said, rubbing her hand on the glass. "We made it in the stairwell behind the stage."

Abby raised her eyes.

"Nice to know."

"C'mon, darling. No secrets between friends."

"So you made it with Sal?"

"As soon as I could..."

Abby laughed so hard she almost spilled her drink.

"And I can tell you," Frances went on, walking over to put the picture back, "it's true what they say about Italians."

"Which is what exactly?"

"They've got the strength of a steer, the stamina of an ox—"

Suddenly, a knock.

Frances opened the door, keeping her glass hidden because alcohol wasn't allowed.

"Someone's here for you," a girl said.

From where she sat, Abby couldn't see her, but she sounded panicked.

"Send her up—"

"It's not a *her*."

"A man?"

"He doesn't seem right," she whispered. "Something's wrong."

"Then let him up."

The girl walked away, leaving them both confused. Moments later, Frances exclaimed, "Harold?!"

When she opened the door wide, he staggered in, and Abby was shocked. He looked like a vagrant, his pants stained and his hair a mess. As they hugged, all Abby could smell was booze, but his condition seemed worse than drunkenness.

They helped him off with his coat and took him over to the couch. He sat with his head down and hands clasped, his body shaking like he was having a seizure.

"Calm down, darling. Tell us what happened?"

"Ro...Robert..." he said, struggling to speak.

"Your brother?"

Finally, he looked up, his eyes bloodshot and face gray.

"I got a telegram. Robert's been killed."

CHAPTER TWENTY-SEVEN

Thomas went down the narrow hallway, the landlord following behind. The man was a short, chubby Italian with a lazy eye, and each time Thomas asked a question, he would grin but not answer.

The rooms of the third-floor walkup were empty, the floors clean but scuffed. On the walls, Thomas could see the holes from where pictures or paintings once hung. All the windows had blackout curtains, now required for new rentals, and he could tell they were homemade because they were different fabrics. In the small kitchen at the back, he saw pencil marks on the door jamb, reminding him of how he and his siblings used to do the same thing to track their growth.

When they got back to the foyer, he looked out to the street. Just outside Maverick Square, the neighborhood was a dense stretch of triple-deckers with flat roofs and no yards. It was rundown and too close to work, but he still felt lucky for the opportunity. With thousands of workers flooding into the city for war jobs, rents had skyrocketed. Apartments were impossible to find, even in bad areas, and Thomas knew the landlord had only called him back because he was a cop.

"You like?" the man asked with a wide smile.

"I like."

"Twenty-five dollars."

The price seemed high, especially for a place with peeling paint and no driveway, but Thomas didn't balk.

"I have two more places to look at."

As he turned to go, the man stopped him.

"Twenty-three for policeman."

Thomas smiled.

"Thank you," he said, and he walked out.

The staircase was steep, and by the time he reached the bottom, he was winded. He wasn't used to going up and down three flights.

Outside, boys were playing kickball in the street, girls in hand-me-down dresses skipping rope. The moment they saw him, they all stared, which was one of the reasons he didn't bring his police cruiser or wear his uniform. In the backstreets, everyone was suspicious, and even if he only lived a half mile north, he was still an outsider. If they were trying to intimidate him, he couldn't help but feel sentimental, remembering the endless summers when he was young.

He had only gone a block when he heard a car approaching. Whether it was the speed or something else, it seemed like it was lurking. His instincts were right because the moment he turned, Labadini rolled up alongside him.

"Nolan," he said.

Thomas always thought of him more as stocky, but sometimes when he smiled, he looked chubby.

"Vin."

Thomas kept walking, but he glanced over long enough to see three other guys in the car. With their slicked-back hair and cheap suits, they looked like grown-up versions of George's hoodlum friends from high school.

"Need a lift?"

Thomas nodded to the station, which was just a block ahead.

"Almost there," he said.

"I need a favor."

Thomas cringed. He never wanted to get involved with Labadini, and this was why.

"A favor?" he asked.

"Gas cards."

Rationing had just started, and already there was a racket for fuel, something the department told officers to watch out for. Even if he owed Labadini, a few dozen steaks was a lot different than taking government property.

"You got the wrong guy," Thomas said.

As he walked faster, Labadini sped up.

"They say there's gonna be a coal shortage this winter. We can get it."

"Maybe we burn wood."

Labadini chuckled.

"One hand washes the other, Nolan."

Finally, Thomas stopped. If he was going to be seen talking to thugs, he at least wanted to make it look like he was in control.

"Gas cards?" asked.

"Just a couple books."

Looking around, Thomas felt torn. He didn't want to say yes, but he was hesitant to say no. Law enforcement was messy, and everyone made deals.

"Let me see what I can do."

......

Thomas sat parked in front of the G.E. plant, a plain brick building that spanned two city blocks. The area around Porter Street was a mix of homes and factories, narrow streets lined with tenements, the brick and corrugated steel buildings of textile companies and machine shops. On the sidewalk, children played barefoot while freight trucks rumbled by. Thomas wasn't a father yet, but he got nervous just watching them.

Suddenly, a whistle sounded. Workers started pouring out, men from different doors than the women. The sexes were still kept apart, some hangup from an earlier era of industry that now seemed old-fashioned.

As Thomas watched, there was none of the eager excitement of previous shift changes. Women hugged each other, waving to their friends, a farewell that was as emotional as it was bitter. For anyone who wasn't an American citizen, it would be their last day, a humiliation made worse by the fact that the War Labor Board had just forced the company to give all employees a five-cent raise.

Moments later, Connie broke from the crowd and walked over. She got in and sat with her arms crossed, and he pulled away. For the first few minutes, she was quiet, and he didn't try to talk. He knew she was upset, maybe even humiliated. Losing a job was hard and losing it for being an immigrant was even worse.

"Did you see the apartment?" she asked.

"I did."

She lit a cigarette, blowing out the smoke like she was exhaling all her frustrations.

"And how is it?"

"It needs some paint."

He could have said it was a slum, but he didn't want to disappoint her. Since their wedding, everyone had been waiting to see what they would do next. He didn't want to leave his family, and she had similar feelings about her own, although not as strong. With his mother and sister at the cottage, they finally had some privacy, sneaking off to his house to have sex. But their days of happy freedom wouldn't last. Marriage came with responsibilities, and they couldn't put off telling everyone she was pregnant much longer.

As they drove up Bennington Street, packs of teenagers lingered on the corners; men in loose-fitting shirts and hats stood in front of pool halls. Even for July, it was quiet, and while poorer people were stuck, anyone who could get out of the neighborhood did, and not just for recreation. With blackouts, air raid sirens, and all the other military activity, the threat of a German attack felt more real than ever, and no one wanted to be in East Boston if it happened.

Thomas passed their street, but Connie wasn't going home yet. A few nights each week, he had been taking her to the cottage for dinner with his mother and sister. Seated around the picnic table, they would watch the sun set while Mrs. Nolan sipped lemonade and Abby filed her nails.

With all the uncertainty in their lives—and in the world—it was one step toward bringing them all together.

As they crossed the neck to Point Shirley, Connie took his hand, and he smiled, relieved that she was no longer sad. Leaning back, he was struck by a feeling of contentment he hadn't had in a long time.

But it didn't last. The moment they came around the bend to the cottage, he saw something and gasped.

"Thomas?"

"Hang on!" he said, and he hit the gas.

He drove onto the front lawn, skidding to a stop, and jumped out. When he ran inside, the house was filled with smoke.

"Ma?" he shouted, then he looked over at Connie. "Open all the windows. Quick!"

Covering his face with his shirt, he walked into the kitchen and saw more smoke billowing from a canister. Connie came in behind him and went over to the sink.

"No!" he shouted. "We need baking soda."

She dashed into the pantry and came out with a box of *Arm & Hammer*. Thomas didn't know if it was enough, but he poured it over the fire and then found some mitts from the drawer. Closing his eyes, he dragged the canister out the back door. When he got it down the steps, he kicked it over, and black, smoldering sludge ran across the ground.

"Is it out?"

He looked over and saw his mother standing in the doorway with a handkerchief over her mouth.

"Where were you?!"

"I just went to Pulsifer's for some bread."

"What the hell is that?" he asked, pointing at the hot container.

"It's grease. For the war effort."

"Grease?"

"To make glycerin for..." she said, hesitating, "...things."

While everyone was willing to help, no one wanted to admit that what they were doing would make explosives.

"I cooked some bacon for lunch," she added.

He just shook his head, exasperated. Connie squeezed by Mrs. Nolan and walked over. But when she tried to come close, he put up his hand, and she stopped. In all their time together, they never argued or got snippy, and it was mainly because they each knew when to leave the other alone.

"Ma," Thomas said, still out of breath. "We can't keep grease next to the stove!"

To his surprise, she nodded in agreement, and she even looked ashamed. Lowering her eyes, she retreated into the house, and Thomas wished he hadn't yelled at her.

But she was getting careless, something he blamed more on distress than her age because she was only fifty. Although her mood had improved since coming home from the hospital, she wasn't as sharp as she used to be. George was the first one to notice, unusual for someone who, in the past, was oblivious to everything. Either way, it gave Thomas one more reason not to move out, or maybe he was just making excuses.

He walked over to Connie and put his arm around her waist. Leaning forward, he kissed her on the forehead, some small show of apology for his outburst.

"What a close call," she said, and he had to chuckle.

Every day she seemed to pick up more American slang.

"Are you hungry?"

She gazed up, nodding with a timid smile.

"Let's eat," he said, and they walked back up the steps into the house.

CHAPTER TWENTY-EIGHT

While Frances drove, Abby sat in the passenger seat holding a bouquet. Thomas only let them take the car because he was working, and they had to have it back by noon. When he said he had an appointment, Abby had to bite her tongue. She couldn't understand why they still hadn't told everyone about Connie. The only thing she could think was that they were trying to give it enough time to appear like the pregnancy had happened *after* the wedding.

They cruised down Blue Hill Avenue in the rain, the wipers so worn out they were scaping. With no rubber available, they couldn't be replaced, and some people were tying rags to their blades.

Abby pointed, and they turned into Boston State Hospital. The grounds looked nicer in the spring, the grass green and flowers in bloom. Still, she had a subtle dread, remembering her mother's stay there and the horrible incident that led to it. Abby often forgot about her suicide attempt, mostly because they never talked about it.

Harold had been there for over a week, sent by doctors for alcoholic psychosis. The night he came to Frances' apartment, he had been drunk for days, stumbling through the streets in a stupor. When he found out Robert had died, he came straight to Boston, although he couldn't explain why. He and his father had had an argument or, as he called it, a *bloody fierce row*. Considering they usually all went home for summer, it was a miracle he even thought to go by Frances' dormitory. They were both thankful he did because he could have ended up like his brother.

The night Harold showed up, he was too incoherent to speak, so Abby and Frances got the full story later. Robert had died in a plane crash with twenty other soldiers in the desert outside Fresno, California. They were all fresh out of boot camp and on their way to San Diego. Harold said it was in the papers, but with all the fighting in Russia, Egypt, and the Far East, it probably wasn't front-page news.

With tens of thousands of troops being mobilized across the country, not a week went by without some fatal accident or incident. In April, three soldiers died in a race riot at Fort Dix; in May, an entire platoon was killed by a train when their truck stalled on a railway crossing. Only a few days before, a bomber had crashed outside Boston, and ten servicemen lost their lives. Abby only heard about it because a local MWDC unit had arrived on the scene to help, something that was announced at their meeting.

When they walked in, the lobby was busy, with staff running around in white smocks, visitors on the benches. For many, the mental hospital was the last resort, the place they were forced to go to by their family or the courts. Even in a time when people everywhere were stressed out and frightened, no one wanted to admit they were weak.

Abby went over to the desk, and an older woman with gray hair looked up with a faint smirk.

"Yes?"

"We're here to see Harold Merrill."

Without replying, she flipped through a binder and then picked up the phone.

"Someone will be out shortly," she said.

They walked over and waited by the windows. Outside, patients stood on the lawn with umbrellas. Frances lit a cigarette and smiled, but neither was thrilled to be there.

"Miss Nolan?"

They turned, and Abby gasped when she saw Doctor Berman.

"Doctor?"

"Come with me, please," he said.

They followed him through the doors and down the corridor. Abby remembered the smell, that pungent mix of cigarettes and Lysol. There was perfume too, although it could have been Frances'.

"This must be a surprise," Abby said, and the doctor glanced over.

"I made the connection when he said your name. He's told me all about you."

"I'm sure he has," Frances said, her heels clicking on the parquet floor.

"And how is Katherine?"

"Back to her old self."

Doctor Berman gave her a cautious smile. Even if her mother had improved, they both knew she wasn't the same as before.

"How is Harold doing?" Abby asked.

"Well, we've got the tremors under control. But he'll need to stay away from alcohol, I'm afraid."

"For how long?"

"Indefinitely."

Abby looked over to Frances, who just raised her eyes. Of all the orders, it was the least likely one he would or could obey.

Halfway down, they turned left into a different wing than Mrs. Nolan had been in. Abby didn't know if it was a good sign or bad, but the rooms looked much the same.

When the doctor stopped, they peeked in to see Harold on a bed in slippers and a silk bathrobe, the newspaper wide open.

"Girls!" he exclaimed, leaning up.

"Aren't you dapper," Frances said, strutting in. "I didn't realize you were so tanned."

"That's what a month in Bermuda will do."

It was a relief to hear because the night he showed up, they were sure it was from liver disease.

They all hugged, and Abby handed him the flowers.

"My love, these are gorgeous," he said, his face beaming. "If only we had the weather to match."

"Rain is good for plants," Frances said, which sounded awkward.

Even if she knew anything about gardening, Abby doubted she had ever done it.

"How're you feeling?"

"My body is better. My heart, unfortunately, still aches."

"We're so sorry."

Harold nodded, looking down, his lips quivering. There was a long and poignant silence, interrupted only when Doctor Berman said, "I'll send the nurse in with his things."

"Things?"

"Yes. His clothing. And discharge papers."

"Discharge papers?"

Abby looked over at Frances, who looked as stunned as she felt. Neither of them knew he was getting out.

"Don't look so befuddled," Harold said, putting the flowers on the table. "I'm a free man."

"Hurray, the gang's back together," Frances said.

"I've always considered us more of a *cadre* than a gang."

Abby was touched by their playful back and forth; Harold could always cheer up a room. But she was also concerned. For someone who had just survived an alcoholic seizure, he seemed far too casual about it.

"Before you leave, stop by the pharmacy," the doctor said. "His prescription will be ready."

With that, he shook Harold's hand and walked out.

"A regular Hippocrates, he is. Now, somebody help me outta this."

As he strained to get up, Frances ran over.

"Don't struggle, dear. You'll stretch your robe…"

……

Abby stood in the darkness under the trees. The rain had stopped, but the ground was still wet, her shoes muddy from the walk over. After

NIGHTTIME PASSES, MORNING COMES

work, she had gone straight to Wood Island and was the first one there. She knew she would be early, but she never expected to wait so long, and being alone made her nervous.

As a girl, she was terrified of fairies, the Irish *Pookas* her father used to spook her with. In her teens, she was more worried about criminals. She had known girls who were robbed, stabbed, and raped. Her biggest fear now was the enemy, and every breeze or creak of a branch made her flinch. After the capture of German spies off Long Island, all of New England was on high alert.

"Abby?"

She spun around, and Angela came out of the shadows.

"Did I scare ya?"

"Hardly," Abby said, but her heart was pounding.

In the distance, she saw the silhouettes of more girls coming over the road from the mainland.

"How long you been here?"

Abby cringed at her gutter slang.

"Not long," Abby lied.

Soon, most of the unit had arrived, the silence now broken by chatter and quiet laughter. Some of the women had come from work while others had just made dinner for their families.

The crowd parted, and Lieutenant Hastings came through, her big hips swaying. Behind her, three girls struggled to carry the crate of flashlights and flares, one of them Nina DiMarco.

When Abby saw her, she had to grin, thinking how her brother and Sarah had snuck away at Thomas' wedding. She didn't know if anything became of it and would have been surprised if it had. In summer, most encounters on Point Shirley were just flings, and despite any heartbreak, they were no less magical.

"Troops," the lieutenant called out, and everyone circled around. "We've received new orders from the *Office of Civilian Defense*. Under no circumstances may there be any light emanating from dwellings within one hundred yards of the coastline. No more warnings. Any questions?"

A young woman raised her hand, and the lieutenant pointed.

"Miss—"

"Lieutenant."

"Lieutenant," the girl corrected. "How do we know what a hundred yards is?"

"A yard is three feet. A foot is twelve inches."

There was low laughter all around, but she wasn't joking. Like most of the officers, she was strict and hardly ever smiled. Considering she was a WASP from Upstate New York, Abby wondered why she didn't want to lead a unit in Back Bay or Beacon Hill with people who were more like her.

While the lieutenant held a flashlight, Nina squinted to read off the names for roll call, members responding with a salute and the word *present*. It sounded like attendance from Abby's high school—*Carracci, Russo, D'Agostino, DiNapoli, Mortali, Vincenzo*, and the occasional Irish names, *Flaherty* and *Dunn*. She understood why her mother said Italians were taking over, although she didn't see them as a threat.

When they reached the end of the list, Abby realized Frances wasn't there.

"Now," Lieutenant Hastings said. "I'll need two girls to watch the equipment."

Everyone looked around, no one stepping forward to volunteer. The lieutenant was about to choose when a figure crept toward them in the darkness. It was eerie enough that Abby could have been scared, but she knew Nazis weren't 5' 1".

"Name, Private?!"

"Frances Farrington."

"Okay, Private Farrington," the lieutenant said with a slight snicker. "You'll stay behind and guard the equipment."

Frances accepted the order without a complaint or remark, which wasn't her style.

"I'll stay, too," Abby said.

"Very well," the lieutenant said, and then she turned to everyone else. "Fall in!"

The women got into columns, chins up and arms tight to their sides. The march back across the salt marsh was as orderly as a military formation. But once they broke into groups and went to their separate patrol areas, all discipline was lost.

Abby was glad Frances made it, excited they could be alone for a couple of hours. But when she turned, her friend stood with a cold pout.

"Is something wrong?" she asked.

"Sal just told me he joined the Navy. He leaves in a week."

CHAPTER TWENTY-NINE

The only time Thomas went into headquarters was to pick up the checks on Friday. In the past, a patrolman would deliver them to the precincts, but with a shortage of officers, everyone had to pitch in. Either way, he liked driving into the city, and he missed the excitement of downtown, his days as a street cop and with the harbor patrol.

After two months in District 7, he was starting to get bored. The day shift was always quieter, but between the MPs at the shipyard and the soldiers at Fort Dawes, East Boston was almost too secure. While gambling and loansharking never stopped, robbery and theft were down, mainly because everyone was working. For all its horror and destruction, the war had pulled the country out of a depression, which seemed a cruel tradeoff.

Most crimes now concerned things that only a year before no one cared about. Scrap metal was a big racket because it was everywhere. With government price controls, the black market for beef was thriving, especially for prime cuts, and gas ration books were being sold on the streets. Any violation was seen as a betrayal of the war effort, and authorities were starting to make examples of people. In Newburyport, a young man had just been sentenced to fourteen years in prison for stealing tires.

When Thomas walked into the office, Lieutenant DiMarco was hunched over his desk with a pen. He always seemed to be doing paperwork, one reason why Thomas never wanted to go any higher than sergeant. The room smelled like smoke, but he knew it was from someone else. In high school, their boxing coach hated cigarettes and made all his students vow to stay away from them.

"Thomas," the lieutenant said, getting up.

As they shook, he looked down at Thomas' hand.

"Where's the ring?"

Thomas frowned. It seemed like something a woman would notice.

"At home on my bureau. Don't wanna get it scuffed up."

"From all those arrests?" DiMarco joked, walking over to the filing cabinet. "Speaking of bureaus. You find a place yet?"

"Not yet."

"My aunt is looking to rent. Top floor. Putnam Street. Right beside the high school."

DiMarco took out a pile of checks, wrapped in a rubber band, and gave them to him.

"Thanks," Thomas said, so anxious he didn't respond to the offer. "Do you have any gas cards?"

The lieutenant shot him a sideways glance.

"What?"

"Gas cards. Do you have any?"

"Did you check at the station?"

"I think they're out," Thomas said, vague enough that it wasn't an outright lie.

When DiMarco hesitated, Thomas felt his heart beating.

"Who're they for?"

"To be honest, I got George's car now and..."

He stopped when the lieutenant's face broke into a wide smile.

"I gotcha, pal," he said with a wink.

He went into his desk drawer and took out a couple of booklets.

"This should help," he said, slapping them into Thomas' hand. "Just don't drive like Ted Horn."

Thomas grinned.

"It's a jalopy."

"The chief is gonna announce *Victory Speed* next week. 35 MPH for the whole city. No exceptions."

"Victory Speed?"

"Yeah, save gas, save rubber. And save lives."

With restrictions on lights, the streets were more dangerous than ever before. Blackouts were the worst, even when they were announced, and the sudden darkness left many people panicked and confused. When the tests started, car accidents had spiked, and the only good news was that now, with gas hard to find, they were down again.

DiMarco walked Thomas to the door.

"Keep that under your hat," he said, looking at the ration cards.

Thomas shoved them into his pocket.

"Between us."

"Congrats again on the wedding. Do we expect to see some little Nolans running around soon?"

Thomas let out a nervous chuckle—it was the first time someone had asked.

"Soon, I hope."

......

It was ironic that with a pocket full of gas cards, Thomas couldn't find any gas. From the North End to Maverick Square, he had passed five stations, and they were all out.

When he pulled up to his house, Connie was on the steps in a flowered summer dress he had never seen before. One side of her hair was up in a clip while the other hung loose. She always surprised him with little changes, whether it was a new color lipstick or fingernail polish. Sometimes they were small enough that he suspected she was trying to make sure he noticed.

She smiled as he got out, but he couldn't help feeling bad for her.

Since coming to America, she had always worked, from the small factory where he met her to the General Electric plant. Now she had no job, and as an "alien enemy," he feared she wouldn't find another.

As happy as he was to see her, the front yard was too public for any affection, so he took her hand, and they walked up the steps to the front door. The moment they got inside, she threw her arms around him and pressed her lips to his.

"Whoa," he said.

"I missed you."

Thomas raised his eyes, as amused as he was excited. At two months pregnant, she seemed hornier than ever, and he wondered if it had something to do with her body chemistry.

He undid his belt and lowered it to the floor, careful not to drop his sidearm. Even if no one got hurt, he would have had a hard time explaining an accidental discharge.

As she kissed him, he could barely catch his breath. Then she rubbed his crotch, and he felt a surge of arousal. He was just about to take her up to the bedroom when someone knocked, and he froze.

Opening the door slightly, he looked out to see a man in a striped shirt and tie.

"Can I help you?" he asked.

"I'm with First Defense. I'm here for the inspection."

"Inspection? What inspection?"

"To be a certified *V Home*."

Thomas frowned, and the man looked down at his clipboard.

"Mrs. Noland called—"

"It's Nolan, no 'd,'" Thomas said. "What's it for?"

As he talked through the crack, Connie massaged his arm, and he heard her giggling.

"We make an assessment of your participation in the war effort—salvage, conversation, air raid preparedness, and other things. If you pass, you get to fly the *V Home* banner in your window."

"Wonderful," Thomas said, not trying to hide his sarcasm. "Can it wait?"

Suddenly, Mrs. Ciarlone came up the sidewalk, and when she turned toward Thomas's house, he sighed in disappointment.

"Okay, come in."

"Zia!" Connie exclaimed.

She greeted her aunt, and the man continued into the house, leaving Thomas standing alone at the door. The two women spoke in a flurry of harsh Italian that only added to his frustration.

"She asked if you could put these in the safe," Connie said, giving him a stack of war bonds.

Mrs. Ciarlone smiled, mumbling something he knew was *thank you* but sounded more like a grunt.

He took the bonds into the dining room and opened the drawer of the china cabinet. The lock box was hardly a *safe*—everyone in the family had a key, including George—but he put them away and secured it.

When he came back out, his mother had arrived and was fanning her face with a folder.

"I thought I lost you," she said to Mrs. Ciarlone.

Like most days, they had been out selling war bonds door to door with the ladies from church. Mrs. Nolan had asked her at the wedding, and now they were like old friends.

"Thomas," she said. "Some water, please."

He went into the kitchen, got a glass, and started to fill it under the sink. But before he could finish, she ran in and grabbed it.

"Sorry. I can't wait."

As she guzzled, the inspector came out from the basement door. With her head back, Mrs. Nolan glanced over at Thomas, and he said, "First Defense."

"Oh, I'm so glad," she said, wiping her mouth.

Hearing another voice, Thomas looked down the hallway and saw Chickie talking to her aunt and Connie. For a house that was usually empty all summer, it felt like a party.

"Almost done," the man said, walking in the back door. "I see the scrap metal pile. Do you save rubber too?"

"In a box beside the shed."

"How about grease?"

Mrs. Nolan gave Thomas a guilty look.

"At our cottage. We're there all summer."

The man nodded, writing something on his clipboard.

"I'll put you down for it," he said.

As Thomas listened, he got impatient. More than anything, he had wanted to sleep with Connie, still worked up from the brief foreplay. But any hope was lost when his mother turned to him and asked, "Can you drive me back to Point Shirley?"

"Sure, Ma."

CHAPTER THIRTY

"Men are sons of bitches!" Frances exclaimed.

As they stood together on the beach, Abby looked over with a sympathetic smile. With Arthur gone, she could relate, but that didn't mean she agreed with the remark. She had reached an age where she knew that both sexes had their quirks. Blaming either one was like blaming the clouds for the rain.

"They think the war will be over by March," Abby said.

"Who?"

"I read it somewhere."

She couldn't remember where, and it might have been hearsay. With civilization destroying itself, people were desperate for answers and explanations, any way to bring some certainty to a world that, only two years earlier, had been steady and predictable. Every week there were new rumors, from that Hitler's Army was now in South America to that the Japs had destroyed parts of the west coast and the military was covering it up.

"I can't believe he would do this."

"He'll be safe," Abby said.

Frances turned to her.

"But how do you know?"

"Because I know Arthur will be safe too."

Just his name seemed to calm Frances, or at least remind her she wasn't the only one suffering. Abby could understand her sadness, but not her outrage. She knew why Sal had joined. Even though he had been born in America, Italians were still looked upon with suspicion, and there was no better way to show his loyalty. He didn't have to go—as someone with a dependent mother and sister, he wouldn't have been drafted—which made his enlistment all the more admirable.

Down by the water, Chickie splashed through the shallows, the bottom of her dress wet. With Sal leaving in a few days, Mrs. Ciarlone had taken him to visit an aunt in Chelsea, their only living relative, and Thomas had driven them.

Abby offered to take Chickie who, at thirteen, still didn't have many friends. The girl was always alone in the summer, playing on the swing set or braiding her dolls' hair on the lawn. Just the sight of another person got her excited, and she would say hello to anyone who walked by. She was such a feature of all their lives that Abby could never imagine a day when she would leave the house and not see her smiling from the porch.

Now Chickie spent her days looking for scrap metal and rubber on Bennington Street or in the empty lots beside the train tracks. She seemed to understand the seriousness of the war, which made Abby realize she was smarter than most people thought. In hard times, everyone had to find some new purpose or reason to go on.

"Such a darling little girl," Frances said.

In their two hours at the beach, it was the first time she had mentioned someone other than Sal.

"A bit of a rascal too."

"I just can't see it."

Chickie would go out salvaging for hours, sometimes not coming home until after dinner. While Mrs. Ciarlone had scolded her for it, she got so worried that, two nights before, she had asked Thomas to drive around looking for her. He found her on Saratoga Street, barefoot and carrying a bunch of scrap in a newspaper boy's bag she had found in a dumpster.

"Abby," Chickie said, walking up with something in her hands.

"What's that you've got?"

"*Stah fich.*"

"Starfish," Frances said with a smile.

When Chickie peered up, Abby saw she was getting sunburned.

"Here, put this on," she said, giving her a hat.

A car beeped, and they turned to see Thomas. He was parked on the seawall, looking over with sunglasses. Abby put up her finger, and they started to collect their things.

"Can I keep?"

"No, dear," Frances said. "Starfish belong in the sea."

Chickie nodded and didn't argue, scurrying down to the waterline to put it back. Even as a child, she never threw tantrums, and the worst she did was pretend not to understand.

Thomas beeped again, and Abby threw up her arms.

"Someone's impatient," Frances said, dusting off her legs.

Abby folded up the blankets and put them in the bag. They still had two of the egg sandwiches her mother made, but they had been sitting out so long that she tossed them on the sand. Instantly, a flock of gulls descended, flapping and screeching, and it was the most excitement they had all morning because the beach was empty.

Chickie grabbed the pail and shovel that Mrs. Ciarlone made her bring. But she hadn't used them, and one of the problems with her condition was that even her mother didn't know whether to treat her like a child or an adolescent.

They walked up to the road, the sand hot against their feet. When they got to the car, they put everything into the trunk, including some sea glass Chickie had collected. While Abby put on her shoes, Frances had another cigarette.

"C'mon," Thomas said, revving the engine.

"What's the hurry?"

"I gotta pick up, Ma."

"Sorry," Abby said, and she got in.

As the only one with a license, Thomas had to drive everyone, and she was sure he hated feeling like a cabbie or chauffeur.

"You hear the news?" he asked.

"We haven't heard anything. We've been here all morning."

"We attacked the Japs in the Aleutians."

"Aleutians?" Frances asked, leaning forward from the back seat. "Isn't that where your brother is?"

As Abby stared at Thomas, she got a sickening feeling.

"Yes."

......

Abby and Frances sat at the picnic table in the backyard, sipping lemonade spiked with some gin leftover from the wedding. In the past, Mrs. Nolan never kept alcohol in the cottage, at first for her husband's sake and later for her own. Or if she did, it was usually just a few cans of Schlitz for when Mr. Loughran came by.

Except for parties or events, Abby never drank during the day, which she saw as the first sign of a problem. But after hearing about the fighting in the Aleutians, she needed something to calm her nerves.

"It sounds like it's just a bombardment," Frances said, leaning over the newspaper.

Abby had been so panicked she made her brother stop at Pulsifer's market to buy it.

"What's *just a bombardment*?"

"Like planes and boats. They've been bombing the island of Kiska to shake up the Japs."

Abby had been with the MWDC for almost four months but was no closer to understanding war than when she was a child. She could put on a tourniquet and brace a broken bone; she could take a pulse and carry a stretcher. They had been learning Morse Code and would even get to test the signal lights. But anything that had to do with combat, anything beyond first aid and evacuations, was a terrifying mystery.

Chickie walked around from the front where she had been skipping rope, looking for playmates in a place that, unlike previous years, was deserted. She reached for her glass, the only one without alcohol, and drank it with both hands.

A car pulled up, and Abby could tell it was Thomas by the sound. Moments later, her mother burst out the back door.

"There's fighting in the Aleutians," she said, flustered.

"It's *just a bombardment*," Abby said with a hint of sarcasm.

"It's true," Frances said. "Air attacks, cannons, things like that. It doesn't say anything about soldiers."

Mrs. Nolan nodded, but she didn't seem reassured. She smiled at Chickie and sat down, folding her arms the way she always did when she was worried or uneasy.

"Won't you stay for dinner?" she asked Frances.

"Not tonight, Mrs. Nolan. But thank you."

"Are you sure? We're having steak."

Abby gave her mother a sharp look.

"My mother's coming up for a visit. We're going to the Somerset Club."

"*Somerset Club?*" Mrs. Nolan said with emphasis.

It sounded elegant, but Abby knew the truth. With Frances' father having an affair, Mrs. Farrington needed to get out of the house.

"We're taking Harold. He leaves this Friday."

"Harold? How is that poor boy?" Mrs. Nolan asked.

"Better," Abby said.

"He's had such a rough go."

After they had told her what happened, she seemed to focus more on his grief than his drinking as the explanation for his breakdown. Abby didn't know if it was out of guilt or regret, but she was sure it brought back bad memories.

Chickie wandered off, and Abby got up to use the bathroom. Entering through the backdoor, she noticed the counter was covered with chopped carrots, celery, and potatoes. It was barely lunchtime, and her mother was already getting dinner ready.

She went upstairs and washed her face, putting on a clean dress. Even when she didn't go swimming, she still felt sticky from the beach.

She came back down, and as she passed through the kitchen, her eyes caught the icebox, and she stopped. Crouching, she opened it to see four or five filets of beef wrapped in wax paper, all prime cuts. Hearing Thomas' voice in the yard only added to her outrage, so she stormed out the backdoor.

"Don't you look fresh as daisies," Frances said.

Before Abby could respond, she saw her mother reach for a glass. In a flash of panic, she lunged for it, and it spilled across the table.

"What in God's name!" Mrs. Nolan exclaimed, jumping up.

"It's okay," Frances said. "It's just Chickie's lemonade."

Abby looked down, relieved but embarrassed. She always hoped her mother wouldn't drink again, but she didn't know. Before her father quit, he had stopped many times, always causing chaos in between.

Abby was about to apologize when she noticed them all smiling.

"What?" she said.

Thomas stepped forward and held out a letter.

"I was at the house today. This was in the mailbox."

She stared at it like it was an artifact. All her life she tried to be tough, and her mother always said emotion was a sign of weakness, even for a woman. But when she saw Arthur's handwriting, her body started to tremble, and she knew she couldn't control it. Afraid to break down in front of everybody, she snatched it from his hand and ran into the cottage.

CHAPTER THIRTY-ONE

Thomas sat next to Connie on the couch, careful not to let their legs or arms touch. Even though they were married, Mrs. Ciarlone was old-fashioned, and he didn't want to offend her. He had only been to her house a couple of times and was surprised at how similar it was to their own. It had Sears Roebuck wallpaper, floral carpets, and faux-leather club chairs. While there was a modern console radio, there was also an old gramophone with a horn. All the windows had blackout curtains, but Mrs. Ciarlone kept the regular ones up too. The only thing the first floor didn't have was a mirror, and Thomas recalled Connie saying something about Italians being superstitious about them.

The wall was covered with pictures of relatives, many dressed in traditional outfits and peasant clothes. At the center was an oval frame with a man in a bowtie and mustache. Realizing it was Mrs. Ciarlone's deceased husband, Thomas wondered why his mother didn't have more photographs of his father.

Mrs. Nolan was in the rocking chair, a glass of iced tea in her hand. Abby was standing in the corner with Mrs. McNulty who, even on a ninety-degree day, wore long sleeves. There were more people in the parlor, friends of Sal's from high school and some coworkers from the nightclub. All day, Chickie wandered the rooms in a white dress, a bow in her hair. She was the only child there but was no less excited. She spent most of her life around adults.

The farewell party for Sal was small but significant enough that he had worn a suit. As he walked around with Frances, she smiled and shook hands, but it wasn't always obvious they were a couple.

Mrs. Ciarlone called from the kitchen, and Connie ran in to help her. Moments later, they brought out a big white cake. Connie put it on the coffee table, and Thomas saw CONGRATULATIONS! written across the top in red icing. It seemed a strange message for someone going off to war, so he assumed it was a bad translation.

Connie called for people to gather around.

"We would like to thank you for coming out today," she said.

As she spoke, Thomas looked at her stomach, always afraid that, at any time, she might start to show.

"Salvatore has made a brave decision that makes us all very proud. All the time he is gone, we will worry, of course. But we know he is safe in God's hands."

Sal blushed.

"Like *Concetta* said," he said, saying her name with an Italian flair. "Thanks everybody for coming. After Pearl Harbor, I wanted to join up right away. But I didn't wanna leave my mother. Now that Concetta is here, I know her and Chickie will be alright."

Everyone clapped, and Connie, Mrs. Ciarlone, and Sal hugged and kissed on the cheeks. Chickie ran in at the last minute and put her arms around all of them, and the room erupted in *oohs* and *aahs*.

Mrs. Ciarlone cut the cake, put it on plates, and handed out slices. All was quiet while they ate, but when the conversation resumed, it wasn't as lively. Even with the windows open, the house was hot, and after drinks and cake, everyone was sluggish.

Not long after, Sal walked his friends to the door and said goodbye. Mrs. McNulty and her husband thanked Mrs. Ciarlone and left. Somehow Mrs. Nolan had convinced a lady to buy war bonds, so they went back to the house and didn't return.

By mid-afternoon, a few guests still lingered, but the party was winding down. Connie walked out from the kitchen, wiping her hands, a slight sheen on her face. She looked funny wearing an apron; Thomas only ever saw her in work clothes or a dress.

"Can I do anything?" he asked.

She looked up with a cute smile.

"It's done."

He felt guilty not helping, but he knew they wouldn't have let him anyway.

Moments later, Mrs. Ciarlone came out too, and when she approached Thomas with her arms wide, he tensed up. He could never tell if she liked him, and most times she wouldn't even look him in the eye. So he was stunned when she reached out and gave him a big hug.

"Thank you, Thomas," she said in clear English.

Then she turned and spoke to Connie, who said something in Italian that made her smile.

"What did you say?" Thomas asked.

"I told her you were taking me to watch the sun set."

......

The inside of Point Shirley was a meandering stretch of rocks and seawall, built to withstand the constant wake from boats going in and out of Winthrop Harbor. At low tide, some areas had enough sand to sit on, but it didn't attract many visitors. As kids, Thomas and his siblings spent most of their time there because it was across from the cottage. It was only when they got older that their parents let them walk the half mile to the public beach.

What the shore lacked in comfort was made up for in beauty. Overlooking the city, it was one of the best spots to watch the sun go down.

"Don't cut your feet," Thomas said.

Standing in the water, Connie looked over her shoulder.

"It's soft," she said, but he knew she meant *sandy*.

He leaned back against the grassy embankment on his elbows. Over at the airport, a fighter was on the runway, and it was still light enough that he could read the numbers on the tail wing. It took off in a heat wave and circled the harbor before banking west.

"It goes to watch for submarines?" she asked, squinting.

Thomas smiled, but only to hide his frustration. There wasn't a place they could go where they weren't reminded of the war. At least they were together, he thought, a luxury a lot of people didn't have. At Sal's party, he saw that look in Frances' eyes, the same one Abby had after Arthur left, that his mother had when George went away.

Everywhere, families were being torn apart, and young men were dying. If he thought about it, he got bitter; if he thought about it too much, he got angry.

Boom!

The ground shook, and birds scattered from the trees. Thomas jumped up and looked around.

"What the hell was that?" he shouted.

When he looked over, Connie was standing knee-deep in the shallows, her hands over her mouth. He ran into the water and went toward her, his shoes slipping on the rocks.

As he got closer, he realized she was crying.

"Are you hurt?"

She shook her head.

"What's wrong?"

Slowly, her head dropped. Then he looked down, and his heart sank. All around her pelvis was blood, and there was more dripping down her legs. When he tried to hug her, she started to shriek and flail, her mouth open and eyes wide.

"Connie, please!" he said, but she was beyond hysterical.

"Thomas?!"

He looked back and Mr. Loughran was standing on the road with a rake.

"What was that noise?"

"I think they just tested the guns at Fort Dawes. Is she okay?"

"No!" Thomas said, so panicked he struggled to speak. "Call an ambulance…"

Before he finished, Mr. Loughran had dropped the rake and was gone.

Thomas grabbed Connie by the wrists, and this time she didn't resist. But when he looked into her eyes, he saw a devastating sadness that took his breath away.

CHAPTER THIRTY-TWO

Frances drove with Abby in the passenger seat. Harold sat in the back with his arm around his suitcase, staring out the window and smoking one cigarette after the other. Thomas had let them borrow the Chevy again, which was generous because, between going to work, seeing Connie, and taking their mother places, he always needed it. For a family that had never owned a car, it was amazing they had ever got by without one.

"You both really must come visit," Harold said. "Bermuda is marvelous, aside from all the bases."

"Bases?"

"The island is swarming with soldiers. It can be a nuisance, but I can't say it's altogether unpleasant."

Abby grinned, and when she glanced over, Frances finally smiled. The whole way she had been silent, speaking only to ask directions or get a light from Harold. Abby had never considered her an emotional person; Frances had that rare gift of being feminine without all the sentiment and soppiness. But since the day Sal left, she had become almost gloomy, and the only time she laughed was after a couple of Martinis. She never mentioned him outright, but her bitterness came out in small remarks about how the war was *crushing people's dreams* or *tearing the world apart.*

Sometimes Abby got tired of her brooding, but she knew what it was like to lose a man. After hearing from Arthur, she at least had some hope. From Texas, his squadron had been sent to Hawaii, which made her panic until she realized it was unlikely the Japs would strike a second time. He didn't say where they would go next, and he probably didn't know. But with American forces battling their way across the Pacific, she was sure he would be with them. He had ended the letter *Forever yours* which, although not as strong as *Love*, was heartfelt enough to know he cared.

"Stop here!" Harold said.

When Frances turned, she cut off a taxi. The driver punched his horn and raised his arms, and Harold waved an apology. They stopped in front of South Station, a giant granite building with Greek columns and a clock at the top. It was always busy, cars pulling in and out, people pouring out the front doors. And while most were morning commuters, there were soldiers too, young men in uniforms with duffel bags at their sides. In the intersection, two cops stood blowing whistles, and across the street, some MPs leaned against a jeep.

Standing on the sidewalk, Harold and Frances shared a cigarette while he looked for his ticket. At one time, planes left East Boston Airport for Bermuda; one of Abby's high school teachers used to go every summer. But with the Army now in charge, most civilian flights had been suspended, so Harold had to take the train to New York and leave from LaGuardia. He was going back to stay with his father, a man who, in a drunken rage, had called him a *fairy*, and then, ironically, threw a vase of roses at him. They never got along, and Harold even admitted he *loathed the man*. But with his mother and brother now gone, it was the only family he had.

"Can you read that?" he asked.

Abby squinted to see the small print.

"10:15," she said.

"Good. Enough time for a late breakfast."

"Stick to orange juice."

"Too hard on the stomach. It'll have to be coffee."

"Would you like company?" Frances asked, even though she knew they had to have the car back by eleven.

"Thank you, my dear. But I've gotta get this eulogy wrapped up."

Abby got choked up, and she could see that Frances did too. But Harold seemed more at peace with his brother's death than they were.

"My girls," he said, leaning forward to hug them. "You've helped me more than you could ever possibly know."

"Don't forget to take your medicine," Abby said, wiping her eyes.

When he tapped his chest pocket, it was only a gesture because she knew he didn't keep it there.

"And write," Frances said.

"First chance I get. Although with all these mail delays, let's hope the war is over before it arrives."

As hard as it was to part, it was a good note to end on, and Harold seemed to know it. Reaching for his suitcase, he blew them kisses, turned around, and headed toward the station. Before he walked in, he waved one last time and then was gone.

"Do you think he'll be okay?" Abby wondered.

Frances turned, blinking as if coming out of a spell.

"Do you think any of us will be?"

......

The ride back to East Boston was like a quiet meditation on all that had happened. Abby didn't mind the silence, since she wanted her friend to pay attention to what she was doing. Frances was the kind of person whose driving reflected her mood. And considering she seemed so anxious and distracted, Abby was worried.

As they came out of Sumner Tunnel, she went into the wrong lane, and they were lucky no one was in it. They heard sirens, and when Abby looked back, she saw a police car.

"Drats!" Frances said, stamping out her cigarette.

She pulled over, and an officer got out and walked up to the window.

"Morning, Miss."

"Good morning, officer," she said with a hint of flirtation.

"License, please."

She went into her purse, fumbling through a clutter of lipstick cases, makeup, and jewelry.

"I seem to have misplaced it," she said, and Abby cringed.

"Registration certificate?"

Rushing to get it, Abby opened the glove compartment, and something fell onto her lap. When she saw a stack of gas ration cards, she gasped, but she didn't have time to cover them up.

"Hey! What're those?" the officer barked. "Lemme see them."

She handed them to Frances who gave them to the officer.

"'*E*' cards? Where the hell'd you get these? This don't look like no emergency vehicle."

Even as someone who didn't drive, Abby knew the cards with "E" on them were prized. Reserved for police cars, fire trucks, ambulances, and other official vehicles, they allowed unlimited gas. But anyone could use them, and most stations weren't interested in enforcing government regulations.

She had been suspicious about the steaks, and now she was sure her brother was involved with bad things. The power police officers had was tempting, and everyone knew that many of them lied, stole, and cheated. In the bars and pool halls of East Boston, cops and crooks mingled like they were opposing teams at a charity baseball event. There was nothing more shameful than corruption, something she and her mother both agreed on, and she never expected it from Thomas. But as angry as she was, she could never snitch.

"We borrowed the car," she blurted, an explanation that gave them an excuse without implicating him.

"Let's see the registration."

Abby reached back in and got it.

"Thomas Nolan? Is that *Sergeant* Thomas Nolan?"

Abby hesitated, but she couldn't lie.

"He's my brother."

"So you're his sister?"

Abby thought she had misheard him until she saw Frances smirk.

"That is...correct," she said, holding back her sarcasm.

"Listen, lady," he said, shoving the cards into his jacket and looking around. "I'm gonna let you go on the infraction. But I can't let you have these. They're government property."

"Thank you, officer."

He tipped his hat and walked away.

"Why, that was exciting," Frances said. "What do we do now?"

"We go."

She put it in gear, and they drove off. When they pulled over across from District 7, Abby was surprised to see Thomas standing out front.

"Want me to ask if he'll take you home?"

"Hardly, dear," Frances said as they got out. "He's been kind enough already. Plus, I have to stop at Filene's."

After they hugged, she waved to Thomas and walked off toward Maverick Station. Once she was out of sight, Thomas came over like he had been waiting for her to leave. In his uniform, he looked sharp, but his expression was cold.

"Keys," he said, holding out his hand.

"Could you drop me at the cottage?"

He opened the door and looked over.

"Take the bus. I've got an appointment."

Whether it was his tone or attitude, Abby got suddenly enraged, and she couldn't hold it back.

"Is it to sell gas cards or buy baby clothes?!"

He slammed the door and ran towards her. When she jumped back, it was only a reflex because neither of her brothers had ever hit her.

"What did you say?"

"I saw the gas cards," she said, but she wasn't ready to tell him they had been confiscated.

"Those are issued."

"What about the steaks at your wedding? Were they *issued* or is that another lie?!"

She started to tear up, the second time that morning. But she was more disappointed than sad. Unlike George, Thomas had always been honest, and it hurt to think he would cheat or steal.

"Another lie?" he said.

"When were you gonna tell everyone Connie is pregnant?"

All at once, she watched his head drop with a sigh. When he looked back up, he seemed beyond devastated.

"She ain't anymore, Abby. She lost it."

CHAPTER THIRTY-THREE

"Please understand," Doctor Wyman said, leaning forward with a look of clinical compassion "This could not have been caused by a loud explosion."

Seated on the couch, Thomas and Connie nodded. She stayed quiet, so he asked all the questions.

"Then what?"

"Anything, really. Sometimes a genetic abnormality, sometimes a bad embryo."

His explanation was straightforward, but it didn't make the loss any easier. If Thomas still had any doubts, it was something he got from his mother, who never trusted doctors. The only one not born at home was George because he had been premature, something Mrs. Nolan always blamed for his bad behavior.

"It shook the ground," Thomas said.

"I'm sure it was quite jarring. But short of nutrition, outside factors play very little role in the stability of a pregnancy. Women give birth every day under horrendous circumstances. Think of all those mothers in London last year."

Everyone remembered the Blitz, Hitler's attempt to demoralize the British. For many Americans, pictures of destroyed schools, churches, and buildings, the smoldering ruins of entire city blocks, were their first introduction to the savagery of war.

"What can we do now?"

"You are both young," the doctor said. "There will be more opportunities for children."

When he smiled, Connie did too, and Thomas was relieved because she had been stone-faced the whole time. All he wanted was for her to be happy, and the tragedy would have only been made worse by her despair.

Doctor Berman handed her a tissue, although she wasn't crying. They sat for a minute in silence, and whether it was his manner or his expertise, he was a comfort to be around. But as patient as he was, they had been there for almost an hour, and Thomas knew he had other people to see.

"Thank you, Doctor," he said.

"Thank you, Doctor," Connie said too, and they both got up.

The doctor walked them to the door where he shook Thomas' hand and then bowed to Connie.

"Be well," he said.

The moment they left the office, it all felt so final. As they waited for the elevator, Thomas was struck by a vague grief, more the loss of a dream than a baby. They had never talked about names, but if it was a boy, he would have wanted to call him Barry after his father. But with the pregnancy a secret, they hadn't been able to plan much for the future. For Thomas, one of the hardest things was knowing that a child had, for a brief instant, lived and died without a name.

The doors opened, and the lobby was busy. Thomas put his arm around Connie, and they walked out. The sky was clear, the sun bright, but the beauty of the day did nothing to ease their sadness.

With the streets around the hospitals so tight, he had parked in an illegal spot, leaving his badge on the dash so he wouldn't get towed. After Abby found his gas cards, he felt guilty abusing his power, but everyone did it. If the feds could deal with Labadini, one of the shadiest guys in East Boston, Thomas didn't mind taking a few risks.

As they drove, Connie didn't speak, and he left her alone to grieve.

But when they got stuck in traffic, he could no longer hold back his concern.

"Are you—"

"I am fine," she said, but her sour smile wasn't convincing.

When the light changed, he hit the gas hard enough that she grabbed the seat. Thinking about that day on the rocks still filled him with fury. After they had gotten back from the hospital, he went straight to Fort Dawes where he shouted at the sentries and even threatened the base commander. If he wasn't a cop, he would have been arrested, and he was lucky that one of the lieutenants was from East Boston.

Thomas wasn't the only one who was outraged. The military had received complaints from as far away as New Hampshire. The test of the 90-millimeter guns had been done without warning, a "miscommunication" between Army and Coastal Artillery units. The blast was strong enough that it shattered windows, and there was a rumor that an old man in Winthrop had died of a heart attack.

However shocking it was, it still didn't explain Connie's reaction. She had shaken and convulsed like a lunatic, her eyes filled with a blank terror. When Thomas finally calmed her down, she looked like she was going to pass out, but by that time the ambulance had arrived. She didn't even remember most of what had happened until he told her.

Throughout their relationship, they never talked about the past, which was easier for her because she knew his family and friends. But for him, she had always been a mystery, showing up out of nowhere to live with her aunt. She was smart enough that she could have gone to college, and yet she worked in menial jobs. He never got the feeling she was lying, but he was sure there was more to her life than he knew.

"What happened to you?"

She looked over, narrowing her eyes in confusion.

"I am alright," she said as if she had misunderstood.

"No. I mean, *what happened to you?*"

"Thomas, I—"

"Tell me," he said.

After a long hesitation, she bit her lip and nodded.

"Let's go to the beach."

. . .

……

Thomas sat on the grass above the shore with his arm around Connie. With her back against his chest, he could smell her hair, feel her breathing, a closeness that was as intimate as sex. The tide was in, all the sandy inlets gone, and the waves lapped against the seawall. It was the same spot where they had heard the cannons go off, and he wasn't surprised she wanted to come back. While it wasn't a gravesite, it would always be a place of remembrance. Thomas had asked the doctor about the remains, a question that was painful but necessary, and they were relieved to know she had been too early in the pregnancy for there to be anything resembling a child.

"We lived in Malta," she said.

"Malta?"

"In the Mediterranean. A small island. My husband was from there."

"Another foreigner," Thomas joked, and she smiled.

"His parents were from Rome. There are many Italians on Malta…"

She got distracted by a sound, the low hum of a trawler as it headed into port. The sea was clear to the horizon, the first time in weeks there weren't troopships or Navy vessels blocking the view. If it wasn't for the row of Army P-40s over at the airport, Thomas might have believed the war was over, or even better, that it had never started.

"The day after Mussolini declared war, he sent planes to attack."

"His own people?"

"Malta is British," she said, and he was embarrassed he didn't know. "The first night, they bombed the harbor. A few nights later, the city—Valletta. We were asleep when it happened. The building beside us was hit. My mother-in-law was killed."

"I'm sorry."

"On warm nights, she slept in the garden. We found her the next morning under the rubble."

"And her husband?"

"He is a fisherman. He was at sea."

"When was this?"

"June of 1940."

Thomas remembered that summer. He had just finished his junior year, and a boxing match against Brighton High had left him with two loose molars. At the time, he was dating his first girlfriend, Maribelle, whose parents were from Valencia, the only Spanish people he had ever met. On weekends, she would take the bus out to Point Shirley where they would wander the beach, have sex beneath the stars. Thinking back to those carefree days, he felt guilty knowing Connie was just trying to survive.

"We tried to stay," she went on, "but it was impossible. Malta is small, and Hitler wanted it. There were attacks almost every day. So my father-in-law took us to Sicily in his boat. We left in the middle of the night."

"Was it far?"

"Not far. Sixty miles. But dangerous. We landed in a small town. We were only there twenty minutes when we were stopped by soldiers. They asked for identification. I am, of course, Italian. My husband also had an Italian passport. They didn't arrest us as spies, but they took him for the *Regio Esercito...*"

Thomas gave her a curious look.

"Italian Army," she explained. "All male citizens over eighteen must join. I couldn't do anything. I went to back Rome and stayed with my cousin. She got me a job at the American embassy."

"Why'd you come here?"

Her eyes got tense, her voice bitter.

"That winter, I got a letter. It said my husband had been killed in Greece—"

"What was his name?"

"Name?" she asked, hesitating like she had to think. "His name was Joseph."

It wasn't as exotic as Thomas expected, but he still got a twinge of jealousy.

"When I found out, I thought I would die too. I was sad. I was angry.

I was crazy. I couldn't eat, couldn't sleep. My mother was worried. She knew what happened in Malta. So she wrote to my aunt Maria and asked if I could come to Boston. Because I worked at the embassy, I got a Visa. Otherwise, it would not have been possible. But I had to leave from Portugal. I took a train to Marseille, a plane to Lisbon, then a ship to America."

Her expression changed, almost like she had come out of a spell, and she turned to him.

"And then I met you."

Thomas squirmed, feeling as bashful as when, in first grade, Nellie McLean said she loved him in the schoolyard. But as touched as he was by the remark, he was also stunned. In all their months together, it was the most honest and open she had ever been about her life. And while he hated to hear about the hell she had gone through, he was glad to finally know the truth.

"Dinner!"

Glancing back, he saw Abby waving from the yard. He got up and reached down to help Connie. As they walked, he felt a slight dizziness, which he attributed to standing and not sorrow.

They crossed the road, and Abby was still waiting.

"Can I talk to you?" she asked, and Connie was polite enough to keep going.

A minute passed before Abby finally looked up.

"I'm sorry."

"It's—"

"No," she said firmly. "I'm sorry. I didn't know."

Thomas swallowed, overcome by a wave of emotion that was like the accumulation of all the things he ever feared, regretted, and despised. He didn't tear up, but inside he felt the tremors of some great struggle that, in the end, left him shaken but also relieved. As twins, he and his sister always shared a special connection. He could have said nothing, and she would have understood. But he wanted to hear it, if only for himself.

"I'm sorry, too."

CHAPTER THIRTY-FOUR

As Abby, Frances, and Angela walked through the streets, it was so dark they couldn't see more than a half block ahead. They all had flashlights but were told not to use them unless absolutely necessary because the batteries didn't last long. The Army had been extra strict this time, ordering the blackout of shipyards and other facilities that had previously been exempted. Lieutenant Hastings had said they were using new technology to measure the *skyglow*, which German warplanes could use to guide them.

By now, the tests were so common that everyone knew the rules. But they were harder to enforce on warm summer nights, which could sometimes feel like the wild west. They passed groups of teenagers who shouldn't have been out and saw cars speeding through the streets with their headlights off. When three drunk guys whistled at them, Angela berated them until Abby convinced her to walk away. People were already frustrated with all the military measures, and Abby didn't want to get into an argument or fight. They were air raid wardens, not police officers.

"Ow!"

Abby and Angela stopped.

"You alright?"

"This area is like a pothole hell," Frances said.

"Shoulda worn flats," Angela said.

Frances' shoes weren't stilettos, but they were too high for walking.

"Don't you have oxfords?"

"I've lots of shoes," Frances said, hurrying to catch up.

"I'm sure you do."

When Angela glanced over, Abby smirked. It was the second time that night she agreed with her, the first when Frances wanted to skip a street because it smelled like sewage.

Over the weeks, Abby had gotten to know Angela and even liked her. She knew her brothers were trouble, but so was George, and neither of them was responsible for their families. As the daughter of a fisherman, Angela was rough, her gutter Boston accent so heavy that, at times, she sounded like she was slurring. But she had a tender side too, like the night they found a cat with a broken leg, and she wouldn't leave until someone rang the police box for help.

"Light!"

Abby looked and saw a glow coming from the first floor of a triple-decker. While Frances waited on the sidewalk, she and Angela walked up to the porch, and Abby peered in. Over on the mantel, she saw a heap of candles burning beneath a picture frame.

"Hello?!"

An elderly woman in a nightgown appeared in the window.

"No lights, Ma'am. Per order of the Office of Civilian Defense," Abby said.

She raised an eyebrow and gave Abby a confused look.

"Senza luce!" Angela barked. "È una violazione. Chiudi la tenda o spegni le candele."

They had a short exchange, a rapid-fire of Italian that almost left Abby dizzy. Finally, the woman frowned and pulled down the shade.

"These guineas," Angela said. "They think they can just play dumb."

As harsh as it was, Abby wasn't shocked or even surprised. Italians, like most ethnic groups, were always hardest on their own.

"What was it?" Frances asked.

"Candles, like a shrine."

"Superstitious old goat," Angela said.

They went to the end of the road and turned onto Saratoga Street where, at times, the silence was more disturbing than the darkness. In the alleyways, things darted between the barrels, rattled chain link fences. Abby knew it was rats, and maybe squirrels, but she didn't say it because Frances would have been horrified.

When they got to the next corner, they stopped and looked at each other.

"Are we done?" Angela asked.

"I am done," Frances said, collapsing on a stoop.

With cigarettes forbidden, she had taken one out but didn't light it, making Abby wonder if she got some satisfaction by just holding it.

"Can we go?"

They had never finished their patrol before the all-clear alarm rang and didn't know what to do.

"How about my house for tea?" Abby asked.

"I could use a whiskey on the rocks," Angela said, and Abby doubted she was joking.

"Lovely," Frances said. "It'll be like Paris during the invasion."

"If anyone asks, we'll say we retreated to high ground."

They chuckled and started to walk. As they approached Abby's street, a faint hum sounded in the distance, and they all stopped. It got louder and closer as the network of air raid sirens rang throughout the region.

"Isn't that about time?" Angela said.

Slowly the streetlights came on, the most magical moment of any blackout.

"Make that two whiskeys," Frances joked.

Something caught Abby's eye, and she noticed a shadow.

"Abby?"

She ran toward it, her heart pounding, and as she got close, she saw a woman lying on the sidewalk. Kneeling down, she turned her over and froze when she saw Mrs. Ciarlone.

……

. . .

Abby sat in the emergency room at Boston City Hospital and stared straight ahead. Even with Angela and Frances on either side of her, she had never felt more alone. The lighting didn't help, that cold and sickly glow of fluorescence. On the far wall was a poster that said BUY WAR BONDS with a handsome soldier smiling. With his dark hair and cheekbones, he looked a little like Arthur, and Abby couldn't decide if that made her feel better or worse.

They had been there almost three hours and still hadn't heard anything. Abby had always been told *no news is good news* but didn't think it was true for a medical crisis. They weren't the only ones waiting, and people had been arriving all night, some hobbling in and others on stretchers.

Most cases weren't related to the blackout, which politicians said wasn't a risk to the public, but some were. A society that relied on light and electricity for everything couldn't be shut off like a radio. There was an old man who had broken his leg taking in his trash barrels, a woman who burned her arm boiling water in the dark. Beyond the injuries, there were illnesses, including a Polish woman coughing up blood.

Even if nothing they saw was life-threatening, it made Abby realize how little she knew about trauma and triage. They had all been trained in first aid, but trying to resuscitate a dummy was a lot different than a human. Some things had to be learned through experience. Either way, seeing all the suffering made Abby's problem seem a little less significant, but it also reminded her that awful things did happen.

When they found Mrs. Ciarlone, she was lying on her side, unconscious. Abby thought she heard a groan, but it could have been the wheeze of her own gasping. The street was empty, and even with the streetlamps back on, it felt dark and gloomy.

Frances got hysterical, running around in circles screaming, but somehow, Abby and Angela stayed calm. Abby pulled the nearest alarm box, and with the police and fire departments already on alert, they were there in minutes. One of the officers was the man who shoved her at the bakery, something that even in all the confusion, she noted. A friend whose brother was a cop told her that Thomas had knocked him out. Abby had pleaded with him not to do anything, but men settled things differently than women. As much as she hated violence, she couldn't deny she got some small comfort in knowing she was protected.

When Frances squeezed her arm, Abby looked up. A young doctor with glasses and a white jacket was at the desk. There were dozens of people waiting, but somehow they knew he was there for them. He walked over, his expression hard to read, and as he approached, Abby got nervous.

"Are you a relative of the deceased?" he asked softly.

Her heart sank, but she didn't have time to be sad. She stood up and pointed at his chest.

"We weren't told she was deceased, you son of a bitch!"

"What the hell?!" Angela said.

Frances just hissed and looked away in disgust.

"Miss, I am so sorry," he said, fumbling to apologize.

A couple of nurses ran over and tried to calm them down. The entire waiting room went quiet. The news was horrific, but Abby would always remember how they got it as the real tragedy.

"This is an outrage!"

With her hand on her chin, she started to choke up, and Frances was already crying. Angela somehow kept it together, walking in circles and shaking her head.

"We did everything we could do," the doctor went on.

Abby nodded, but she had stopped listening. After five years of living next door, she had finally gotten to know Mrs. Ciarlone, and now she was gone. She had the same gut-wrenching hollowness she got when her father died, which somehow made her jealous. She only ever thought she could feel that way about him. She realized then that the pain of loss was universal, that it only differed in intensity.

"Abby?!"

Turning, she looked toward the door. The moment she saw her brother, she ran toward him and into his arms.

"How'd you know?"

As he held her, she could feel him trembling.

"Someone came to the house," he said, and she knew why he didn't want to say who.

With no phone at the cottage, Angela had called her father, who was staying on the other side of Point Shirley. After the fight at the beach the summer before, Abby never imagined he would walk over to tell her family, but he did. If there was any upside to war, it was that it ended a lot of the petty feuds and grudges of the past. Even with all the recent American victories, the threat of defeat was still real. Some people helped each other out of kindness and others for survival.

"Did she make it?"

Looking up, Abby shook her head, and she watched him cringe.

"Where's Connie?" she asked.

His eyes watered, his face twitched.

"She's watching Chickie."

CHAPTER THIRTY-FIVE

"Of course, I'm furious, goddammit!"

"Thomas, please. Calm down," DiMarco said. Sitting behind his desk, he mostly just listened, and the fact that he also seemed upset was some consolation.

"We need more patrol cars on the street!"

"I know, I know. But we don't have the manpower—"

"No one should have been out driving!"

Even as Thomas said it, he knew it was naïve. With millions living in the blackout zone, it was foolish to think everyone would comply. Cities and towns were cracking down, giving fines and even jail time. But there would always be scofflaws and exceptions.

"That's why we tell people to stay in their homes," DiMarco said. "It's dangerous."

Thomas dropped his head in defeat. He still couldn't believe Mrs. Ciarlone was dead. The hit-and-run had happened at the corner of their street, which, despite its tragedy, seemed a fitting end for a woman who walked everywhere. He sent half the station out to interview people, and there were no witnesses. The closest they got was a woman who had heard a screech, but there was also an accident on Bennington Street around the same time.

"Listen," DiMarco said gently. "I know it ain't much. I'm gonna give you a week off for grief. Take Connie somewhere nice."

"I don't—"

"That's an order."

Thomas sighed.

"Thanks."

For some reason, his anger had subsided, or maybe he was just worn out. When the lieutenant looked at his watch, Thomas knew he had to go. They had been talking for almost an hour and were no closer to an explanation for what happened or a remedy for preventing it in the future. Thomas hadn't been a cop for very long, but he knew that sometimes there was no justice.

"We get any tips, you'll be the first to know," DiMarco said, and they got up.

They shook hands at the door, and Thomas walked out. As he went down the stairwell, he saw some men from the harbor patrol, and they just nodded. Headquarters was too big and too busy for everyone to have heard about the accident. People were killed every day on the streets. And considering a lot of officers had brothers fighting overseas, Thomas couldn't expect an outpouring for the death of an in-law who shouldn't have been out in the blackout anyway.

At the station, it was different because they got the call. Even Jeremy Collins had pulled him aside to say he was sorry, something made more poignant by the fact that Thomas could still see the mark from where he hit him. The secretaries bought him flowers, which he gave to Connie. As someone who had already experienced the brutality of life, her aunt's death wasn't the hardest blow, but more like one in a series of hits that left her stunned but still standing. As a boxer, it was the best analogy Thomas could think of.

The most heartbroken one was Chickie. After they told her, she ran up to her room and wouldn't come out. She had snuck out that night to look for scrap, probably getting lost in the blackout. They assumed Mrs. Ciarlone was out looking for her when she got hit because, with the curfew for Italians, she never went out after dark. It was a cruel irony, and one Thomas was sure Chickie understood despite her mental deficiencies. Even infants had the capacity to feel guilt.

Thomas walked out the back door into the parking lot. What was once reserved for cops and employees was now a mix of vehicles, and sometimes it was hard to find a spot. With the country at war, public safety and civil defense overlapped in a mess of organizations that all worked together. Some were official like the *Office of Civilian Defense, Aircraft Warning Corps,* and, of course, all branches of the military. Others were volunteer like the *American Women's Voluntary Services,* the *United Service Organizations,* and the *Civil Air Patrol.* In the corner, Thomas saw a green truck with an MWDC insignia on the side.

Getting into the cruiser, he started it and revved the engine, which was much smoother than George's Chevy. He always felt powerful in the patrol car, and after his months as a rookie, he finally felt like a cop. Whatever happened in the war and in the world, he knew he had to protect his family. He hit the pedal and sped off into the city streets.

......

"We need to tell Sal," Connie said.

Sitting at the table, Thomas fidgeted with his hands. Being in Mrs. Ciarlone's kitchen made him uneasy, and he didn't know if it was the sadness, guilt, uncertainty, or all of it.

"I called the Red Cross. They handle these things for the Army. They can put in a request. They can't guarantee it."

"Could we call him?"

"No," he said with a smile. "He's in basic training."

Her blue linen dress was shorter than her others, more like a stylish nightgown. As serious as the conversation was, he couldn't help but try to catch a glimpse of her legs, her bare feet. Outside, it was ninety degrees and the house was sweltering. With all the windows open, they could hear Chickie playing in the yard. The Braga girls had come by in the morning, and Mrs. McNulty brought her six-year-old granddaughter over for lunch. The visits were thoughtful, but they were temporary distractions because Chickie always ended up alone.

"Some tea?" Connie asked.

"No, thank you."

He never understood hot drinks on a hot day, something his grandparents used to have. He had been thinking about them more lately, as well as all their relatives who were no longer living. His aunt and uncle had died when he was in middle school, ending their trips to Maine. When they were very young, their mother's oldest brother Walter lived at the top of the street. A lifetime bachelor, he wore a top hat and used a cane, and whenever he came by, he would flip Thomas and his brother a few nickels. For some reason, Thomas missed them all now more than ever.

As Connie lit the kettle, he looked around. The kitchen was a lot like their own, with a hand-painted cupboard, modern stove, and checkered valances, which were now just decorative because there were blackout shades. The only thing Mrs. Nolan wouldn't have had was the picture of the Virgin Mary because, as devout as she was, she was never one for saints or symbols. Other than that, their tastes were the same, and Thomas knew they could have been good friends.

He was startled when Chickie came in the door. Her hands were dirty, her face red, and she had scuffed one of her knees.

"Mux-uh," she said.

Connie smiled—they both knew what she wanted. Moxie was her father's favorite beverage, and she had been drinking it since he died.

Connie got a bottle from the pantry and popped off the cap. As she filled a glass, Thomas sensed Chickie watching him, but he didn't turn. He could never look her in the eye without experiencing the same crushing sorrow he had felt in the weeks and months after his father's death. The fact that the feeling was the same made him realize that, as hard as the past year had been, he and his siblings had never really had much loss.

"Chickie, go play."

She ignored Connie and stared at Thomas, drinking the Moxie with both hands. When he finally looked over, she smiled, and he choked up.

"C'mon, Chickie," Connie said, followed by something in Italian.

She made a pout and skipped out the back door.

"What are we going to do?" Connie asked.

"What can we do?"

After pouring some tea, she walked over and sat down.

"I read that the war might be over by Christmas."

Thomas frowned.

"Where'd you read that?"

"I…I didn't read it," she said, stumbling. "A girl…a woman at the shop did."

Thomas scoffed; he was tired of naïve gossip.

"For god's sake, no one knows when it will end, Connie."

"I didn't say I know it. I said I heard it."

"You said you *read* it."

It was the tensest conversation they ever had, and he could tell she was mad by the way she stirred the spoon.

"Look, if Sal…" he said, before correcting himself. "*When* Sal comes home, who knows what kinda state he'll be in? Chickie needs special care."

She looked up, her expression sharp.

"She will not go into an orphanage."

"No, no…I didn't mean that."

"Then what did you mean?"

"I just mean…she's different."

"Isn't that a blessing!"

"She needs to be taught."

"And I can teach her!" she shouted before lowering her voice. "I have to try. You have to try. The girl lost both her parents. We can't just—"

Connie stopped, and when Thomas glanced back, Chickie was in the doorway. She hesitated and then pointed at her glass.

"Muh Mux-uh, please."

CHAPTER THIRTY-SIX

Abby stood beside Frances and Angela, all holding umbrellas in the drizzle. At some point during the service, Frances had let go of Abby and was now clutching Angela's arm. Considering their backgrounds, they were an unlikely pair, a girl from the slums and a girl from the suburbs. But since the accident, they had become friends, and there was nothing like a traumatic experience to bring people together who wouldn't normally meet.

Before them was the tall stone obelisk Abby's great-grandfather had bought around the time of the Civil War. Whether he had planned to start a legacy, she didn't know, but etched into the sides were the names of her mother's ancestors going back four generations—Mildred O'Leary, Brigid O'Leary, John O'Leary, James O'Leary, Catherine O'Leary, etc. Their father was on there too, *Bartholomew Francis Nolan: 1889-1941*, the cold finality of life. While no one could dispute the date of his death, he was never sure of his birth year. After his parents died of typhus, he and his siblings were separated, and his birth certificate had gotten lost.

With its rolling hills and trees, Holy Cross Cemetery probably didn't look very different back then except with fewer graves. But over the years, Malden had grown around it, a blue-collar city of forty thousand with businesses and factories, dense streets lined with triple-deckers.

Aside from a few extra parks and a lake, it wasn't much different than East Boston.

The crowd was small, and not just because of the weather. Mrs. Ciarlone didn't have a lot of family in America. With her husband buried in a rundown municipal graveyard in Somerville, Abby had suggested they could put her in their plot, and Connie didn't object. Mrs. Ciarlone's only other surviving relative was an elderly cousin who, when asked, just shrugged his shoulders and said *they never slept in the same bed anyway*.

The burial service was over in less than twenty minutes, with two gravediggers standing by in raincoats. Father Ward had been busy that day, so he sent one of the younger priests, and Abby was happy to find out he was Italian, even saying an Italian prayer.

Once it was over, everyone turned to each other, hugging and shaking hands. Thomas stood next to Connie, who wore a black dress and a hat with a veil. A group of his colleagues had come, all in uniform, and Abby saw Nina DiMarco's brother.

Several of Sal's friends had shown up, but he did not. Two days earlier, they got a telegram from the Red Cross that said, "Request for Bereavement Leave Indeterminate," and no one knew what it meant. With millions of men mobilizing across the country, things were chaotic, and Mr. Loughran, a veteran of the Great War, said they probably just couldn't locate him in time.

People trickled back to their cars, all parked in a line on the road. Abby and her friends stopped to wait for Thomas, who was pointing at something on the gravestone. Like his siblings, he never cared much about the past, but lately, he had been more interested in their family's history.

"You're coming back to the house, right?" Abby asked.

"I can't. I have to help my father fix fish nets," Angela said, and Abby thought she meant the stockings.

"Fish nets?"

"Gillnets, they're called. For the boats. He does it for money."

Abby looked at Frances.

"I wish I could, my love. My mother is coming up to visit."

Thomas ran over, covering his head because he had been too stubborn to bring an umbrella. The rain was picking up, the trees swaying, and the dreary weather was fitting for the occasion. They got in the car, and there was plenty of room. Their mother had driven over with Mr. McNulty, whose wife and some other ladies were watching Chickie at the house. The young girl had already seen one parent buried, and no one wanted her to go through it again.

As they pulled away, Abby glanced back to the monument, now wet and gray. The last time she was there was when her father died, a day that, to her surprise, now felt like a long time ago. She had only been to a few funerals in her life but leaving the cemetery always seemed like the saddest part. And when they went out the front gate, she didn't realize she was crying until Frances handed her a tissue.

......

"What on earth will we do with two houses?" Mrs. Nolan said.

"Ma, she still lives there!"

With Chickie around, Abby was careful not to say her name.

"She can't live alone," Mrs. McNulty said, sipping her tea.

They sat on the couch with the windows wide open. On the glass of the middle one was a large "V," the sticker that indicated it was a certified *V House*. While not as poignant as the gold star, it still showed they were doing their part in the war effort.

The rain had cooled things down, but it was still stuffy. Some women from church had come back, as well as Mrs. Ciarlone's cousin, who brought a bottle of homemade wine. But otherwise, the gathering was small and quiet.

"I can watch her. But who will take her to school?"

"She has a brother!" Abby said.

Her mother raised her eyes, and Mrs. McNulty was polite enough not to respond. The consequences of Mrs. Ciarlone's death were almost as difficult as her death itself. With her mother gone and her brother in the Navy, Chickie was now alone.

"She could move in with us."

"Then what'll you do with next door?"

"I guess we could shutter it," Mrs. Nolan said. "Turn off the water, drain the toilet, close the chimney vent. Like we do with the cottage."

"Maybe we could just shut Chickie down?!" Abby said.

She stood up and stormed into the dining room. Reaching for a plate, she got some cheese and crackers, and celery. She had no appetite, but she knew it would calm her down. As upset as she was, she couldn't blame her mother or Mrs. McNulty. Having lived through the Great War and the Depression, women from their generation were always more practical.

Thomas walked in the back door, his suit still damp, and she wondered why he hadn't changed.

"What's wrong?" he asked.

"Nothing," she said, but she knew he didn't believe her.

"I've gotta go into the city. Chickie's on the porch with Connie."

"Where are you going—"

Someone knocked, and they both ran to get it. Any time there was a visitor, it was always a race to the door, one of the last playful antics Abby and her brother had carried into adulthood.

Thomas got there first like he always did, and when he opened it, they froze. Standing on the porch were two men in tuxedos. And in their arms was a giant flower bouquet that looked almost too heavy to carry. Mrs. McNulty and Mrs. Nolan walked over, and everyone just stared. It was the most elegant arrangement Abby had ever seen, a heap of snapdragons, orchids, tulips, and roses, all draped in an American flag. Just the sight of it got her emotional, but when she saw the message underneath, she burst into tears.

TO THE CIARLONE FAMILY
OUR DEEPEST CONDOLENCES
FROM YOUR FRIENDS AT THE COCOANUT GOVE

CHAPTER THIRTY-SEVEN

Thomas walked out of the courthouse and down the granite steps. He had worn his police uniform, which at first confused the judge until he explained he was on his lunch break. DiMarco had given him a week off, but he couldn't use it, and with Connie out of work, they didn't have the money to go away. With so many officers quitting to join the service, the shortage in staff was becoming a crisis, and everyone worked overtime even when they didn't want to. The department had already lowered the requirements for recruits, but it was getting to the point where they were taking men who were half blind and had clubbed feet.

As he walked over to the car, the sky was clear and the sun bright. At midday, it was hot, but he could sense some subtle change in the air. With Labor Day a week away, fall was approaching, and the nights were cooler. He didn't dread the end of summer like he used to, maybe because he always associated it with his father's death, and now with Mrs. Ciarlone's. Beyond that, something about having a wife and a job made every day important. He could no longer live his life in anticipation of beach days and campfires.

If he liked anything about August, it was that it was the slowest month of the year. Even in wartime, people took time off and went on vacation. He got to Sumner Tunnel in two minutes, and with no traffic, was in East Boston in less than ten.

He found a spot across from the station, and as he backed in, the tires screeched. By now they were bald, and new ones were impossible to find. As a cop, he could get all the fuel he wanted, but that wasn't the problem, and even Governor Saltonstall admitted the main reason for rationing was to conserve rubber, not gas.

Thomas was about to cross the street when a black car rolled up. Realizing it was Labadini, he sighed, but didn't cringe. The night of the accident, Labadini's father had walked over to the cottage to tell them what happened, and for that, Thomas at least owed him his attention.

"Vin," he said, nodding.

"I'm sorry about your girl's aunt."

"Thanks."

"You find out who hit her?"

It was a bold question, but Thomas couldn't lie or ignore it. On the streets of East Boston, rumors and deceit spread fast.

"No, we haven't."

"Want me to ask around?"

"Ask around?"

"Yeah. Maybe I can find out who it was."

Stepping closer, Thomas stared him straight in the eye.

"No more favors," he said.

Labadini chuckled and looked over at the guy in the passenger seat.

"You got me all wrong, Nolan. Ain't no favor. We'll call it a gift. That could've been my sister. My mother, even, God rest her soul."

The fact that Labadini worked at the shipyard had always put him in a higher category than real criminals, but Thomas still didn't trust him.

"Sure. If you hear anything, let me know," he said, and he turned to go.

"Her husband was from Avellino," Labadini said. "Same town as my father. That makes us family, sort of."

Thomas glanced back with a sour smile.

"Yeah. Sort of."

......

The moment Thomas walked into the cottage, he could smell something cooking. He went over to the kitchen, and a pot was simmering on the stove. Through the window, he saw his mother and Connie at the picnic table. Chickie was playing between the rows of vegetables, which was a surprise. Now that it was a *Victory Garden*, Mrs. Nolan never let anyone near it.

"Thomas?"

Startled, he spun around, and Abby was in the doorway.

"When did you get home?" she asked.

"Just now."

"What's that?"

He looked down at the envelope in his hand, which he had been holding so long he sometimes forgot he had it. All afternoon at work, he wouldn't let it go, even taking it into the lavatory.

"Just something," he said.

She frowned, and he walked out the back door.

"Thomas!" his mother exclaimed.

Connie got up and ran over, giving him a peck on the cheek. Even though they were married, neither was comfortable kissing on the lips in front of family members yet.

"Are you hungry?" Mrs. Nolan asked. "The chowder should be ready."

He smiled but didn't answer, sitting down with Connie in the shade of the elm tree. In the distance, the harbor was calm, which made him feel calm, and the sun was descending over Boston in a white and yellow haze.

"How was your day?" his mother asked, sipping her iced tea.

When Thomas glanced at Connie, she gave him an encouraging smile. He held out the letter, and his mother put her glass down.

"From George?"

He shook his head, and she opened it. As she read, her hand began to tremble, and when she looked up, tears were rolling down her cheeks.

"Temporary guardianship?"

Thomas just nodded, too choked up to speak.

"If Sal does not object when he comes home," she said, "then the adoption will be final."

He could knock out most men with a punch, but when it came to matters of the heart, Connie would always have him beat.

Chickie skipped over, her hair in pigtails and wearing the flowered dress Connie had sewn from an old gown.

"Wuh wrong?" she asked Mrs. Nolan.

They all looked at each other, and then Connie said something in Italian. Chickie started jumping up and down, flapping her arms.

"Sì!"

In a burst of uncontrollable joy, she went running across the lawn in wide circles yelling, "Sì, sì sì, sì…"

"What…what did you say?" Mrs. Nolan asked, wiping her tears on her sleeve because she didn't have a tissue.

"I asked her if she would like to be our daughter—"

"Why is everyone upset?"

When they looked up, Abby was standing on the porch in her uniform. Before anyone could answer, Mr. Loughran walked into the yard, and Thomas was relieved by the interruption. He could never handle too much emotion at once.

"They are adopting Chickie," Mrs. Nolan said, and Abby's face dropped.

If anything had changed about her since her breakdown, it was that she was now more direct.

"Sounds like cause for celebration," Mr. Loughran said.

"A beer?" Mrs. Nolan said, getting up. "Or ginger ale? I think there's still some in the pantry."

As Mr. Loughran stood thinking, they all waited. He was one of the only people Thomas knew who could pick between alcohol and soda with the same enthusiasm.

"Ginger ale?" he asked.

"They were Barry's."

Thomas smiled. It was always good to hear his father's name.

"If it was Barry's, I'll take one. He would've wanted it."

CHAPTER THIRTY-EIGHT

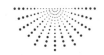

"Abby?!"

When she glanced back, Eve was in the doorway.

"I need those cinnamon rolls!" she said, then she blurted something in Italian.

Connie grinned, and Abby knew it was either sarcasm or a joke. Eve got a thrill talking to her, which was strange for a girl who used to insult Italians all the time. Connie had only been working there a week, and everyone loved her.

"I gotta get more powdered sugar," Abby said.

As she walked back to the storeroom, Carlo was coming up from the basement, a bag of flour on his shoulder. She gave him a cute wave, and he smiled. His arrest in June had horrified everyone, and while he had only been detained a couple of hours, Abby knew it was humiliating. He had to go before a judge, explain why he hadn't registered, and then swear his loyalty to America. He had to give up his radio too, and for a man who loved opera, it felt cruel.

But things were getting better for Italians. There was a bill in congress to remove their status as *alien enemies*, and even Attorney General Biddle said they weren't untrustworthy like the Germans and Japs. They still had to carry registration cards, but the curfew was no longer enforced, mainly because, in a city of immigrants, it was impossible to do.

Abby grabbed a box off the shelf, and when she got back, Connie had already scraped enough sugar out of the shaker to finish the sheet. She was a hard worker and smart, and Abby felt guilty having to train her. Only a few years older, she had a seriousness and maturity that went far beyond her age. Thomas said she had seen some terrible things, but he wouldn't say what.

Loretta walked in the back door in her white uniform. Although still in training, she was one of the thousands of nursing students who had answered the call to volunteer at local hospitals.

"The leaves are starting to turn," she said, hanging her bag on the hook.

"Where are there any leaves in East Boston?" Eve asked.

"Wood Island."

"Are the barracks done?" Abby asked.

"They're getting close."

"I hear it's gonna be all *darkies*," Eve said.

Tying her apron, Loretta looked up with a sneer.

"I don't care what color they are. They're serving our country. All you do is serve bombolonis!"

Abby and Connie looked at each other, and even Carlo noticed the tension. With the rolls done, Abby quickly carried them over to Eve so there wouldn't be an argument.

"The nerve of that bitch," Loretta said.

The Army had been clearing Wood Island Park for months to build a small base, and there were rumors it was going to house black troops. Some people were outraged, and others quietly disapproved. For a neighborhood of immigrants, many of whom were looked down on and mistreated, it seemed hypocritical.

Carlo took two more trays of pastries out of the oven and put them on the table. Abby glanced over at the clock and realized she had to go.

"Ice the Danishes first because they're hot," she said. "The tarts need to cool for ten minutes before you take them out of the pan. Croissants get an egg wash, not too much...

As she spoke, Connie stood with an amused smile. Abby knew she was being frantic, something she got from her mother. But it was her first day back to school, and she was anxious.

"Go. I will be fine."

Abby stopped.

"Okay," she said, nodding and out of breath.

She took off her apron, grabbed her bag, and flew out the door.

......

Sitting on the cold bench, Abby stared out into the darkness. Whenever the train went under the harbor tunnel, people were silent, something that never used to happen. Or was she imagining it? More and more, she found herself blaming everything on the war, even the small peculiarities of daily life. With so much fear and uncertainty about the future, it was easy to romanticize the past, forgetting that only a decade before, a quarter of the country had been out of work. Still, when she thought about everything that happened in the last year and a half, she had to laugh. Humor wasn't the best response, but it was always the best remedy.

If all the hardship and sadness had done anything, it was to make her finally realize what she wanted. Like any young girl, she once had big dreams, a fancy home in Marblehead or Swampscott, a husband who was a banker. Now her only wish was for her brother and Arthur to come home safe. Anything else she ever achieved or attained would be a benefit. She would be satisfied with a simple life, a couple of children and a small house in East Boston, maybe Point Shirley. Knowing about all the death and destruction going on in the world, it was hard to ask for more.

Soon the train pulled into Scollay Square station. She got in line to exit, and when she reached the doors, a young soldier with a duffel bag stopped to let her go first. Short with blonde hair, he looked nothing like

Arthur, but every serviceman reminded her of him now. With a smile, she stepped off and headed upstairs to get the streetcar.

When she got to BU, the courtyard of Marsh Chapel was busy, welcome banners strung between the archways. Students walked around in new clothes, their bookbags full, and Abby could spot the freshman because they looked so nervous. But even with all the activity, it was quieter than the previous September.

She turned into the Arts & Sciences building, her syllabus in her hand, and for once she wasn't in a hurry. Her first class didn't start until nine, and now that she was a sophomore, she could make her own schedule. With many of her required courses done, she had even picked a few electives, including Irish History. All her life, she had heard her father talk about his homeland, but she knew nothing about it. And considering her mother's ancestors were from there too, she wanted to learn more.

She went down the corridor, looking at all the notices on the wall. What used to mostly be for clubs, societies, study groups, and concerts was now mixed with posters about the war. Some were for recruitment like JOIN THE US ARMY AIR CORPS and NAVY: ENLIST TODAY, while others were about secrecy and defense like LOOSE TALK CAN COST LIVES and AN ENEMY EAR MAY BE NEAR. Pinned to a corkboard was an announcement about a former student who had been killed in the Aleutian Islands, something that gave her a chill.

"Abigail?"

Hearing his voice, she froze. She turned to see Professor Bauermeister walking toward her.

"Professor?"

"Welcome back."

"You are...here?"

"I am," he said with a wide smile.

He had on a brown tweed suit and bowtie. From the last time she saw him, he had put on weight, which looked better because he had been too thin.

"I didn't know..." she said, still stunned.

"I've been reinstated."

"I'm delighted."

As they faced each other, she got a feeling of warm gratitude. She didn't know if what she said to Ms. Stetson had led to the administration reconsidering his case, or if they had done it on their own. Either way, she had only wanted to help, and she was never looking for credit for it. At a time when all of society was consumed by fear, suspicion, and hatred, stopping one small injustice seemed like a great victory.

"You're taking German II?" he asked.

"I am."

"Good. I'm teaching it. 11 am. Don't be late."

With a smile, he tipped his hat and walked off.

"I won't," she called out.

She continued down the hallway, so excited she wanted to skip. As she went down the stairs to the cafeteria, she could smell bacon and other things cooking. Even with all the pastries at the bakery, she never ate when she was working, and she was hungry.

"Abby?!"

Standing in the doorway, she looked over and saw Frances at the same corner table they always sat at. And there beside her was Harold, dressed in a light-colored suit, his hair longer than the last time she saw him.

"Don't you look happy as a clam?" he said as she walked over.

"The professor is back."

Harold looked confused.

"Bauermeister. The German," Frances explained.

"Ah, right. Cheers to that!" he said, and he raised his glass of orange juice.

When he smiled, his teeth shined, and his eyes were clear. More than that, his voice sounded different, and he radiated some new joy or optimism that Abby had seen somewhere before.

"Harold, you look...wonderful," she said.

"Thank you, darling. That's what putting down the hooch will do."

She looked over at Frances.

"He's been *dry since July*," she said, emphasizing the rhyme.

"The 23rd to be exact. I got in with this great group of fellows. We meet twice a week, talk about our weaknesses. Some of it is blather, but it's all in good form."

"Alcoholics Anonymous," Abby said.

Harold gave her a sideways glance.

"Now I can't really say, can I? Or it wouldn't be anonymous."

When he winked, she smiled, remembering how her father used to go to meetings.

"Can I get anyone anything?"

The food line was short, and she knew it wouldn't last.

"I'll have toast, no butter," Frances said, reaching for her purse.

Abby held out her hand; she wouldn't let her pay. She put down her bag and was about to go to the counter when a dozen soldiers walked in. If anyone turned to look, it was only the freshmen. The Army had been on campus for so long that most other students didn't notice or care.

"Outflank them," Frances said, lighting a cigarette.

"On the double!"

As Abby hesitated, she had to grin. By now, military jargon was part of everyday conversation. But when she looked over at the men, their young faces and eager eyes, she couldn't help but feel tremendous sadness. With thousands of American casualties already, all the chest-thumping enthusiasm was gone, replaced by the solemn acceptance that many more would die before there was peace.

"What's the matter, Private?" Harold joked. "Did you forget there was a war on?"

"Never."

Enjoying *Nighttime Passes, Morning Comes*? The story continues in *Onward to Eden,* keep reading below for the first two chapters. Click the link below to pre-order now.

www.amazon.com/B0BWBZ9PWV

Sign up for Jonathan Cullens newsletter to stay up to date on new releases.

https://liquidmind.media/j-cullen-newsletter-sign-up-1/

I'd love to hear your feedback! Consider leaving a review by following the link below and scrolling down to the review section.

www.amazon.com/B0BDSNB11W

JONATHAN CULLEN

ONWARD TO EDEN CHAPTER ONE

October 1942

It was strange that, despite all the shortages, sacrifices, heartaches, and hardships, Abby Nolan woke up some mornings forgetting there was a war.

The world had changed but, in many ways, her life had not. She still lived at home in the house her Irish great-grandfather had built, the same place her mother and grandmother had grown up. She still slept in the same small bedroom at the end of the hallway. When she went out, she would wave to Mrs. McNulty across the street or Mr. Braga a few doors down. She was still surrounded by the people she had known all her life.

If anything seemed different about East Boston, it was how quiet it had become. Most of the young men were gone. Timothy Enright, who owned Enright's Dairy, had joined the Navy, so now everyone had to walk to the shop to get their milk. Jimmy and Anthony Ianocconi had left for the Army in July. Libby Franchette was in Northampton training with the Naval Women's Reserve, and one of the Costello boys was missing in Guadalcanal.

After Pearl Harbor, the casualties had trickled in over the winter.

Now it was like a flood. Every Sunday at Mass, Father Ward would read out the names of the dead or missing, eliciting cries and moans from the pews.

"Abigail!"

Abby opened her eyes. While her mother's voice was jarring, she didn't cringe like she used to. The only good that had come from the stress of the past ten months was that they had all become more forgiving of each other. Her father had died two summers before, and her brother George had joined the Army. The shock of death and war made any family bickering seem petty. Somehow they all knew, now more than ever, they had to stick together.

"Abigail!"

Abby yawned and pushed herself up from her bed. With no work and no classes, she could have slept till noon.

"Be right down," she called.

This was the first year Boston University had closed for Columbus Day. The official announcement made it sound like an act of patriotism, but it was probably to save money. With so many boys gone, the student body was a fraction of what it was before the war. If the college hadn't been hosting various Army training programs, it could have gone bankrupt.

Abby shivered as she got dressed. The nights were getting colder. Soon she would have to start wearing her wool gown to sleep. She put on a dress and walked out to the bathroom to fill the sink. As she washed her face, her eyes fell on George's toothbrush and she froze. Its frayed bristles and splintered wood handle were like a metaphor for his own troubled life.

Abby had never gotten along with her older brother. As a boy, he was mean and restless, always causing problems. By the time he was eighteen, he had been arrested twice. She had assumed he would end up in prison like some of his friends. But after their father's death, he had changed, even softened. For someone who only cared about himself, he'd surprised everyone by joining the Army. Now she worried about him more than anyone.

Abby reached for the Phillips toothpaste, its tube bent and split at the edges. With tin limited by the War Department, every container, from vegetable cans to shaving cream, was cheap and flimsy.

"Abigail!"

"Oh, for Christ's sake," Abby muttered.

She dried off her face and ran downstairs.

In the kitchen, her mother stood at the oven. She wore an apron over her nice dress, her dark hair in a pompadour. At fifty, Mrs. Nolan had the figure of a woman much younger.

Her mother glanced back, her face damp and frantic as usual.

"Were you gonna sleep all day?" she asked.

"What time is it?"

"Nearly eleven."

Mrs. Nolan took a tray of buns out of the oven and dropped them on the counter.

"I need more butter," she said. "The German market should be open today."

"Are you certain?"

"I saw Mr. Schultz yesterday."

"Okay."

"And be quick! The announcement is at noon!"

……

Abby walked out to Bennington Street. Although most of the stores were closed, every window had an American flag. A neighborhood that had once been Irish and Jewish was now largely Italian. As a people viewed with suspicion, they were more patriotic than anyone. One deli even had an effigy of Adolph Hitler hanging from a noose until the police ordered them to take it down because it was scaring children.

As she crossed the street, she glanced over at Gittell's Tailor, a small shop between a pool hall and a paint store. It was where she had first met Arthur who had worked there for his father. He had been in the Air Force a year, and she hadn't seen him since Easter. Mr. Gittell was only open three days a week now.

Abby walked over to the German market. Mr. Schultz had owned the place for years, and everyone knew him. But it still didn't protect him from prejudice. As she opened the door, she could still see the word "Kraut!" someone had tried to scrub off the wall.

A bell jingled, and Mr. Schultz looked up from the counter.

"Abigail," he said in a heavy accent. "Happy Columbus Day."

"Same to you, Mr. Schultz."

As a girl, Abby always thought he was old. Now that she was an adult, he looked more like a distinguished gentleman. He had white hair and a handlebar mustache, the ends twisted with wax. Although short, his shoulders were broad and muscular. Most men Abby knew over fifty were hunched from hard work, but he was still fit. Rumors were that he had been a champion swimmer back in Germany.

The shop was small, with low ceilings and plank floors. In a neighborhood where most people didn't own a car, it sold everything from bread to bath salts. After the Rexall in Orient Heights closed during the Depression, Mr. Schultz got a license for a drug counter. The pharmacist was a young Romanian woman who Abby never saw because she only worked two days a week.

As she went down the aisle, she noticed some of the shelves were bare. At the back, she opened the cooler and wasn't surprised there was no butter. Food shortages had been on and off since the start of the war, and one never knew what to expect. A month before, pork chops were impossible to find. Sugar had been scarce since summer.

She grabbed a package of Nucoa instead. Her mother hated the stuff, saying it was lard with food coloring. But it was better than nothing, and Abby didn't have to waste a ration stamp buying it.

She walked back to the register, and Mr. Schultz said, "Margarine?"

"I didn't see any butter."

He held up his finger and went out back, returning a minute later with a block of butter.

"For your lovely mother," he said.

"Oh, thank you, Mr. Schultz."

At a time when everyone was struggling, his kindness meant a lot.

"Eighteen cents, please," he said, and she went into her purse. "Did you hear the good news?"

"What news is that?"

"We destroyed three Japanese boats in the Solomon Islands. That makes eleven this week."

Like any man, he viewed the war like a sport, something to be measured in a series of gains, losses, and comebacks. She tried to keep up with it all, but it only made her think about Arthur. The last letter she'd received from him was in September, around the same time they'd heard from George. He was somewhere in the Far East, although he hadn't said where. While she didn't know the Solomons from Siberia, she panicked anytime she heard about an incident in the Pacific.

"Hopefully it's one step closer to peace," she said, handing him two dimes.

He handed her the change with a smile.

"Tell Mrs. Nolan I say hello."

......

Abby walked up the Ciarlones' steps and stopped on the porch. She was still uncomfortable with her brother living next door. That summer, Thomas had married Mrs. Ciarlone's niece Connie, an Italian girl whose first husband had died in the war. Two months later, Mrs. Ciarlone was killed by a car during a blackout and not long after, her son Sal left for the Army.

The door opened, and it was Connie.

"Have you been waiting out here?" she asked.

Abby shook her head and gave her the butter.

"For the rolls."

Connie had on an apron over a red dress, her hair in pin curls. Although flustered from cooking, she was no less beautiful. She had an exotic charm, and it wasn't just her accent. Mrs. Nolan said her eyes were too close together, but Abby knew her mother was just looking for a flaw.

"Can I help with anything?" Abby asked.

"No, thank you. The ham should be out shortly."

Abby walked in to see a dozen people, mostly neighbors and women from church. Thomas was kneeling by the radio, trying to get a signal. He had on his police uniform.

In the dining room, their mother was at the table with some older ladies. For a woman who used to complain about "all the foreigners," she now had more Italian friends than anyone.

Mrs. McNulty sat on the couch beside her husband, a tall man who always wore a bow tie and had a permanent grin.

"Hello, Abigail," she said, sipping wine. "Any news from George?"

Abby and her family hadn't heard from George in six weeks.

"He's still in the Aleutian Islands as far as we know."

"Let's pray he's safe."

Abby appreciated the sympathy, but it was easy for them to say. The McNultys' son Paul worked for the Department of State in Maryland, and their daughter Teresa was in the Women's Army Auxiliary Corps, stationed somewhere in New Mexico. Even if they were doing their part for the war, they were far from the battlefields.

"I hear the new barracks at Wood Island Park have been completed," Mr. McNulty said.

As a member of the Massachusetts Women's Defense Corps, Abby knew things other people didn't. But she couldn't say anything. She was saved from having to lie or avoid the question when Chickie came running down the stairs.

"*Uh-buh!*"

She had on a flowered dress, one sock pulled up to her knee and the other at her ankle.

"Hi, Chickie," Abby said, and they hugged.

At fourteen, Mrs. Ciarlone's daughter still acted like a young girl. She got easily excited and spoke in broken sentences. It was never determined exactly what was wrong with her. The doctors said she was *delayed*, and everyone else just called her *different*. After Mrs. Ciarlone's death, Thomas and Connie had adopted her.

"Play?" Chickie said, taking both of Abby's hands.

"Maybe in a little bit."

Suddenly, the radio got loud.

"Shhh!" Thomas said.

Connie ran in from the kitchen, and people gathered in the room. Moments later, the voice of Attorney General Francis Biddle came on:

"Here in America some six-hundred-thousand Italians...are working side by side with other millions who have in them the blood of the French, the Norwegians, the Belgians, the Dutch, the Poles, the Greeks....In each division of the United States Army, nearly five hundred soldiers, on the average, are the sons of Italian immigrants to America... Many more are of older Italian origin. I do not need to tell you that these men are abundantly represented in the list of heroes who have been decorated for bravery since December seven, nineteen forty-one."

"It is for this reason...I now announce to you that beginning October nineteen, a week from today, Italian aliens will no longer be classed as 'alien enemies.'"

There was a burst of heartfelt sighs. A few of the older Italian ladies wept. It was a speech everyone had expected the AG to make, but hearing it was a relief. After ten months of restrictions, curfews, and overall humiliation, Italians in America were finally free.

Thomas put his arm around Connie, and they kissed.

"C'mon," she said, wiping a tear from her eye. "Let's eat."

ONWARD TO EDEN CHAPTER TWO

Thomas raced down Border Street past dockyards and warehouses. When it came to crime tips, speed and timing were everything. He kept the sirens off, but with another cruiser behind him, the raid would have hardly been a surprise.

"If anyone tries to run, crack 'em," he said.

Officer Carroll grinned, glancing down at his shiny baton. He was only two years younger than Thomas at eighteen, but with his head shaved and pimples on his chin, he looked like a kid. He had only been on the force for a month, which wasn't unusual. Their precinct was full of new officers.

They passed the entrance of East Boston Works where, even in the urgency, Thomas got sentimental. His father had worked there for thirty years until his crane collapsed in a windstorm and killed him. Since the start of the war, the facility had doubled in size. The fence had barbed wire, and MPs now guarded the gates. With so much military activity, all the shipyards had become like bases.

They stopped in front of a plain brick building and got out. Sergeant Silva and two patrolmen parked behind them, and they all walked up to the door. Thomas knocked three times, waited a few seconds, then knocked again. Finally, he heard someone undoing the lock. A bald man with a mustache opened it and peered out.

"Yeah?"

Thomas showed his badge.

"We've got a warrant to search the premises," he said.

"For what?"

"For mice."

When the man started to close the door, Thomas shoved it in.

"Hey, take it easy!" the guy said. "It's got a chain lock. I had to shut it to open it—"

Thomas ignored him, and they burst inside. Two other men stood up, and one even raised his arms.

The small office was shabby, with three desks and some old filing cabinets. The air was dank and oily, the overhead lamps emitting a dull light. Thomas could hear machinery somewhere in the back.

"What is this place?" he asked.

"Why don't you check your warrant?" the bald guy said.

Thomas frowned and looked over at the other men.

"We're a small manufacturer," one of them said.

"Of what?"

"We have a contract with the Department of Defense to produce cadaver pouches."

Thomas squinted in confusion.

"Body bags," the man explained.

The grim silence was broken only by voices behind the wall.

"Who's back there?" Thomas asked.

"We've got about a dozen guys on the line. Italians mostly. They've all been cleared."

"Look around," Thomas said, and the patrolmen began to search the room.

He still wasn't comfortable giving orders. With so many men leaving for the service, officers moved up fast. He had only been on the force a year and was already a sergeant. He was proud of the promotion but still felt guilty for not enlisting like his brother.

"Sarge?"

Thomas looked over and officer Carroll was standing by an open drawer, holding something up. When he walked closer, the sight of gas ration coupons made him smile. There were hundreds of them, all stamped with the letter "B", the most valuable kind. The spaces for the license numbers were blank, so he knew they were either forged or stolen.

"Are these counterfeits?" he asked.

With their heads slumped, the men just glanced at each other.

"Where'd you get them?" Thomas pressed.

They remained silent.

"You know this is a violation of the regulations of the Office of Price Administration?"

"I wanna talk to my lawyer," the bald guy said.

After a long day, Thomas didn't have the patience to interrogate them. Dealing contraband in wartime was a serious crime, but judges had been lenient, mainly because they sympathized. Everyone hated the restrictions. He knew the men probably wouldn't be prosecuted anyway. Or at least, that's what he told himself.

"Consider this a warning," he said, and he shoved the rations into his coat pocket. "Next time, we'll shut you down. Understand?"

The men hesitated.

"Understand?" Thomas barked.

"Yeah, yeah," the bald guy said.

Thomas nodded to Carroll, Silva, and the others, and they left.

......

Each time Thomas turned the wheel, the front of the car rattled. It was impossible to find new tires. The used ones he had put on over the summer were already flat. As a sergeant, he could've taken a cruiser home, but he liked the old Ford. George had given it to him before he left for the Army, a gesture that had surprised everyone. After years of tension and spite, Thomas finally respected his brother. He might have even loved him.

He stopped in front of a corner shop on the ground level of a triple-decker. The sign in the window said, "Betty Ann Food Shop," but everyone called it Betty Ann Bakery. Although the owners were Cornish, they sold a mix of traditional and Italian pastries, from custard tarts to cannoli. Abby had been working there since high school and had gotten Connie a job after she was fired from the light bulb factory for not being an American citizen.

Moments later, Connie walked out. She had her pocketbook slung over her shoulder and a box in her hands. Thomas jumped out to get the passenger door for her, something his father had taught him. Thomas had never listened as a boy, but his father's life lessons continued to affect him. He had been gone over a year but in some ways, Thomas felt closer to him than ever.

"Hello," Connie said, kissing him on the cheek and sliding into the seat.

As he shut the door, he glanced over to the shop to see the counter girls looking out. He grinned to himself, walked around the front, and got back into the driver's seat.

"How was work?" she asked.

Thomas could control his emotions, but he could never hide his frustration.

"All the usual."

"What's all the usual?"

"What're those?" he asked, looking at the box on her lap.

She opened it, revealing cookies filled with chunks of red fruit.

"Victory cookies."

"Victory cookies?"

"Made with cranberries."

"How're we gonna win the war with those?"

She smiled.

"Cranberries makes sweet to them," she said, her English sloppy after a long day. "Only one cup of sugar for each batch."

Pulling out, a horn blared, and he hit the brakes. Connie gasped, and they watched an Army truck speed by. As it turned the corner, he saw black soldiers in the back.

"Where do they go?"

"The new barracks on Wood Island Park," he said, distracted.

They continued down Bennington Street, the traffic so heavy that it took fifteen minutes to go a mile. By the time they turned onto their street, it was already dark outside.

Thomas parked, and they got out and walked up the front steps. When they reached the porch, the door swung open, and Chickie ran out.

"*Conn-ah*," she said, jumping into Connie's arms.

They had discussed asking her to call them Mom and Dad, but they still weren't officially her parents. Until her brother Sal returned from the war—and they all hoped he did—her parental status was in limbo.

Mrs. Nolan walked out smiling, but Thomas could tell she was exhausted. Except for when Connie had off work, she picked up Chickie every day at school and watched her until they got home.

"Care to escort me back?" she asked, holding out her arm.

While she was only being playful, his mother really did need the help. She wasn't as steady as she used to be. After their father had died, she'd had a breakdown. No one was sure whether her drinking was the cause or just a consequence. Since getting out of the hospital, she had stayed dry and her mental state had improved. But she still wasn't like she used to be—none of them were. All his life, Thomas had dreamed of leaving East Boston. Now, he was glad he never had. He had come to realize that, especially in a time of war, there was nothing more important than family.

When they got to the porch, Mrs. Nolan walked up to the post box, a rusted iron relic from the last century. Thomas was surprised because she usually got the mail the moment it arrived.

"You didn't get the mail already?"

Her hand came out empty, the hatch closing with a ding.

"I did, but I figured maybe…"

The mailman never came twice, but Thomas understood her angst. They hadn't gotten a letter from George since September and were all starting to worry. But correspondence in wartime was unreliable, and his brother, who had dropped out of high school in tenth grade, had never been much of a writer. They knew people who hadn't heard from their sons at all yet. Even Abby's boyfriend Arthur had only written to her a few times.

"Maybe tomorrow," Mrs. Nolan said.

"Maybe, Ma."

Opening the door, he put his arm around her back, and they walked in.

Enjoying *Nighttime Passes, Morning Comes*? The story continues in *Onward to Eden,* keep reading below for the first two chapters. Click the link below to pre-order now.

ALSO BY JONATHAN CULLEN

The Days of War Series

The Last Happy Summer

Nighttime Passes, Morning Comes

Onward to Eden

Shadows of Our Time Collection

The Storm Beyond the Tides

Sunsets Never Wait

Bermuda Blue

The Jody Brae Mystery Series

Whiskey Point

City of Small Kingdoms

The Polish Triangle

Love Ain't For Keeping

Sign up for Jonathan's newsletter for updates on deals and new releases!

https://liquidmind.media/j-cullen-newsletter-sign-up-1/

ABOUT THE AUTHOR

Jonathan Cullen grew up in Boston and attended public schools. After a brief career as a bicycle messenger, he attended Boston College and graduated with a B.A. in English Literature (1995). During his twenties, he wrote two unpublished novels, taught high school in Ireland, lived in Mexico, worked as a prison librarian, and spent a month in Kenya, Africa before finally settling down three blocks from where he grew up.

He currently lives in Boston (West Roxbury) with his wife Heidi and daughter Maeve.

Made in United States
North Haven, CT
22 June 2024